W•CLARK
PUBLISHING

Still Feenin'

A Novel By
Sereniti Hall

Wahida Clark Presents Publishing, LLC
60 Evergreen Place
Suite 904
East Orange, New Jersey 07018
973-678-9982
www.wclarkpublishing.com

ISBN 13-digit 978-09759646-4-4
ISBN 10-digit 0-9759646-4-X

Library of Congress Catalog Number 2010937836
1.   Urban, Lesbian, Gay, B-Sexual, Miami, Strippers, AIDS, Augusta Georgia, African-American, Street Lit – Fiction

Cover design and layout by Oddball Design
Book interior design by Nuance Art.*.
Contributing Editors: Linda Wilson and R. Hamilton

Printed in United States
Green & Company Printing, LLC
www.greenandcompany.biz

My Inspiration

As always my two beautiful daughters, Rockell and Cleopatra. You still give me reason to press on and be the best that I can be. I want you to know that no matter what obstacles you go through in life, you can still come out on top if you strive to do the best that you can do and be the best that you can be. Your life is in your hands. I strive to teach you girls to know better so you can do better in life.

The art from which comes a great mind is destined to do great things.

—Dorothy Hall.

Acknowledgments

God grant me the serenity to accept the things I cannot change, courage to change the things that I can, and the wisdom to know the difference.

All my praise and glory goes to the Messiah, the beginning and the end, my maker, for without him there would be no me. I'm humbly grateful for the life you have given me and the storms that you have carried me through.

To my mother and father, Vermell Fargas and Artic Hall, and my step parents Harvey Shelton and Pamela Williams, much love and respect. I love you guys.

My grandmother Ms. Mary Hall, the spine in my back, you have all my love.

To my cousin Stephanie Smith that I said was full of shit the first time; you've redeemed yourself. Now you hold the title of my sister not my cousin. You're doing an excellent job over at Murphey Middle School with your students, and it was a pleasure to come and speak with them. Keep up the good work.

To my auntie Bernice Green, forgive me for not mentioning your name in the first novel. You know it wasn't intentional.

To Reginald Smith aka Slanga, the storm is almost

over for you. You're almost out of the belly of the beast as some call it. We miss you dearly. Waiting on your story too.

To Arlinda Tray Johnzzzzz, my jail house lawyer, you know that you ain't nothing but the truth. I hope you get the opportunity to get on someone's stage one day and be the comedian that you are.

To Sandi Collins, we had our ups and downs, but we had some good days too. I am a woman of my word. I hope you go out and do wonderful things with your life.

To Jeffrey Tyrone Hall, I wouldn't trade you for anything.

To Robert Elam, there's not a day that I can say you're not a damn good father to the girls. You could put your foot down sometimes, but you may think that would kill you. A girl can't complain, not even when you piss me off.

To Wahida Clark, you're the fuckin' best. Thanks for taking a chance on me. Now I'm on my second novel and I can't even believe it. Much love to the team over at WCP. They work hard for their money.

To Ms. Linda Wilson, my editor, you're phenomenal. We have a long road ahead of us. I've learned a lot from you and I thank you for your time and patience.

To my Ethiopian Queens, Sarah, Makda, and Lorna, you're the sisters that I never had. Go to www.arayamusic.com and listen to Makda's latest song. Feel free to leave any comments.

To Lana Hampton, it's time to get that book done. You have a story to tell, girl.

To Paulene Pelmon, thanks for your help on that old ancient typewriter. Deb Dalton, I swear you're the fastest typist I've ever seen. Thank you so much for your help.

A major thanks to all the people and book stores that supported me on my first novel. I aim to get better as I go further into my writing career.

To Ninth Ward in Augusta, Georgia, some of you guys have me cracking up when you ask about the characters in the book. So much shit happened on Ninth Street back in the day that I don't even know who's who half the time. Thanks for the support. Ninth Street ain't what it used to be anymore. I think when Charlie McCain left it was over. Now Mr. Jay's gone, what people gone do now?

To my brother Harvey Hall and his wife, Randrill Hall, you guys are the truth. Keep up the good work and I hope your marriage lasts for a lifetime. Love will carry you guys through any storms. I learned that from a wise man by the name of Donnell Kelly. He is the man of all men.

Shouts outs: My sis, Jackie and Talia Shelton, thanks for the support. Doeretta Davis, Pamela Hollins, Sonya Owens, Pamela Mays, Valerie Hollins, Kiera Reeves, Joseph Riley, Toni Wilkes, Kathy Mosley, Rosalyn Rhymer, Rebecca Drake, Marva Nash, Crystal Bazzell, my white sister, Cammie Armour, Nicola Brown aka

CoCo, Acquanetta Richardson, I am so sorry for your loss. Daphney Tingle, Tonya Larry, Gloria Hernandez, Shelly Perkins, Melinda Fisher, Towandalyn Jordan, Ms. Linda Zech, Vernon Gardenhire, Ms. Melinda Thee Hill. Stephanie Holmes, there's no way in hell I can forget you. I wouldn't forgive myself. Akosua Animpong, Marcus Henry, thanks for the encouragement. Melinda Tyner, thanks for all the uplifting talks we had. Valerie Knowles (you've earned the name Dusty Foot; it's officially yours.) Carla Graham, my deepest sympathy about your mother. Demita Clark, my friend till the end. Tasha Croom Lewis, you my number one B$###. And last but not least, to everybody on lock that supports me and doesn't support me, especially the girls that were at FPC Pekin before they turned it into a men's facility. Thank you and always keep your head up. Your mind can only be locked up if you let it.

God bless and much love.

Chapter One
DIGGING UP OLD BONES

D o you remember the first time we met?" Infinity asked Tanisha.

"Yeah," Tanisha answered, wondering if Infinity was speaking of the time in front of Church's Chicken when she was cracked out and Infinity was looking for Roscoe. Or the time at the apartment when she told Tanisha how the business was going to be run and what her place was.

"When I saw you standing there in that lingerie it triggered an unwanted flashback. You were looking sexy, and all I could think of was the first time I'd caught Roscoe cheating. I mean, I'd heard that he had cheated before, but to catch him in the act was something totally different. It felt like I'd been hit by a bus." Infinity paused for a few seconds. "There was this friend, a family friend named Teresa." She let out a deep sigh. "I let her and her two small children come stay in my house. I can't believe I trusted that bitch." She beat her fist once against the steering wheel. "How in the fuck could I be so fuckin' stupid?" Infinity bit her bottom lip and went completely silent.

Tanisha waited patiently for her to continue, thinking, *I know she said she caught him in the act, but I want* details.

"This is my first time ever telling this to anyone. Roscoe doesn't even know that I saw him. I could never bring myself to confront him. It was too embarrassing to even let him know that I knew." A small puddle of water formed in her eyes.

"Why did she have to come and stay in your house? Why didn't she get her own place?" Tanisha inquired.

"Girl . . ." Infinity caught a tear falling with the back of her hand. "She did have her own place in the beginning. That is, until she and her husband started having problems." She sniffled. "He was an alcoholic and he became abusive. The marriage went south and she filed for divorce. Shortly after the separation, that fool threw Molotov cocktails through the windows of their home. The house immediately caught fire and she and her two kids barely escaped. Her husband was arrested and sent to prison."

"Damn! That's messed up. So was she all right?"

"She was safe, but they had nowhere to go. I felt more sorry for the kids than her. I should've been thinking more about myself and what could happen if I let a woman I barely knew live with me and my husband. Being a family friend didn't mean shit to her, so it shouldn't have meant shit to me."

Tanisha reached over and stroked Infinity's arm slightly as her own guilt kicked in.

"Two weeks after I let her move in—just two fuckin' weeks after—I came home early with a migraine from one of my meetings at the refuge house. Roscoe's SUV was parked in the driveway and I was excited, hoping to snuggle and get some good loving since things had been going so well for us. It had been six months straight, no fussing, no fighting, and no cheating. I rushed to the door, stuck my key in and as soon as I opened it, I was smacked in the face with the aroma of good old-fashioned fried chicken. I knew Roscoe loved fried chicken, but I also knew that he had never touched a stove in his natural born life.

"As I headed to the kitchen, the chicken smell got stronger. Now the sizzling sound was clear in my ears. But it wasn't the only sound I heard. I didn't panic, but my heartbeat accelerated. My body temperature heated up and my hands trembled as I prayed the faint sounds of a woman moaning wasn't what I was really hearing. I wanted to turn back, but in my heart I knew it was something that I needed to see. The sound grew louder and stronger as I came closer.

"Oh papi, fuck me harder, harder papi," Teresa moaned in pleasure. I couldn't believe my ears. I'd let this woman into my home. Not only was she fucking my husband, but she was cooking his favorite meal on my stove.

"I remember thinking, I can't believe this shit. They're fucking in my goddamn house and frying my chicken! Sons of bitches! I should get a gun and blow their muthafuckin' heads off! I still didn't move; I couldn't move."

Tanisha's eyes bucked. "Did you say anything to them?"

Infinity continued as if she never heard Tanisha ask her a question. "Teresa pushed Roscoe's head from between her legs, hopped off the counter, and dashed for the stove. Her pussy juices ran down her thigh and her tight miniskirt was pulled up over her big, over-sized ass that Roscoe seemed to love so much. He laid his head on the counter with his dick still rock hard, waiting to fuck, I guess. 'Fuck the chicken, girl; bring me that pussy so I can put a bruising on it.' He laughed. Teresa shut the stove off after she removed the chicken from the skillet. 'Come here, girl.' He smiled as he stroked his dick. She went to him, blushing; her face was lit up like a Christmas tree. She unbuttoned her blouse, threw it to the floor and did the same to her bra.

"Roscoe touched her breasts and then grabbed her around her small waist. His eyes roamed over her body. I leaned against the door ledge.

"Lose the skirt too," he insisted as he sucked one of her breasts, then the other. She dropped the skirt and he lifted her from her feet as she locked her legs around his back. Roscoe fucked her and howled like a werewolf and didn't give a fuck who heard him. I heard the bitch moan, "It's better than the last time."

Tanisha gasped and then said, "So it wasn't the first time they fucked?"

Infinity let more tears fall as she cursed and then pounded the steering wheel, breaking one of her false nails. Tanisha jerked at Infinity's sudden outburst. She knew not to ask anything else about Roscoe's affair.

Oh my God. This woman has gone through so much and now I've added to her pain.

"He told her it was gonna get better every time he laid his boa constrictor in her pussy. He continued eating her, then slipped his tongue inside her asshole and asked her if it was good. The bitch barely got the word yes out as she gasped for air. Then he told her, 'Girl, you better not give this pussy to anybody, but me. Shit, this pussy good.' After standing there and watching their marathon of anal and oral fucking, it took all of three minutes and he

4

exploded in her mouth and told her to swallow. Teresa's three-year-old daughter interrupted them because she had to pee, but the bass in Teresa's voice scared the child out of the kitchen. The bitch begged Roscoe to finish, and he did until she came again. Then he popped the wine bottle and they drank from it as they giggled and fondled one another."

Son of a bitch! But why is she telling me all of this? The bitch may wanna kill me. Tanisha's mind raced with possibilities.

"I slipped back out the door as if I'd never come into the house. My heart was crushed and my mental state was torn to pieces. I didn't know what to do. For a while, I sat in my car with my head collapsed on the steering wheel. Then I pulled out my nine millimeter and thought of going back into the house to kill Roscoe, Teresa, then myself. Then I thought about just killing myself. As soon as I put the gun to my head, it began to thunder outside and the bottom dropped out of heaven. The rain was pouring. In an instant, sudden darkness covered the sky."

"I sped off, headed straight to a liquor store where I purchased a bottle of Patron, downed my troubles and decided to let it go. After all, I still loved him, and I thought if he had no clue I knew about his malicious infidelity, it wouldn't hurt for me to keep it to myself. But what does he do? Go and do the same old shit with somebody new—you."

* * * * *

"What now, Infinity?" Armani answered the phone, holding a martini.

"Hello? Can you hear me?" Infinity asked.

"Yes, I can hear you. There's just a little static in the phone. Where are you?" Armani shouted.

"Did you forget already? I told you I was picking the bitch up from rehab—the bitch that slept with my husband."

"Yeah, I remember you said that, but I don't see why you even bother to dig up old bones. Why don't you just let sleeping dogs lie? You know in your heart of hearts you will never forgive her for what she did with Roscoe," Armani said.

"Why are you questioning me? You know I want this bitch to pay for what she did to me and my husband. I hate this fuckin' drug addict bitch!" Infinity roared.

"So what does she have to say about all that?" Armani asked sarcastically. "Oh, I forgot. She doesn't know. Does she?"

"That's the object of the game. Duh!"

"Where is she now?"

"Down at the beach pouring out her faggot ass friend's ashes."

"What? At the beach? What fucking beach? Hold up. What friend?"

"Miami beach, girl. Her friend, Roscoe's brother, Frenchy. Do you forget everything I tell you?" Infinity asked.

"No, I don't. I guess I'm just puzzled because you're way down in Miami with a girl who you consider to be your worst enemy. Oh my God! What the fuck are you trying to do? Kill her?" Armani asked.

"I'm not trying to kill the hoe. Besides, that would be too easy. I want the bitch to suffer in the worst way possible."

"What way would that be?"

"You let me worry about that. You already seem to have cold feet."

"I don't have cold feet. I'm down with you for whatever. I just want to get Roscoe out of your heart. I know you're in denial and you're still in love with him." Armani knew how sensitive Infinity was when it came to Roscoe, but she wouldn't spare words about the situation. Infinity needed to move on with her life.

"Denial?" Infinity asked, fuming with anger. "I told you I'm over that no good ass nigga. I don't know why you don't believe me! Besides, you're the one that think you see Cliff's ass every time you get a Martini or two in your system. The husband that didn't want your ass, so don't get on me with no bullshit about me and mine."

Armani sighed loudly and rolled her eyes heavenward. "Maybe it is the alcohol that makes me think that I see Cliff from time to time I'll take that, but he was a huge part of my life, but, if you're not in denial then why are you still pursuing this resentment you have for this woman? It's not like it was all her fault. You know crack causes people to do many things out of character. Just like being under the influence of alcohol. You do know about that, don't you?" Armani responded.

"Don't you even breathe it. I swear you better not say it. I don't want to hear it. I can't bear to think about that. I'll tell you what you do. You just call Venom and Jazzy to make sure everything is a go for the party. Remember, don't tell Jazzy my plans. That bitch is still the police. I don't care how you look at it. Make sure you tell Venom she doesn't have to tell her girlfriend everything, no matter how good she licks her clit. I don't want any fuck-ups. We'll be heading back up I-95 North tomorrow evening." She paused briefly.

"I'll tell you, girl. It's a beautiful day in Miami today." Infinity peered into the horizon from the balcony of her hotel room. "You should've come with me. But since you didn't, I'll see you when I get there." Just as Infinity put her hand on the phone to close it she then remembered something.

"Hey!" she yelled just before Armani hung up.

"I'm still here," Armani answered.

"I only agreed to bring her to Miami because I thought it was a nice gesture. The faggot didn't do anything to me, and it gave me a chance to win her trust. Trust is the key, you know. When I get her right where I want her, kaboom!" Infinity closed her phone with a deceitful smile.

Forgetting a most important detail, Infinity redialed Armani's number.

"What, Infinity?" Armani answered after two rings.

"Did you get the ecstasy I told you to pick up?"

"Yes, I did. I bought six of them."

"Good. When I ask you for the drinks, put two in her first drink, and two when you bring the second."

"I don't know about this, Infinity," Armani said reluctantly.

"Bitch, you don't need to know about it. Just do as I tell you and don't forget to set the fuckin' cameras up. Call me back in an hour so I can get the ball rolling on his bitch, and don't be late."

Armani hung up without responding.

Chapter Two

A SCORNED WOMAN

I n the corner of her mind, Tanisha thought that if Infinity was faking at being so forgiving and kind to her, she was doing a damn good job.

Tanisha was so thankful to Infinity for agreeing to take the trip to Miami so she could pour Frenchy's ashes into Miami Beach. Frenchy was her first one true friend. The least she could do was grant her wish after her stupid ass brother, Roscoe had her body cremated. Tanisha was definitely sure Miami Beach was where Frenchy wanted to be. A year ago, she and Frenchy had one of their best times there. Frenchy did most of her shopping and met most of her down low brothers at Miami Beach. A grin spread across Tanisha's lips as thoughts of Frenchy filled her brain. She could hear Frenchy now, complaining about some clothes she had on that didn't meet her standards.

"Ms. Thang, I don't know where you think you're going dressed like that." It made her smile to still have Frenchy's footprints etched on her heart.

Overwhelmed by Frenchy's memory, Tanisha inhaled and exhaled deeply. She both loved and missed Frenchy so much, but her memory alone left her content. AIDS had taken Frenchy's body captive, and there was no escaping. She'd rather Frenchy be in heaven, free of heartache and pain, than to be on earth suffering all over again.

Tanisha glanced over at Infinity, who remained silent and gazed awkwardly ahead as if searching for a peace of mind. But maybe her observation was off and she had completely read her the wrong way. Looks could definitely deceive at times.

During the drive, Infinity claimed she took the money Jimmy Jr. gave her and made a miraculous come up. She was so nice that Tanisha couldn't believe it. Tanisha began the trip wearing a white T-shirt, blue jeans, and a pair of white Keds. But before they continued to Miami, they stopped at an outlet store and picked up some designer clothes and matching shoes. Later, the two shopped non-stop all around South Beach in designer couture boutiques until the arches in their feet were begging for a rest from the stilettos they wore.

Once the shopping spree ended, Infinity and Tanisha decided to go out and display their bikinis, trying to look cute and seductive for the deliciously attractive men that flourished in South Beach. Tanisha remembered Frenchy putting her down on the queer and down low men of South Beach a long time ago. She definitely didn't want to be fucked up with a nigga who wanted the same thing that she wanted. A good hard dick! Just watching their masculine, sculpted perfect bodies would have to do.

Along with the hot bodies, Infinity instantly fell head over heels in love with the beach. The fresh breeze blew through their hair, and the sun, which was barely shining through the swaying palm trees, thrashed warmly against their skin. They were enjoying the luxury of nature that God bestowed upon them.

"I've never enjoyed the beach like I am at this very moment," Infinity blurted as they lay out on a beach towel big enough to wrap around them three times. "This is truly relaxing. I know where to go when I want to get away from everything and everybody." Infinity exhaled, lying on her side with her cell phone beside her. She faced Tanisha while stroking her jet black wavy hair along the side of her neck. Her cell phone rang, disturbing her peaceful reflection. "Hello," she answered and listened to the caller. Then she lowered the phone and stared at Tanisha.

"This is one of my girlfriends. We're having a party this weekend. Would you like to come?" she asked, wearing a thoughtful smile.

"Of course," Tanisha responded without question. "Why not? I don't have anything else to do." An excited grin formed at the corners of her mouth. Tanisha wasn't sure where she was going after this trip anyway, considering she didn't have a place to go back to, to lay her head.

"Okay cool. I'll explain everything later," Infinity whispered and continued her call.

Infinity's behavior both puzzled and amused Tanisha. The Infinity she was dealing with now was foreign to her. Even her vernacular was different. She seemed to have changed so much from what Tanisha remembered. But if her guess was on point, this was a scorned woman reeking of a hardened heart, and trying deeply to cover it up, even when it was so transparent. Otherwise, why mention catching Roscoe cheating with a family friend, or how sexy Tanisha looked in lingerie a year ago when they first met? Why bring all of that up now? It obviously still bothered Infinity a lot more than she wanted to admit.

After their overnight rendezvous in Miami, it was time to go back to the peach state, Augusta, Georgia. Little did Tanisha know, the state of forbidden fruit had much to offer her once again.

Chapter Three
IN A NUTSHELL

I t's been said that big things come in small packages. Like Augusta, Georgia, Tanisha's hometown, a place much smaller than Miami. Augusta is home of the Master's, a prestigious golf tournament and home of the Godfather of Soul, James Brown. A two hour drive from the capital of Atlanta, Augusta is commonly called "Baby ATL." Despite its low key status, it continues to thrive. Tanisha could relate to her place of birth because despite her previous troubles, she eventually wanted her life to thrive as well. She just didn't know which step she was going to take first.

"Do you mind if we get to know each other a little better?" Infinity asked, interrupting Tanisha's thoughts as the Range Rover cruised up I-95 North. Infinity lowered the volume on the radio.

"Of course not. There's not much to know about me," Tanisha replied, giving a light shrug.

"Hmph! There's always a lot to get to know about a person. Everybody has a book of their own, a story to tell. What may not be interesting to you—" She glanced at Tanisha. "Might be interesting to the next person."

Infinity smiled.

"So what you want to know?" Tanisha looked at Infinity's side profile and fidgeted in her seat.

"Let's start with your family. If you don't mind."

"No problem. What about them?" She knew the bitch had a motive for asking. Tanisha pulled the lever on the seat of the Range like a reclining chair, awaiting to be cross examined.

"Where's your mom? Why didn't she come to your rescue when you were in the streets and on drugs?"

Damn, she got right to the point, up front and personal, Tanisha thought. "She did. But it's not like that was the first time I was out in the streets on drugs. For some reason I couldn't shake it. Once I turned to smoking crack, it was all downhill for me. It completely took over my being."

"What do you mean by that? Took over how? In what way?" Infinity bombarded her with question after question.

"I didn't know what I was doing half the time. All I wanted was that five minute high that could've cost me my life every time I went in the streets to get it. The crack controlled me so much I wouldn't dare spend a dime unless it was with a dope man. That was my mall."

"So your mom tried to help you out, but you kept going back out to smoke?" Infinity asked. "Did it ever cross your mind of the pain and anguish your mother suffered each time you went on your sprees? Worried sick about her child and wondering if you were dead or alive? Didn't you even care that she would be hurt by what you were out there doing?" Tanisha felt slightly uncomfortable, but since Infinity opened up, Tanisha thought, What the hell? What would be wrong with me opening up just a little.

"I resented my mom for a lot of things that happened to me as a child. When I needed her most I couldn't bring myself to go crawling back to her as bad as I wanted to. Shit, she didn't protect me back then, so why would I think she could protect me now?"

"Didn't protect you from what? Or who?" Infinity asked curiously.

Tanisha ignored her question.

"You don't have to answer if you don't want to," Infinity said.

Tanisha looked out of the window. "She didn't protect me from my uncle molesting me. So there you have it, all in a nutshell."

"Damn girl, you really had a hard life. I'm sorry to hear you had to go through so much." Infinity glanced over at Tanisha too long and the car veered slightly to the right and half off the road.

"Bitch, watch where you're going instead of studying me!" Tanisha said, jerking the wheel left.

"My bad," Infinity said, straightening the vehicle and focusing back on the road. Silence took over for a few minutes, but Infinity wanted to know everything about the woman sitting next to her. "Tanisha, were you afraid being out there in the streets and getting involved with different men?"

Tanisha frowned. "Hell yeah, I was afraid. At least at first I was, and then I learned the ropes." She exhaled and decided to turn up the radio to end this unwanted interview.

"Learned the ropes in what way?" Infinity turned the radio off.

Tanisha glanced out the window but spoke her heart.

"Anything you do on a daily basis can get you fucked up. Granted, some people put themselves in worse situations than others, but when it's your time to go, it's your time to go. Can't nobody predict that but God. My mentality was: Give the niggas what they want so I could get what I wanted. Everyone walks out a winner."

"That simple, huh?" Infinity tilted her head.

"Yeah, that simple," she answered, not proud of her past actions.

"You mean to tell me that all you did was suck them niggas dicks? You never fucked any of them?" Infinity pried deeper.

"Yeah, I've slept with some. Mostly, I just gave head... That's what I did best." Tanisha squirmed in her seat. "I never liked nobody penetrating me unless they had a nice sized dick. I'm just hard to please when it comes to penetration." She couldn't believe she'd just told Infinity how she got down in bed.

Infinity smiled.

"Why are you smiling?" Tanisha asked skeptically.

"It's just funny that you said that about being penetrated because I'm the same way. If the man isn't directly caressing my g-spot, I can't cum. He has to get my clitoris aroused to make me pour like Niagara Falls. I just can't cum from penetration alone."

Tanisha looked at Infinity, mildly in awe. "Damn, me too. I thought I was the only one like that. That's some crazy shit. I wonder why it happens like that? I guess it doesn't matter because I just moan and groan and act like I caught an orgasm when they start nutting." She laughed, thinking back on all the times she faked an orgasm.

"So tell me—" Infinity tried to keep her focus on the slowing cars ahead, but stole a quick glance at Tanisha.

"All the times you were out tricking . . . I'm sorry. I didn't mean to say it like that."

"That's fine. It is what it is." Tanisha didn't let her past get her emotional. *I know the bitch meant it exactly the way she said it,* she thought.

"What I was trying to say was, did you ever get horny? Regardless of what you were doing, you're still a woman."

"Mostly, I just wanted the crack, but I got head too. Other times I just masturbated and got myself off. That's the easiest thing in the world to do."

"What about Romelo? Did you just suck his dick, or did he fuck you and eat your pussy, too?" Infinity tightened her grip on the steering wheel.

Surprised by the Roscoe question, Tanisha felt this was what Infinity was getting around to all along. She didn't know what to say. "Out the middle of nowhere you ask about Roscoe. Damn, I don't mind the indirect questions, but you hit home base with this one." Tanisha crossed her arms.

"Infinity, I don't think this is a good subject for us to be talking about," Tanisha said.

"Why not? We're talking about everything else? We're both adults here. What's the problem?" Infinity shrugged.

"It's just the fact that so much happened back then. Things are going so good for us now. I don't want to spoil it by digging up old bones," she explained, hoping Infinity would give the fuck up on the questions.

"It's okay. I'm just curious about how these dirty ass niggas try to play women. For instance, Roscoe said you just sucked his dick and licked his asshole!"

Tanisha reared her head back. "You must've licked

his asshole 'cause I don't do no asshole licking. That's totally out of the question. We fucked, I sucked his dick, and he ate my pussy. I sucked his dick more than he ate my pussy, but he still did it while he was acting like he didn't know I was the same girl that sucked his dick in the alley. It was the same night I saw you at the corner of Ninth Street and Laney Walker Boulevard," she blurted without even thinking twice. "I'll be damned if I licked his asshole. Who that nigga think he is? Michael Jordan or somebody? That nigga's paper wasn't that long. Fuck that shit!"

"Damn, you sure do look different than the girl I saw that night. I remember that night like it was yesterday. You damn sure did a one-eighty, quick. You were looking like shit!" Infinity laughed.

Tanisha rolled her eyes.

"Excuse me, but girl you had it bad back then!" she joked.

"It's okay. Frenchy took me under his wing and helped me pull myself together. I take it there's a lot about your husband that you didn't know."

"Ex-husband, that is. It doesn't matter now. I'm just glad he didn't give me AIDS. All I miss from his no good ass is the way he licked my pussy and laid that pipe. I can't be mad at you. Fuck that nigga. Fuck all those niggas!" Infinity shouted out of her window, doing ninety miles an hour. She passed cars on I-95, handling the candy apple red Range Rover with snow white leather seats like it was the only car on the road.

Tanisha couldn't believe some of the things Infinity was asking her. She didn't want to seem defensive, but at the same time, she didn't want to revisit the past. For some strange reason Infinity didn't mind bringing up old bullshit. Why did she want to know how intimate Roscoe was with her? Was she searching for closure? Couldn't have been, because if that were so, she should've been questioning Roscoe, not her. After all, he was the one she married. He was the one she was fucking and sucking, not me, Tanisha thought. She guessed in the beginning, Infinity thought like her: That her beauty would keep the man in her life from going astray. When the shells were released from the eyes and reality set in, even the most naïve could see that a dog always went sniffing in somebody else's backyard. Curiosity always killed the cat.

Tanisha didn't know if Infinity got what she was looking for or something she didn't want to hear, but Infinity took the information and handled it like a real trooper. If she didn't, she sure as hell didn't let it show.

During the rest of their drive, Infinity caught her up on all of the hood and celebrity gossip. Then she said, "Out of all the head you gave, wouldn't it be better to have a man jump at your command instead?"

Tanisha's mouth turned downward. "What do you mean by that?" she asked.

"Remember the call I received while we were at the beach?" Infinity kept one hand on the steering wheel and put in Usher's CD with the other.

"Yeah, I remember."

"Some of my girlfriends and I made a pact to get together around this time of the year to do something wild and out of the ordinary. The first day of summer is the start of a new beginning, as we put it. This year we decided to have an exclusive exotic male review party to get the summer started off right! Oh yeah, baby!" Infinity ran one of her perfectly manicured hands through her hair.

"Friends? When did you get friends?" Tanisha asked with a perplexed look, not ever remembering any friends around her but Madison's stank ass.

Come to find out Infinity had met three women at the support group she attended a while back. Some people had different names for places like these. Some might even call it a house of refuge. However it went, it was a place for the battered: mentally, verbally, and physically abused women. Infinity spoke of these women like they'd created some type of bond while in treatment.

Whatever's best for you to make it 'more tolerable' to be married to a man like Roscoe, so be it, Tanisha thought.

"So, you really thought I was that big of a fool for Roscoe, huh?" Infinity laughed out loud.

Really! Not this damn Roscoe shit again, Tanisha thought. "Yeah, I did. That's what it looked like to me," she answered honestly.

"Well, mami, don't believe everything you hear. You know how the saying goes: Never let your right hand know what your left hand is doing. I'm not green by far. I knew long before JJ told me about you fucking my husband and sucking his dick what kind of man I married. I thought maybe he'd change after I forgave him the last time. He didn't change; he only got worse. Seriously, I didn't want anybody to think I knew, so it wouldn't look bad on my part. The shame of people knowing I knew would've killed me alone."

Just like you're doing to me by bringing up this same old Roscoe shit. I wish you would leave it where it belongs—in the past.

Chapter Four
PARTY TIME

T alk about a woman scorned. If somebody looked that up in the dictionary, they would find Infinity's likeness and name there. She continued her sob story about Roscoe, bringing Tanisha's mood completely down. Tanisha had, had a hard life too, but she wasn't going to keep complaining about it.

Tanisha rolled her eyes heavenward and thought of tuning Infinity out, but she couldn't help but hear her. Not even Usher's smooth voice could drown out this woman's pain. "Besides, no man gets any love from me at this point in my life. My mentality about men now is totally different than it used to be, and I'm sticking to it. I'm only out for personal gain now. That's why my girls and I get along so well. We're all on the same page." Tanisha wondered what page that was.

If it wasn't for Infinity's hair and complexion, Tanisha would swear she was just a light-skinned sistah. Her attitude and demeanor reeked "black sistah." Every now and then her accent would roll off her tongue. This had only happened once in the past.

"When do I get to meet these girls? Also, why are you being so nice to me?" Tanisha asked. She knew Infinity had to have some type of resentment on the inside.

"Hey, hey, hey, one question at a time." Infinity put

her hand up, motioning for her to stop. "It's not that I'm being so nice. I'm doing what my heart says is the right thing to do. I know men, including my ex-husband, used your weakness to their advantage to get you to do whatever they wanted. I can tell you haven't always been the type of woman to trick with men for dope. At least you took the initiative to get yourself some help. Many women these days take their anger and frustration out on the other woman. I'm woman enough to know a woman can't do anything a man doesn't want them to do and vice versa. Technically, my problem was with my husband. He knew the consequences behind his actions. That's who I handled it with. Don't get it twisted." The red hue always seemed to seep through her skin when she was getting worked up.

Tanisha couldn't believe her ears. Was this the same Infinity that slapped her in the hospital for sleeping with her husband and deceiving her all of those months?

There was complete silence for sixty seconds, then Infinity blurted, "Yeah, I may have slapped you in the hospital, but that was out of anger. I shouldn't have been mad at you about the things I already knew. My emotions were all over the place. I acted on impulse. I apologize." Infinity rubbed Tanisha's arm. The touch made her uneasy and she flinched.

Was she reading her mind? Or did that statement just come out of the middle of nowhere? Infinity really threw Tanisha for a loop. She was at a loss for words after that affirmation. Given time to collect her thoughts, she responded, "No need to ponder the past. I had that slap comin' even though it was unexpected!" Immediate laughs from both of them followed that last statement.

Infinity must have realized she was overdoing it with

the Roscoe issue because Tanisha got quiet. Infinity pushed the Kelly Rowland disc into the CD player, selected the track "Motivation" featuring Lil' Wayne and began to gyrate her hips mimicking Kelly in her video. "It's party time, girl! Are you sure that you're ready for this?" Infinity smiled at Tanisha.

"Why wouldn't I be ready? A party is a party," Tanisha responded sarcastically.

"Not the parties that my girls and I throw."

"Hold up. I hope there's no freaky shit going on."

"It depends on what you call freaky. Besides, didn't you invent freaky?" Infinity looked at Tanisha with one eyebrow raised and a silly grin on her face.

"Oh, so now you're trying to be funny."

"When we do it, we do it big! No holding back. We only have one life to live. We intend to live life to the fullest extent that life has to offer."

"I can understand that." Tanisha smiled, feeling the same way. She was down with living life to the fullest.

"You have to be down for whatever," Infinity said with a serious face.

"I am down for whatever with you," she replied like an idiot, not even knowing what she was getting herself into just so she could fit in. She only hoped that whatever it was it wouldn't be that bad. Tanisha kissed her finger, drew a cross over her heart, and silently said, "Cross my heart, hope to die. I'll prove to you that I'm loyal. If for no other reason, it'll be for giving me a second chance."

"That's what I'm talking about, mami!" Infinity's Spanish accent rolled from her tongue.

Silence again. When this happened it made Tanisha feel awkward. It left her wondering what Infinity was thinking.

"Si mi cruzas otra vex te mando a la chingada (If you cross me again, I'll fuckin' kill you!)," Infinity mumbled.

"You know I don't speak Spanish. What did you just say?" she asked, hoping she didn't say anything stupid behind her back.

Giving a mischievous, malicious smile, Infinity said, "Nothin'. I do that when I get excited."

Tanisha shook it off, but it actually aggravated the shit out of her.

After a couple more hours of driving, Tanisha began to recognize their surroundings. She noticed, Boykin Road, Tobacco Road, Pepper Ridge subdivision and then she saw Bobby Jones expressway.

"So where are we headed now?" she asked Infinity.

They had arrived back in Augusta, Georgia. It felt good to be on familiar ground.

"To my place, so we can drop off our things, get a shower and get dressed. Don't take all day. You go shower on the second floor and I'll shower on the third. You only have time for a whore shower. You do know what that is, don't you?" Infinity joked.

"Ha, ha, very funny. Yeah, I know what a whore shower is," Tanisha said, rolling her eyes.

"What is it then?" Infinity folded her arms.

"P.A.T. Pussy, armpits and titties!" She shook her head and blushed.

"Muy bien. That means very good." This was the first time Infinity ever translated Spanish to her.

Twenty minutes later, they arrived at Infinity's three-level plush home. Her house was elegant from the time Tanisha stepped foot in the door. Tanisha knew Infinity was living nice when she was with Roscoe, but not this nice living on her own. Everywhere she looked there was a plasma screen television, Italian leather couches, tropical fish tanks from small to large and fur throw rugs all over the floor. The smell of the cinnamon scented candles reminded her of the times Frenchy used to bake those succulent cinnamon rolls.

"Go on and make yourself comfortable," Infinity shouted, interrupting her thoughts. "You know I was only kidding about the whore shower, right?" Infinity asked.

"Yeah, it's cool." Tanisha waved her comment off.

She directed Tanisha to all the necessities for a shower. Tanisha headed for the second floor to get prepared. Shit, she needs to be on MTV Cribs how she's living. Everything was nice and neat, and put in its own place. Tanisha was scared to touch anything.

Once she entered the bathroom, she found twenty-four karat gold faucets and a mirror directly in front of her. Pure luxury. At first, she couldn't tell which shower she was supposed to go in. She realized one was male and the other was female, but there definitely was no sign of a man in the house. Choosing the shower on the right, it took a while for Tanisha to open the door. Finally, she pressed the flat gold buttons alongside the door and it opened. She was glad she didn't have to make a fool of herself by asking Infinity how to open the door.

Stepping into the shower, she let the warm water spray her body for a couple minutes. As the water soothed her she began to smile, thinking how happy she was to be drug-free and starting a new life. As she caressed her body with the soapy sponge, she thought about how long it had been since she had an orgasm. The thought of feeling the eruption of her inner juices was hard to resist. She couldn't help herself as she washed over her breasts, hardening her nipples. Aroused, Tanisha ran her hand across her clit, and then locked her hand there. She held her head back, winding her clit against her hand, until she could feel the little man in the boat get hard and send signals of ecstasy to her brain. Go ahead and handle your business, it urged her on. With one hand she massaged her clit and caressed her breast with the other as she squeezed her legs tightly together until she came thinking, I haven't had a good, long dick up in this pussy for a while.

The shower door slung open, startling her. Tanisha turned to see Infinity standing there with her hands on her hips. Angrily, she said, "Damn bitch, you think you Halle Berry or somebody? Look at cha'. You're going to take up more time." Infinity stared at the black bush between Tanisha's legs and kept a straight face although she was disgusted.

"Why do you say that? I'm getting out right now." Tanisha turned off the shower, fully embarrassed.

"I don't think so. Not with that hairy pussy. Let me see under your armpits," Infinity said.

Not the least bit bothered with Infinity seeing her naked, Tanisha raised her arms.

Infinity frowned and said, "I only hang with classy bitches. And bitch, right now you're showing your true color."

"What color is that?" Tanisha gave attitude.

"Straight hood rat! Let's get that bush together. You can't go out half-steppin'. The pussy has to be pretty, too," Infinity explained with a disgusted look.

This bitch is really beginning to get on my last muthafuckin' nerve. If she only knew my kettle was about to shoot off some steam.

Infinity's comment about a 'pretty pussy' made

Tanisha ask, "Why does it have to be pretty too? All the men I ever fucked with love hairy pussy." Tanisha crossed her arms.

"Well, that just goes to show you've never been with a man before."

Tanisha's old ways were about to get the best of her. She thought, This bitch is trying to make me feel inferior. At least, that's the vibe I get from what she said. She really wanted to tell her, "Your husband sure used to love to eat out this bush, bitch." Instead she said, "I've never shaved down there." Tanisha struggled to keep her cool, tightly clenching her jaws.

Infinity responded in a way she never expected. "Well, shave your underarms and I'll get down there for you."

"You'll what!" she asked with a shocked look. Is this bitch gay?

"You heard right. What? You scared?"

"No, I'm not scared. It's just a little unexpected for you to even offer to do that for me." Tanisha was completely thrown for a loop.

"We're both women. What's the big deal? I promise you no freaky shit. I'm not gay," Infinity declared.

Tanisha shaved under her arms while Infinity sat there talking to her like it was nothing. She never took her eyes off her. When Tanisha was done shaving under her arms, Infinity escorted her to her bedroom. She stretched out a jumbo size leopard Chanel towel across the red satin comforter spotted with leopard throw pillows. The king-size bed was set in a snow white, pearl marble. Infinity motioned her to lie on the towel spread across the bed.

After gradually getting over the cold feeling from the

shaving cream, Tanisha could feel Infinity's warm breath against her bare skin. She relaxed, looking around the room, enjoying the scenery of the vaulted ceilings, dimmed lights, freshly scented candles flourishing the room and the countless sex toys stacked neatly across the marbled dresser. Had Roscoe fucked with her emotions that much?

In a matter of minutes, she was done shaving Tanisha's pussy. As Tanisha stood to her feet, she could see the perfectly thin vertical line created from her pubic hairs ending at the summit of her clit.

Infinity stepped away from the bed, pressed all five of her fingers together against her lips, gently kissing them away into the air as if she were a chef just finishing a gourmet meal and said, "Eso si es una bonita panocha!"

"Come on, girl. You're doing it again. I never heard you speak this much Spanish as much as you do now."

"I guess you don't know me as well as you think you do. I told you I do that when I'm excited. I said, 'That's a pretty pussy.' You better take a second look. I should've been an artist!" Infinity joked arrogantly.

"Whatever you say. I'll let you think whatever you like." Infinity smiled at Tanisha as she walked over and started rummaging through her closet.

Tanisha returned the smile. Then she got dressed, anticipating this party.

A few minutes later, Infinity came over to Tanisha with a pair of crotchless pantyhose that she previously purchased.

"Here, put these on," Infinity instructed and forced them into Tanisha's hands.

"What the hell am I supposed to do with these?" Tanisha asked with a narrowed brow.

"Like I said before. When we party, we party. Put them on." She gave Tanisha a dental dam, and said, "You're gonna need it."

What the fuck do I need dental dam for? she thought.

Chapter Five
A NIGHT OF ECSTASY

N ot even twenty minutes from where Infinity lived, they arrived at a mini-mansion where the party was being held. Infinity and Tanisha exited the Range Rover with sleeveless designer mini dresses attacking every curve of their bodies. Tanisha turned back to look as she heard a proper woman's voice saying, "Secure Range Rover." Infinity forgot to lock the doors on the SUV. Without turning back, she threw her right hand over her left shoulder pressing down on the keyless remote with her thumb. Consecutive beeps assured the SUV was secured.

Infinity reached into her purse, pulling out a gold plated single key hanging from a chain with a picture of a woman with jet black, flawless skin, big beautiful eyes, and an Egyptian bob.

Walking up to the steps that led to the front entrance, Infinity stopped one step ahead of Tanisha and said, "Brace yourself for physical ecstasy tonight."

As the beautiful night sky complimented Infinity's body she continued to the front door shimmering like glitter. Tanisha followed her through the foyer. Above her head was a stained glass rotunda. Six-feet ahead of her was a bridge styled staircase with fifteen steps to the right and to the left.

Slowly, she trailed Infinity down the corridor. She could hear music playing by the singer Tweet. The music bounced off the walls in the house. There were no speakers anywhere in sight. The sound was clear and pleasing to the ears.

Up the stairs and to the right, Infinity pushed the first door slightly open and there stood a woman bare-skinned, winding her body to the music. She was applying glamorous glitter to her ebony skin. It was the woman on Infinity's keychain. She was in her own world. Infinity held out her hand, motioning Tanisha to stand as still as possible. Tanisha felt like a peeping Tom.

"Pay attention!" Infinity tapped her on the shoulder. The onyx skinned woman caressed herself between her thighs. Her body tensed with each stroke of her finger across her clit.

Damn, I guess I wasn't the only one feeling myself tonight, Tanisha thought, getting hot and wet just by watching her. Infinity stood there like this was a natural thing for her, as if she had no sexual feelings. She has to be feeling sumthin', unless she's turned ice cold on the inside. The woman seductively made love to herself. They could tell by her body language that she was right at the peak of reaching her climax.

Infinity interrupted. "Armani, what are you doing? We're supposed to be having a party; it looks like you're having your own party."

The woman wore a startled look. " Damn' I thought you were Cliff , you scared me."

"OMG, those damn' martini's do it every time." Infinity teased.

"Whatever, you're not going to believe me until you see him for yourself, besides can't a woman get an orgasm in her own home without being spied on? Damn!" she responded in a proper voice with sweat popping from her forehead.

"All that money you have. Can't you pay somebody to come spank that pussy for you?" She slightly chuckled.

"Of course I can, but I know exactly what I want without having to guide someone to what I need for my body."

"Okay. Whateva you say. I want you to meet my friend, Tiny. The one I've been telling you about." Infinity put her hand around Tanisha's waist, pulling her closer to Armani.

"Tiny, this is my friend, Armani." Infinity turned to her as Armani grabbed a towel and wrapped it around her body.

"Hi, I'm Armani. Please forgive me for having to meet you under these circumstances." She extended her hand to Tanisha then quickly snatched it back with a sheepish grin as she remembered what she'd just done to herself. "Some people have jokes." She glanced over at Infinity with a disappointed look. "I've heard so much about you. What is your real name, if you don't mind me asking?"

Yeah, I wonder exactly what she's heard about me, Tanisha thought. "It's Tanisha."

"Do you mind if I call you Tanisha?" Armani asked.

Infinity chimed in before Tanisha could answer. "Damn Armani, must you always be so difficult?"

Infinity turned to Tanisha. "She always wants to be different from everybody else. She thinks she's white, black as she is."

"It's okay with me. I don't mind if she calls me Tanisha. I like that better." She smiled. Armani stood between the two.

"Where's Jazzy and Venom?" Infinity asked.

"They're already getting the party started. You took forever to get here." Armani excused herself, entering the walk-in closet of her bedroom to get dressed. "You can still hear me, right?" she asked.

"Yes," Infinity said.

"Good. You're really going to love the theme of this party. I used a rainforest, jungle type of combination. It looks really sexy and exotic!"

"It better, for the money I paid," Infinity snapped.

"Please girl, you know money isn't a problem for you." Armani smacked her teeth.

"So now you're keeping tabs on my pockets?" Infinity's hands stayed glued to her hips.

"Girl, of course not. I couldn't care less about what you have in your pockets. I can't spend what's in your pockets." Armani came out of the walk-in closet dressed in an all-black tube mini-dress. She wore a diamond choker, along with a pair of peep-toe, black and silver heels. Her jet black Egyptian bob went perfectly with her ensemble. Tanisha imagined her being the spokes model for Cover Girl.

"I don't have time for this back and forth. Let's get this party started." Infinity smiled, showing all thirty-two porcelain veneers.

"Show some hospitality." Infinity glared at Armani. "Get us some drinks."

"I apologize. What would you ladies like to drink?"

"Patron," Infinity answered.

"How about you ladies follow me down to the soundproof room?" Armani walked ahead of them and went down the stairs and down a corridor.

Did this bitch just say the party is in a soundproof room? This is some freaky shit for real. Now I know these women have two damn good jobs or either somebody died leaving a smoking will, or there's some serious illegal activity going on. Whichever one it is, who am I to question? I've probably bit off more than I can chew—for real! Too late to back out now.

Armani secured the rest of the house by activating the security system. She called ahead on the house intercom and announced they were on their way. Tanisha followed her and Infinity to the back of the house and down ten steps to the left where there was a soundproof room. A woman met them at the door dressed in a leopard bunny suit with drinks in her hand. After the woman handed them the drinks with a smile, Infinity leaned over and kissed her on each cheek, but not a word left her lips. The woman turned and walked away. Her entire ass was out and her G-string was visible through her fishnet stockings. Tanisha almost choked on her drink. Infinity smiled wickedly in excitement.

The house was beautiful from the building structure to the foyer, paintings hung on the walls alongside the corridor to the bedrooms, but this room was the most extravagant. The carpeting on the floor appeared to have fresh green grass on it.

"Could you ladies remove your shoes and leave them at the door please?" the assed out lady asked. After removing their shoes, their feet sank into the plush carpet. Artificial palm trees appeared to be rooted in the grass, and the carpeted floor circled the leopard print painted walls behind the matching leather sectional couch. Where each tree stood, there was a mini waterfall next to it. Fluorescent light blue, lime and hunter green, and a touch of yellow light sparkled throughout the room. "Purple Rain" by the artist Prince boomed so loud Tanisha couldn't hear herself think, but she was enjoying the atmosphere. Just as she began to wonder where the male dancers were, two women drinking and talking amongst themselves crossed her path. One was the woman who handed Tanisha and Infinity their drinks, and the other woman had on a red thong with matching pasties. Her breasts stood at attention. Tanisha had to do a double take to see if her eyes were playing tricks on her. Infinity caught her reaction, grabbed Tanisha around the waist, and whispered, "Those are not the dancers for tonight. Don't start thinking stupid. Those are my other two friends, Jazzy and Venom. I'll introduce you to Venom later. Jazzy has to leave for work. She won't be joining us for the rest of the evening, but she'll be back for breakfast." Infinity pointed toward the woman wearing the red thong. "She just came to have a drink and spend a little time with her girl. As you can see, they're a little preoccupied." Infinity smiled. She knew exactly what Tanisha was thinking.

"Where are the male dancers?" Tanisha asked.

"Do you see where the forest trees are standing?" Infinity pointed and beckoned Armani to bring another round of drinks.

"Yeah, and?" Tanisha responded.

"Those are hidden doors. The fun part about this party is all four of us ladies get to choose our destiny tonight by choosing a door. We never get to see the men behind the doors before we choose them. What's more exciting is there are four doors and two of them have two men behind them instead of one. The lucky ladies that pick those doors get a double dose of ecstasy tonight.

"Wait a damn minute now. I'm a little confused. What the hell we gotta pick a door for? All the men are going to dance, right? Aren't we supposed to give them money?"

"Do you have any money to give them?" Infinity asked with one hand on her hip, sipping on her Patron.

"Oh, I guess now the jokes on me?" she asked, concerned with Infinity's sarcasm.

"No jokes, just the truth," Infinity replied.

"You know I don't have any money."

"Well, quit questioning everything. I asked you from the beginning were you down for whateva with me, and you said yes."

"Yeah, I did, but if a girl isn't used to something, can't she ask a question?"

Armani interrupted, giving both of them another drink.

Although Tanisha was only on her second drink, she would swear her body said it was the tenth drink. By the time she took the last sip, she didn't have a care in the world what happened from that moment on. Everything Infinity told her to do she did it with no hesitation. She felt like she was floating on a cloud or some shit.

When the party got crunk, the party got crunk! Tanisha happened to be one of the lucky ladies to pick the double dose of the night. At first she didn't know what to do with the guys she chose, so she mingled a little. She wanted to see what the other girls were getting into. The two identical six-foot tall, chocolate glasses of milk trailed right behind her.

Venom was the first person they looked in on and discovered she was the other lucky candidate with double the fun. Butt booty ass naked, Venom was taming the two men like they were wild animals. Their physiques were very pleasing to the eyes. Tanisha thought Roscoe was fine, but damn . . . She must've been blind for real. People were always saying red men weren't in any more. That was bullshit! One was packing nine and a half inches of pure hard flesh and the other was right at nine with a juicy, thick, pecan brown head on his dick that would make a woman squeeze her thighs together.

A man rushed to Venom's every command. Using her binocular vision to zero in on the action, Tanisha's pussy throbbed so intensely she thought it was her heartbeat pulsing from her crotchless pantyhose. Venom sat propped up in a chair that looked like she was about to have a pap smear in a gynecologist's office. Both legs were relaxed in stirrups and spread approximately three-feet apart. One of the men poured strawberry flavored motion lotion on her as the other guy massaged it across her body and blew gently on her skin heating up the oil, putting a deep arch in her back. Venom commanded the guy named Storm to pick up her tote bag lying on the floor at the foot of the stirrups. Then she said, "Thunder, stroke the shaft of your dick and rub my pussy gently until I tell you to stop." He nodded obediently as he got right to it.

Tanisha was stuck. She couldn't move, desperate to see what would happen next.

Her two hunks didn't complain. They were enjoying the scenery too. As the trio continued to watch, one of the twins came close up on Tanisha, pressing his rock hard penis against her butt.

Venom looked at both Storm and Thunder and said, "How much is it going to be for everything?"

"Do you want the entrée and the dessert?" Thunder

asked as he continued to caress her pussy.

"Yes, I want the full course meal and I want it right now."

"Since you put it like that, you and the rest of your friends are our number one customers. It'll be seventy-five hundred for the rest of the night," Storm said.

Tanisha thought, Holy shit! A piece of dick for seventy-five hundred dollars? Well, two dicks. . . . but still, seventy-five hundred dollars. Clearly, this is nothing new for these ladies. Infinity meant every word when she said they lived life to the fullest extent.

"Let me check these niggas out again," Tanisha mumbled, inspecting the two men. Okay, they both are red bones with sexy bodies, nice and thick and they have an exceptional piece of meat between their legs. But hell no. Fuck that shit. Seventy-five hundred dollars is too much fucking money for a piece of dick! She knew she was staying put for the rest of this high dollar freak show.

Venom agreed to Storm's fee as he stood over her and Thunder continued massaging her soaking wet pussy. Thunder thrust two fingers inside her and with every fierce push her pussy gushed as if it were kissing his fingers. Venom told Storm, "Get the dental dam and magnums from my bag." Storm obeyed and then placed the bag back on the floor. Opening the dental dam package, he walked over and stood next to Thunder still at work fingering Venom.

"We're gonna play a game of Simon says," Venom commanded. "Thunder, you can stop now. I'm going to make the night a little more interesting." She sat up and rested on her elbows.

"It's already interesting to me," Thunder responded, pushing his finger in and out once more as he licked his lips.

"Simon says?" Storm asked.

"Yes." Venom sucked her finger. "This is how the game goes. If Simon doesn't say it, don't do it. If Simon says it, you will have to change positions."

Both dancers said at the same time, "Let's get started."

Venom started the game off. " Simon says place the dental dam on the pussy." She lay with her legs spread eagle. Storm laid the dental dam gently across Venom's pussy.

"Simon says eat the pussy." Both men went down on her at the same time. Venom realized this wasn't going to work, so she got more creative with the game.

"Okay fellas, I see I've created a problem here. To be clear, I'm going to say the name of the person I'm referring to, then I'll say Simon says." The men stood there looking so delicious with their king cobra shaped chests, tightly formed abs and nice, firm asses.

"Thunder, Simon says suck on the clit like you just came out of your mother's womb, hungry as ever." Thunder kneeled down and wrapped his lips around her clit. His lips perked up and his jaws sank in with each suction. He was performing profoundly.

Venom's belly heaved up and down rapidly. She had no control. Gasping for air, Venom was finally able to say, "Storm, Simon says put on a magnum and put your dick in my mouth." Storm put the condom at the head of his dick and rolled it down, finding a snug fit. He pinched it at the top, leaving a little breathing room. He walked over to Venom, being just tall enough for her to turn her head and take his entire dick into her mouth. As wonderfully as everything was going, Tanisha didn't think an argument could occur until Storm said the wrong thing.

"Why can't I take this condom off?" He wanted to feel those bare jaws clinging to his dick.

Venom sat up and said, "I haven't seen no dick yet that will make me suck it or fuck it raw. You can either get with the program and stop fucking my night up, or you can let the door knob hit ya where the good Lord split cha. I'm the paying customer, and what I say, goes. As a matter of fact, if you plan on staying, keep your mouth closed for the rest of the night unless you're licking pussy, and let Thunder do all the talking." Venom lay back down.

Venom was definitely the right name for her. Without hesitation, Storm proceeded to go along with the game and Thunder did the talking when it was necessary.

Thunder was still eating Venom's pussy during the short intermission with her and Storm.

"Now—that we seem—to have everything—under control, let's keep the game going," Venom stated, barely able to get the words out.

Tanisha guessed Storm didn't respond since Venom told him to let Thunder do the talking for the rest of the night. This bitch is poison for real. I see why they call her Venom.

"Thunder, Simon says stop and back away from the pussy. Storm, Simon says take that condom off, put on a new one, and fuck this pussy real good." Once Storm stuck the head in, Venom went to moaning about how she loved to fuck after an argument, and how the dick was so good. At first Storm had a mean look on his face until the sudden change in his expression showed the pussy was getting really good to him. Then he started giggling.

Tanisha took a look around to see what was so funny. Venom raised her head to look at him while he was deep inside of her and trying to go deeper. She didn't know why he was giggling.

Venom said, "Storm, Simon says pull out now." Obviously, Simon's word didn't mean shit this time because Storm giggled even harder with his lips tightly closed. Storm leaned over, putting a deep hump in his back like a bobcat getting ready to strike. He put his hands underneath her ass, lifting her up as her feet came out of the stirrups, and pulled her in closer to him. Soon, Storm howled like a wolf and was cumming like rockets shooting in the air on the Fourth of July. His exhausted body dropped down on her and his head rested on her stomach until she pushed him up and out of her. Tanisha couldn't see anything but the head of his dick from where the rubber burst, and Venom's mouth was about to hit the floor in disbelief. Tanisha tried to turn briskly to walk away.

"Tanisha wait!" Venom shouted in a panic. "Come here for a minute." Tanisha went to her with a shamed look on her face from spying. She took her aside, away from all the men and said, "I knew you were standing there the whole time. I love when someone is watching, but you better not say anything about that condom bursting to Infinity and Armani."

"Girl, your business is your business," Tanisha told her.

"Tomorrow, I'll give you a token of my appreciation, so get with me on that." Venom nodded once.

"Word is bond with me. You don't have to worry," Tanisha tried to assure her.

"Well, you go and enjoy the rest of your night,"

Venom insisted, giving her a crooked smile.

Tanisha really got an eyeful tonight. It's always been said, You can never be too careful, no matter what you do in life.

Chapter Six
PLEASURE ISLAND

Since Tanisha knew what was behind door number one and two, it was time to see what was behind three and four. Yeah, she was very inquisitive, especially when she was brought into an environment not knowing what the hell was going on. Even this wasn't really telling her anything, but she did get a chance to learn a little about these woman's true character. Everything always leads to something. It just takes time. What happens in the dark comes to the light.

Instead of opening the door, Tanisha proceeded to door number four. She guessed her two hunks grew tired of walking around with a hard on and spying on everyone else, so they decided to take a break to get something to eat and drink. While her inquiring mind wanted to know what was going on behind door number four, she realized there was no sign of Infinity. Tanisha guessed she'd ditched her. It wasn't like she'd never been ditched before.

As she stood in an empty doorway, one of the twins swept her off her feet from behind. He carried her over to where the other twin was stretched out on his back and sat her directly on his face. Instantly, she went into a panic attack, blurting all sorts of things. "I don't have any money to pay you. I need my dental dam. Oh no, I'm not the customer. This isn't for me. Let me up, please." Obviously, they didn't understand no means no.

Then BAM! Magic happened. The little man in the boat had been tampered with and was ready for whateva. She didn't know if they were playing games with her or not. As soon as the little man stood at attention, twin backed off. Tanisha looked down at him with a 'what the fuck are you doing' look on her face.

"What is your name?" she asked, hoping he got back on her clit.

One twin answered. "This is Beavis and I'm Butthead!" Exploding laughter followed.

One of them replied, "I'm Hurricane and my brother's name is Tornado." Tanisha went with the flow. She had to figure out how she was going to tell the difference between the two. Hurricane didn't have an empty space on his body for anymore tattoos. Neither did Tornado, and they both had pythons hanging between their legs. As she looked closer, she recognized the city of New Orleans disaster artwork displayed on their bodies. Several names were by tombstones marked RIP.

She had to ask, "Are you guys from New Orleans?"

In unison they answered in a deep, sexy southern accent. "For sho'." Tornado let Hurricane have the conversation while he exited the room.

"I guess the tats gave it away, huh? Or was it the accent?" Hurricane grinned as he sat next to her on the couch massaging her breast with one hand and rubbing her bald, one striped pussy with the other. She didn't even understand why she sat there and let him fondle her, but she was loving every minute of it.

"No, I kinda figured by the tattoos plastered all over

your body," Tanisha said.

"All of these tattoos stand for something or somebody that was, or shall I say, is very important to us because we still hold a place in our heart for them, and their memory will live through us for as long as we have breath in our bodies," Hurricane said, full of compassion.

"May I ask you another question?" Tanisha rubbed her hand across the middle of his chest and down his left arm.

"What's that?" Hurricane asked.

"Why are you selling your body for money?"

"I knew that question was coming next. We're, and when I speak in plural tense I speak for all the guys here tonight. This money helps us to assist our families with rebuilding homes in New Orleans. After Hurricane Katrina, there are still people without a stable roof over their heads.

"We are all professional trainers by trade, but one of our guys came up with this brilliant idea to call guys to go out on dates with very wealthy women. From there, it turned into doing private parties as exotic dancers. During one of the parties, the women propositioned us to give them oral action for more money. We're all single men, so there was no harm done. We all agreed. Ever since then we don't bring in no less that fifteen-thousand for some dick."

"Damn, that must be some super dick y'all selling! You think a girl can sell some pussy for seven thousand with no strings attached. No offense, but damn y'all make some serious come ups in one night!" She had to have another drink; her mouth was as dry as cotton.

"Whatever gets the job done we're down for it. Baby girl, we were born on Pleasure Island and we know how to keep a woman on our hip. If you feel like you got some quicksand pussy, go for what you know." Hurricane kneaded her breast like dough. Tornado re-entered the room and went straight to nibbling on her feet.

"Quicksand pussy? What do you mean by that?" she slurred. She didn't know what had gotten into her, but she was horny as a muthafucka.

"Baby girl, I'm talking about that good, wet, tight pussy to make them niggas go wild when they get in it." Hurricane peered into her eyes.

"Did you say the four of you? When did the other two guys come in here? Hey! Where are you two going?" Tanisha asked when Tornado stopped kissing her toes and left the room again. She was hallucinating, seeing four guys instead of two. Her drink was getting the best of her.

"What other—" Before Hurricane could complete the sentence Tornado came walking back in with a huge piece of black plastic folded up. They both smiled at one another. Hurricane left Tanisha solo on the couch as he gave Tornado a helping hand, lying out the large plastic object he brought into the room. She grew tired of looking.

"What is that?" she asked.

"It's a bondage bed," Hurricane answered, rubbing his hands together and licking his lips like LL Cool J.

"Like I know what that is! What is it for?" Tanisha was fighting to keep her eyelids from shutting. She used her elbow as a prop to keep her head upright.

"You're about to find out in a few minutes. Wait until we get it all set up," Hurricane replied with a mannish look.

"Tell you one thing. I don't know how you're gone

get paid 'cause I don't have no damn money." That statement just slipped out of her mouth. She didn't know what she was saying. She guessed her second mind started talking for her through the crotch of her pantyhose after drinking the Patron.

"We've already been compensated for our services. All you have to do is relax and enjoy." Immediately, her little friend in the boat throbbed. The signal sent to her brain was as clear as day. I thought they were never gone get to it, said the little man in the boat. Anxiously, Tanisha waited for one of the sexy hunks to reach the center of her tootsie pop.

"Did Infinity pay you?"

"Who paid for the services is irrelevant. What's important is that you get your money's worth. And we never leave a customer without leaving a craving in their mouth for another taste," answered Tornado. He looked as if he could see straight through her with big brown eyes that could penetrate a woman's soul. Rolling his thick, pink wet tongue around his thin smooth luscious lips, Tornado beckoned her over to him with his fingers. Submissively, Tanisha went to him, impatient and eager to know what they had in store for her.

Tornado grabbed her around the waist from behind and caressed her neck with his tongue. Hurricane kneeled down in front of her, gliding his tongue slowly down the mid-section of her abdomen and down between her legs and onto her thighs, proceeding with the same level of pleasure making. Her body shuddered. Hurricane stopped and got a tight grip, wrapping his strong, sexy chocolate hands around her ankles.

Before she knew it, Tanisha was floating on thin air as if she'd just stepped out of a spaceship and on to planet

Mars. They carried her over to the bondage bed and gently placed her body onto the velvet layer. They began taking the punishment devices attached to the bed and securing her hands, legs, and waist so she wouldn't resist any sexual pleasures they had to offer. Her head spun violently, making her dizzy. Her body trembled from the sudden cold air, but then her temperature grew extremely warm and sweat beaded all over her. Her ability to speak was lost and she knew the men were unaware to the change in her that had taken place. She tried desperately to release her arms and legs from the straps, with no luck whatsoever. All she could do was listen to the water flowing and watch the room spin right before her very eyes. Although she could see and feel everything going on around her, she couldn't respond to any of it. She'd never felt like this before, not even when was smoking crack. Both men had taken total control.

Hurricane was eating her pussy like crazy. She could feel every inch of his tongue gliding across her clit again and again. He positioned the hood of her clit with his middle finger and thumb sending those signals to her brain once again. It was feeling so good. Her clit felt so much pleasure it wanted to jump from her body and start tongue kissing him. Her legs quivered as juices exploded from her pussy like opening a can of shaken beer. Moving her hips in a circular motion, her temperature rose, increasing her heart beat. She repeatedly licked and smacked her dry lips. Hurricane fiercely beat her clit with his moist, pink rattle that darted from between his lips two hundred times a minute. His tongue was persistent. The sensation hadn't yet allowed her to release the final lava from her volcano. Trying to squirm away but still wanting more, she needed him to back up just a little. As soon as his jaws slowed down and he began to take gentle licks, her pussy erupted like Mount Saint Helen. The circumference of his mouth was soaked with icing from her cake. Hurricane removed himself, changing positions with Tornado.

Tornado stood directly below her like a tamed, welled-groomed black stallion in perfect shape, staring into her dripping vagina. Both of her arms and legs were tied down, pointing in different directions. He pulled out his penis, appearing not longer than three-inches from the base to the tip. Its foundation was covered with silky jet black grass. Tornado stroked himself slowly, rubbing the head in a circular motion and gazing into her eyes waiting to enter the soft, warm, juicy, wet walls. In an instant his dick grew like the Mississippi River, leaving her wondering when the end was gonna come. The size placed fear in Tanisha's heart. She wondered where was he going to lay all that pipe. Without time to take a deep breath, the head was at her opening. He proceeded to push his way through. What a sensational feeling as he thrust the head in and out, teasing her like he was gonna give it all to her. He could tell Tanisha's body was begging for more. But she didn't want it all. Three more inches in, then four. He pulled it back out, teasing her with the head again and again. Tanisha tossed her head from side to side, moaning and purring like a cat. She breathed in and out rapidly. The freak in her no longer wore a mask; everything was out on the table. She wanted it all. She wanted to be in control. With every breath she took, her ribs showed as if a thin layer of skin covered them. Tornado rubbed the head up and down on her sensitive semi-swollen clit.

If she were standing she would've dropped to her

knees. Around and around her clit he stroked with one finger and into the door of her vagina, barely touching her g-spot, evoking an even louder moan from Tanisha. Then Tornado pushed eight and a half long hard inches of pure flesh into her. He was on her like a dog in heat. Her throbbing pussy was slippery wet; he automatically slid deeper into her. She saw the imprint of his dick at the tip of her belly button. Being a big girl, she lay there like a champ taking as much as she could possibly take. All she was able to do was look into his eyes, and moan. With one hand, Tornado wiped away the sweat pouring from his forehead and dripping onto her face as he did pushups inside her with the other. Lying his body flat on top of hers, positioning both hands behind her neck, he went deeper inside with a camel hump in his back. Tanisha felt his dick teasing her g-spot as if she had collagen in it for more sensitivity. The harder and deeper he stroked, the more she came.

A perfect stranger, she thought to herself, is making me have multiple orgasms.

Chapter Seven
WHO'S STABBING WHO?

Tanisha, wake up. Wake up. It's twelve o'clock noon time. I started to wake you when the girls and I were having breakfast, but you were sound asleep, so I decided not to bother you," replied Armani. She stood over her wearing a silk, dark brown Fendi signature scarf tied to the back of her head and the matching robe and slippers.

"Did you say twelve o'clock noon?" Tanisha rubbed her eyes, not wanting to move.

"Get up. Get your shower and get dressed, so you can join us on the patio by the pool for lunch."

"Where am I?" She slowly opened her eyes as she wiped the sleep from them.

"The same place you were last night, only a different room."

"How did I get in here?"

"You were so out of it, Infinity and I had to carry you in here and put you to bed last night."

"My goodness! I have a throbbing headache and I feel dizzy as hell. Will you get me a glass of water? It feels like I've swallowed a bag full of cotton." She smacked her lips.

"No, but I'll get you something else to drink. Cold water reactivates your high."

"What high?"

"Uh—from your alcohol consumption last night."

"Oh yeah, I'm not doing that again for a long time. This was my first time drinking liquor and getting these kinda after effects."

"First time for everything. You get showered and I'm going to fix you an old remedy my grandmother used to give my grandfather when he'd come home in the middle of the night pissy drunk, as she'd call it."

Armani left the room. It took a while, but Tanisha was finally able to gather her things. Her head still ached from front to back, so she sat for a moment until the room slowed its spinning. Armani returned ten minutes later and led Tanisha to the bathroom.

Just as Tanisha was taking a shower, someone knocked on the door.

"Who is it?" she answered. The sound of the water nearly overpowered her voice.

"It's Venom."

"Who?"

"It's Venom. I have something to give you."

"It can't wait until I get out of the shower?"

"No, because I don't want any of the other girls in my business."

"Come in." Venom couldn't take her eyes off her as she stared through the glass shower door. Tanisha stood there soaking wet from head to toe with soap suds sliding down her body.

"Damn girl, you fine as a muthafucker. Do you have implants?" Venom asked, inspecting every inch of Tanisha's body.

She turned to face Venom. "No, it's all natural, baby. Can't you tell! Did you come in here to look at my body or did you have some other reason for coming in here?"

"Do you remember last night when you were spying on me, and what happened with the stripper when the rubber came off?"

"Yeah, but like I told you, that's your business. I couldn't care less."

"I know, but I would really appreciate it if you didn't say anything to the girls, especially Infinity. They can be very judgmental at times." Venom glanced back at the door and closed it. She turned toward Tanisha.

"I'm going to take you at your word, and I'm going to compensate you for your loyalty."

A curious expression lowered Tanisha's brows and downturned her mouth. "Hold up now. I don't owe you nothing. My loyalty doesn't belong to you. I'm just giving you my word."

"Same difference."

"Not even close."

"Whatever. I don't want the girls to know I've been slippin' on my pimpin'," she whispered and took a step closer to Tanisha.

"Everybody makes mistakes sometimes, and everybody should know that," Tanisha replied, and continued lathering her body with shower cream and a loofah.

"Yeah, maybe everybody should, but if they get mad they will throw it up in my face. You don't know them like I do."

"I know Infinity, and that's all that matters."

"Oh, really?" Venom half smiled. "You never take a person at face value unless you really know them. You were fucking her husband, and trust me, she worshipped the ground he walked on. She'll never forget that. I don't care what she tells you. Do you know the saying, keep your friends close, but your enemies closer? The Bible she lives by is a book called the 48 Laws of Power. Do you know how Christians quote scriptures?"

"Yeah, your point?"

"Infinity studies that book for power, always searching for instant gratification. Her favorite part of the book is where it says, Be weary of friends, they will betray you more quickly. "In fact, you have more to fear from friends than from enemies. If you have no enemies, find a way to make them. Never put too much trust in friends. Learn to use enemies."

"And you said that to say what? I'm not Infinity's enemy." Tanisha turned off the faucets and began to reach for a towel.

"Of course you are. You slept with the one man she's loved all her life, and that alone makes you a person she knows will try to prove your loyalty by any means necessary."

"That's not true."

"Okay, you just remember this conversation we had on this day. I see you're already loyal to her, like you have something to prove. I'm going to put this purple Crown Royal bag under your towel. I'll see you down at the patio."

Eager to know what was in the purple bag, Tanisha reached for the sack before Venom was completely out of the bathroom. Dripping wet, she opened it, finding one hundred dead presidents. Venom's gotta be desperate for me to keep my mouth closed. One hundred Benjamin's that are identical. Wow! Ten thousand dollars! "Holy shit!" Tanisha shouted. Using her hand as a muzzle for her mouth, she nervously looked around the room.

Excited, but suspicious, she needed to sit and collect her thoughts about the things Venom told her. I know the bitch is poison. If she wasn't, she'd never have a name like that. But what is she trying to accomplish by dropping salt on Infinity? She already has my word. As long as she never fucks me; her secret is safe with me. Then again, Tanisha thought it could be a setup and Infinity was testing her loyalty to see if she was still up to her old tricks to get money. Or maybe it was a test to see if money would cause her to turn her back on Infinity. She didn't know which it was, but she decided to roll with the punches. Venom could be telling the truth about everything. If it was a setup, she'd have to cross that bridge when she got to it. Nobody could play the hand that had been dealt to her, not even if she showed them.

"You can't allow them whores to beat you at your own game," she whispered as she went into the bedroom and quickly put on her clothes.

Should she take the ten thousand dollars and make a run for it? Or stick around to see who was stabbing who in the back? Finally, making up her mind, Tanisha decided to join the pack of she wolves on the patio.

Chapter Eight

YOU NEVER KNOW WHO TO TRUST

T anisha could sense tension as she entered the patio that sat just above the mermaid shaped pool with a marble, aqua blue colored walkway that centered the pool leading from one end to the other. Four beautiful women sat at the oval shaped oak table having a casual country lunch catered from T-Bones.

"Hi ladies. Sorry I'm late. I hope I didn't keep you from eating," Tanisha said, looking radiant in a peach off the shoulder tailor made linen dress designed by Sergio. She joined the ladies at the table.

"No, we were just sitting here waiting on the food to get cold," Jazzy sarcastically replied.

"Excuse the hell out of me," she politely lashed back.

Armani, being the peacemaker, interrupted, "You will have to forgive her. She lets her mouth get the best of her sometimes. That's why we call her Jazzy. You're just in time for a hot lunch, and here's that drink to cure your hangover." Armani passed the glass to Tanisha.

"What's in it? It smells awful!" Tanisha sniffed the concoction and her face screwed up.

"If I tell you, I'll have to kill you." Armani smiled.

"Seriously, if I tell you what's in the glass you'll never drink it. Don't even think about it. Just turn it up until it's all gone," Armani demanded.

Turning up the glass filled with thick liquid the color of tomato paste, she grimaced. It tasted like she was sucking on a sour lemon, but worse.

"Damn girl, that dress is nice and it's fitting in all the right places," Venom said to Tanisha.

Jazzy let her jealousy get the best of her as it always did, and without notice she dashed a tall glass of juice in Venom's face. "Bitch, don't you ever disrespect me with another bitch! You talking to this bitch like you know her!" Jazzy spat.

Venom half grinned with embarrassment as she wiped the remaining juice from her face and shirt with paper towels. Infinity passed more towels across the table.

"No, baby, I don't know her. My first time seeing her was last night when we were together," Venom said to lessen Jazzy's temper tantrum.

"Together? What do you mean together?"

"I was talking about the party last night. I didn't see her anymore after that." Venom volunteered more information than she was asked. She was scared to death, not knowing if it would feed Jazzy's jealousy and give up her secret.

"So bitch, exactly what did you do last night? I knew not to leave your ass here alone."

"Hold up now. You are getting out of control. You know I don't do men, period, so you can get off that shit," Venom argued. "Now stop accusing me. By the way, I got something for you."

"I bet you do have something for me. That's all the

time when you know your ass is in hot water. What is it?"
Jazzy asked, slightly lowering her voice and glaring into
Venom's eyes.

"Tell me you love me first and apologize to these
ladies. You'll fuck up a wet dream."

"Sorry for what? I didn't do shit." Jazzy stood with
her arms clasped behind her back.

"Okay, I guess you don't want what I have for you."

"Baby, you know I love you. I just get a little jealous
sometimes." Jazzy's anger started to vanish. Venom had
a way with her.

"No, insecure is what you call it. You're forgetting
something." Venom nodded her head toward all of the
ladies.

"Okay, okay. Ladies, I apologize."

"We forgive you," Infinity and Armani chimed in as
Tanisha sat observing.

"Girl, we know about your smart ass mouth, but
everybody's not going to take your bullshit like we do.
One day, somebody's going to tap that ass. It may be one
of those girls at the jail," Infinity said.

Pulling out a small aqua box from Tiffany's, Venom
kneeled on one knee with the box in one hand and held
Jazzy's left hand in the other, looking into her eyes
without a blink. "Jasmine, I want to love you forever. For
many years of my life I've wanted somebody to love me
and somebody to love at the same level as I'm able to
love them. I want infinite peace and love in my
relationship. I've been scorned by men and I've found no
good in them. Before I met you, I'd given up on love and
happiness. When you came into my life you changed all
of that. Now I can feel my heart beat again. I want your
face to be the first thing I see in the morning and the last

thing I see when my head hits the pillow at night. I love you and will love you until the end of time if you let me." Venom opened the box, displaying a sparkling violet emerald cut five karat diamond. All the woman's eyes watered at once.

"Hell yes, I'll marry you. I love you more than words can say," Jazzy blurted as she placed both her hands on Venom cheeks, laying a kiss on her that she'd never forget.

Armani put her two cents in. "You two know I'm your friend to the end no matter what, but there's no good going to come out of this. Marriage! You've got to be kidding me."

"Armani, are you judging us? You don't have room to talk. Ever since your husband left you for a younger woman you've been committing fornication, masturbating . . . look at you. You're looking at everybody in the room like somebody told me that. I don't need rocket science to figure that shit out. I have common sense. You have to bust a nut some kind of way with your sophisticated ass. Sweep in front of your own door first. I don't see any one of us knocking you for what you do. Hell, you gotta get yours too!" Jazzy responded in an angry voice meant to cut deep and pour salt into Armani's wounds.

"Excuse me! I'm not trying to be judgmental. I just want the both of you to be happy. We've all been through so much in the past year. Maybe we're all going into a new way of life blindfolded."

"I'm not blindfolded. I know what the hell I want." Jazzy stood firm.

"If you say so," Armani replied.

"Don't knock it until you try it." Jazzy laughed. "You

jealous?"

"Sorry baby, that entrée isn't for me. You'll never catch me dropping to my knees for anything with a split in it. Never," Armani said.

"Yeah, that's what they all say. There's only two things I've never seen before and that's a UFO and a hoe that won't go."

"You know what? This is getting out of control and I refuse to sit here and keep entertaining this conversation. We're supposed to be adults." Armani heaved and rolled her eyes.

"You're right. We are. And you do have the right to your own opinion," Jazzy said.

"I know I don't have the freedom of speech to express what I'm feeling when you step on my toes. You're always so judgmental about everything and always in other people's business. Maybe if you get a life you won't have time to worry about everybody else. Everybody needs somebody and your five finger discount isn't going to always get the job done. But then again, you can pay someone to come over and fulfill your sexual desires for you, right?" Jazzy added.

"Sounds like someone is jealous because they can't afford to do it," Armani shot back.

"Like you told me, I'm your friend and I'm concerned. Whoever it is that comes over to fulfill those desires is eventually going to have to go home to their mate and where does that leave you? Back to square one. People living a life like yours only have time to pry where their opinion really isn't wanted. If I'm going to fall on my face, you're supposed to be that friend you pretend to be and catch me when I fall."

"You're right, because some people have to learn the

hard way." Armani gave Jazzy the 'take that' stare.

"Infinity, you're quiet. What do you think?" Venom asked.

"To each his own. Like I told you from the beginning of our friendship, I'm down for whatever you're down with. If you like it, I love it. Let's not make a big deal out of it. Can we sit down and enjoy our lunch? By the way, that's a bad ass diamond you bought. I love it! I can't imagine what you had to do to get it."

"What the hell you mean?" Venom wondered why the hell Infinity would make a comment like that, knowing a lot of tension rode the air.

"Don't get so defensive. You know I'm just joking," Infinity replied.

Jazzy was too heated by Armani's response to her engagement that she didn't even pay attention to Infinity's negative comment.

"So Tanisha, how was your night last night?" Infinity asked as if she really didn't know.

"I really enjoyed myself, but this feeling in my stomach won't go away. My stomach is feeling a way I've never felt before."

"What all did you do?" Infinity inquired.

"Everything everybody else did, I'm sure!" She let out a soft moan and slowly changed her position in the chair.

"Are you trying to be funny?" Infinity asked with a bit of an attitude.

"No, I'm serious. My goodness! I feel like I need to go to the hospital," she slurred. As she slouched down, her eyes began to water.

"No, no, we'll take care of you. You need to relax. Armani, take her to one of the guest rooms so she can get some rest," Infinity insisted, knowing she couldn't let her go to a hospital.

"Sure," Armani answered as she walked away leading Tanisha back into the house. She glanced back at Infinity with a worried look of guilt. They made Tanisha feel like she'd been smoking crack or something.

* * * * *

"What's up with that shit? I know y'all didn't do anything to that girl last night." Jazzy showed concern, standing there with her eyebrows slightly raised. Her cop mentality had kicked in.

"What could we have possibly done to her?" Infinity asked.

"I know how treacherous you can be when you don't like somebody," Jazzy said.

"I do like her. What do you mean?" Infinity lied.

"Yeah right. The bitch fucked your husband. I know you'll never forget that."

"No, I won't forget it, but that doesn't mean anything."

"When you get caught up, don't call me 'cause I'm not jeopardizing my job for you. What you hoes eat don't make me shit," Jazzy stated.

"Okay, okay, I just kinda, sorta told Armani to drop two ecstasy pills in her drink. Okay, both of her drinks, and we put hidden cameras in the room to videotape her fucking the men. I needed to have something on her in case she tries to fuck me twice." Infinity tried to justify her actions.

"If she does fuck you twice it's your fault. What the hell you bring her around for? You should've left well enough alone, but no, you couldn't stand the fact that she slept with your husband right under your nose."

"You're probably right. One thing is for sure though. I know she'll do anything I ask her to do," Infinity said with payback in mind.

"I see you're still living by what you call the Bible, huh?" Jazzy lifted the book from the counter.

"What do you mean living by what I call the Bible?"

"That book you live, sleep, eat, and shit by. The 48 Laws of Power." Jazzy shook the book at Infinity.

"Most of the stuff in the book is common sense," Infinity defended.

"Whatever! If that girl finds out what you did, there's no telling what she'll do," Jazzy said, referring to them possibly going to jail.

"Who's going to tell her? You?" Infinity asked.

"Don't try me. I don't have any reason to tell. If that's the case, I could book you right now just for telling me about it."

"You take that cheap paying ass job too seriously for me."

"Damn skippy! What about your job? Where you work?" Jazzy stood there waiting on an answer with her ear stuck out and one hand propped on her hip.

"I thought so. Nowhere, but you sure are living the life of the stars, aren't you? So be careful who you put down when you're on your high horse, 'cause you're guaranteed to see those same people you looked down on when you come tumbling back down on your ass."

"As you've always said. Tell me something new." Infinity sighed.

"I'm going to keep on telling you until I turn blue in the face or until it makes a difference, whichever one comes first."

"Run your life and let me run mine." Infinity got up close in Jazzy's face.

This conversation about Infinity's husband sleeping with Tanisha was like a slap in the face to Infinity. The more they discussed it the faster Infinity's heart pumped. Her belly turned somersaults and her eyes felt as if they had turned fire red. Still, she denied the pain of deception caused by Tanisha and Roscoe.

After putting Tanisha to bed, Armani entered the room and found everyone in uncomfortable positions with disturbed looks on their faces.

"Hmmm, speak of the devil and she will show her face." Jazzy smiled at Armani as she entered the room without a clue about what was going on.

"Who are you calling the devil?" Armani asked, looking at Jazzy.

"Like I've always said, hit dogs will holla! I'm talking to you."

"I thought we were through with this conversation," Armani stated. She frowned until her eyebrows kissed one another.

"Oh, it's not what you think, but your shit sure stinks now!"

"What are you talking about?" Armani turned as Infinity tried to exit the room quietly.

"Infinity, do you know what she's talking about?" Armani yelled, confused and frustrated with Jazzy talking her around in circles.

Infinity stopped in the doorway as she was about to exit the room and said, "Jazzy was concerned about what's going on with Tanisha and I told her."

"You did what? It doesn't surprise me. You're just like a broken refrigerator—you can't keep shit," Armani

64

said to Infinity.

"Why are you mad at her? Didn't you lend a hand? But you're always judging somebody else," Jazzy shouted angrily as she got in Armani's face.

Armani responded with the same attitude, chest to chest with Jazzy. "That's not the same."

"You're damn right it's not the same, it's worse. You could have killed that girl."

"I wasn't trying to kill her. She's not dead, is she?"

"Lucky for you this time. You never put something in somebody's drink without their knowledge. You don't know how other people bodies can react to certain things." Jazzy took a seat at the table.

The conversation was getting heated and out of control, leaving Armani in total disbelief.

Jazzy and Venom left Armani's home, leaving the tension between Infinity and Armani.

The two remaining ladies stood there in total silence. Infinity eased over to the table where lunch was never completed and took a seat in the tall high back oak chair where her feet barely touched the ground. She slouched down with her back facing Armani.

Armani wondered why Infinity would tell Jazzy of all people what happened. Regardless if she was a friend or not, she was still a police officer. Armani walked down to the pool side and sat beside the pool, sticking her feet in while collecting her thoughts.

Infinity gave Armani time to cool off then she went down to the pool and placed both of her hands on Armani's shoulders, massaging her, and wanting her to relax from all the chaos.

"You know I'm sorry that I let this get out of control, right?" Infinity said to Armani. "It won't happen again."

"I know you meant no harm, but I've always told you Jazzy never cared that much for me. That's why I never wanted you to tell her anything personal about me. Did you tell her anything else that happened last night?" Armani asked, looking over her shoulder as Infinity loosened up the tension in her shoulders.

"No, of course not. I would never put your business out like that. I hope that's not what you're sitting out here worried about. That's our secret."

"The thought did cross my mind," Armani replied.

She and Infinity sat beside the pool enjoying the sun and the breeze as they plotted against Tanisha while she lay fast asleep in bed.

"So Infinity, what do you plan on doing with the tape?"

"I'm unsure right now. I do believe it will come in handy in due time," Infinity responded with a vengeful look in her eyes.

Chapter Nine
THREE SIDES TO A STORY

B ack in the guest bedroom Tanisha woke up from a deep sleep, but didn't even know how she got in there. She turned over and wiped slob from her mouth, then looked around hoping nobody saw her.

After stretching and turning over flat on her back comfortably, she relaxed her hands behind her head. A tear rolled down her cheek as she thought back. Frenchy was her best friend in the world. She couldn't believe she'd lost her friend to a silent killer, AIDS. It could have easily been her.

She'd had plenty of time to rest, but still had no place of her own. The lap of luxury and no worries was soon coming to an end.

"Good morning, Tanisha," Armani said as she walked into the room. "Sleepy head, it's time to get up." Armani drew the drapes back so the sun could shine in.

Tanisha stretched out her legs and arms as she rolled over to acknowledge Armani.

"It's morning already!" She yawned.

"Yes, I came in to check on you several times last night, but you were fast asleep."

"Where's Infinity? Did she stay here last night?"

"No, she told me to call her when you woke up."

"Are you expecting her this morning?"

"Yes."

"Well, call her. I don't have anything to put on. All my clothes are still in her car," she stated in a slight panic, not knowing if Armani was being truthful or not since Venom dropped the dime on Infinity.

"Calm down. Infinity is coming, but I'm more interested in how you're feeling at the moment."

"I'm fine. I must've slept off the hangover."

"Well, that's good. If you would like to shower, I'll give you something to put on until Infinity gets here. I know you may want to freshen up.

"Thanks, I would like that." Tanisha rushed Armani off, realizing she'd fallen asleep with ten grand in a strange house that looked like a decorated mausoleum. She searched so hard, that if the money had been a snake it would've bitten her. For a moment she sat down on the edge of the bed thinking she'd been got. Then she felt something neatly tucked in her bra. The ten grand! Tanisha smiled, tickled pink on the inside for being so stupid. She undressed so she could shower.

Three knocks came at the bedroom door. Tanisha started to marvel. Was this a coincidence, or was it every time she wanted to shower someone wanted to talk? With her back to the door and nothing to hide behind she said, "Come in."

Armani entered with her eyes focused on Tanisha's body, not even conscious of where her eyes landed. "I called Infinity. She should be here in the next hour or so."

Looking back over her shoulder with an awkward look, but showing respect, she asked, "Is that all you wanted to tell me?"

"Yes and no."

"Actually, I have a few questions. Infinity told me the story of how you two met, but there's always three sides to a story."

Tanisha turned front and center so Armani could see whatever it was she came looking for.

"Yeah. Your side, Infinity's side, and the naked truth straight down the middle." Armani barely got out her words as she seemed mesmerized by Tanisha's body.

"Which version would you like to hear first? The lubricated version, or the X-rated version?" she joked with a devious smile. "I'm gonna go ahead and get into the shower."

Armani gave a confused look as she followed Tanisha to the bathroom and took a seat on the toilet. She crossed her legs, sitting with perfect posture.

Tanisha stepped into the shower and turned on the water.

"You know it's always been said, Be careful what you ask for," she shouted over the spray. Inside she giggled, still playing on Armani's intelligence. The water warmed up in seconds and she washed her face with the soapy towel. The warm water removed the suds from her face and she proceeded to wash up.

"You almost done?" Armani asked after a few minutes passed.

"Okay, seriously I'll just give you the short, clean version. I met Roscoe when I was out on the streets on drugs. At that time he was hustling on the street corner. I don't know if he had to do it like that or if he was out there just to get his dick sucked and take advantage of women that were on crack. Long story short, he propositioned me one night. I was desperate, so I went along with it." She toweled herself off.

"Roscoe dropped his pants and I dropped to my knees. I didn't know he had a wife at the time. I don't even know if it would've even mattered to me at that moment, to be honest. I was only worried about getting my high on. He then beat me out of money and made a fool out of me. When I got the opportunity to get revenge, I took it. But as it turned out, I got myself in deeper than I thought." Tanisha wrapped her body with the towel.

Armani said, "I know you had to feel like less than a woman."

"The type of man he was and his mentality at the time went hand in hand. But my friend Frenchy took me off the streets and helped me get clean and drug free. Frenchy invited me to the Players Ball in Miami and Roscoe was there. I thought he didn't recognize me, so I took advantage of that. I wanted payback, so I let him peel my peach until the juices flowed like never before. He got some good dick. I have to give props where it's due."

"Damn," Armani said, shaking her head. "I can't understand why Infinity loves him so much."

"I can. The dick is the bomb! But Roscoe was up to all types of dirty tricks. Hell, he even fucked Infinity's sister-in-law, Madison. He's a trifling ass nigga, but the time came when karma beat his door down. And I got a serious wakeup call and decided to change my life. That's why I checked myself into the rehab."

"Not all things good to you mean they are good for you. Infinity said he only wanted you around to suck his dick. She said he never slept with you," Armani instigated.

"Yeah, she would say that. That's her husband. If it wasn't for her stanking ass brother, Jimmy Jr. telling her after his precious wife crushed his heart by cheating with Roscoe, she never would've known. I can understand why everybody put everything on me."

"Hold up! Did you say Madison slept with Roscoe?" Armani asked. It finally hit her that Madison was Infinity's sister-in-law. Infinity had never mentioned Roscoe and Madison fucking around.

"Uh-huh!" Armani said, jumping up and down like a school girl.

"Yes, that's exactly what I said. I guess she didn't tell that. That's a prime example of why they try to put everything on me."

Armani looked up at Tanisha.

"I was the easy target for everyone to blame. Think about it, I was on crack and sleeping with another woman's husband right under her nose. Then it turned out my best friend was Roscoe's brother whom he denied because of his sexual preference. If they put all the blame on me then they wouldn't have to confront the problems they had long before I entered their lives. There's no telling how long Madison had been fucking Roscoe, and they treated me like shit."

Armani stared into Tanisha's mouth as if she were counting how many teeth she had, letting everything she told her register.

Tears began to drip from Tanisha's eyes.

"Why are you crying?" she asked, placing her arms around Tanisha's naked body.

"I just get a little emotional thinking about all the things I've been through and my best friend dying. I try to be strong, but when it keeps coming up, it's like a slap in my face. That's just the tip of the iceberg. I've had to deal with so much."

Armani squeezed Tanisha tightly.

Infinity walked in, halted in her six-inch stiletto tracks and retracted her neck as if she'd found them in what she mistook to be a 'compromising position.'

With one hand placed on her hip and the other slightly up against the doorjamb, she stood with one foot in front of the other, dressed like she'd just signed a contract with America's Next Top Model. "What the hell is going on here? Armani, I thought you were strictly dickly?"

"You better believe it. I haven't seen a woman yet that gets my adrenaline to rush or makes my pussy drool, "Armani responded as she removed her arms from around Tanisha.

Infinity quickly looked both ladies over. "From where I'm standing that's a weird way of consoling somebody."

"I guess that's where the saying, 'Believe none of what you hear and half of what you see,' comes from. 'Cause what you thought you saw, you didn't see. Never assume anything," Tanisha said.

"I don't know who the hell you think you're talking to," Infinity said with an attitude.

"I'm talking to you, but no harm meant by it. I was only trying to explain your misconstrued idea. If I crossed you the wrong way, I apologize." Tanisha kept it cool with Infinity, knowing she needed to get on her feet first.

Infinity and Armani exited the room so she could get dressed. She knew she had to beat them at their own game.

Chapter Ten
WHEN SHE LEAST EXPECTS IT

I nfinity lashed out repeatedly at Armani. "What the hell were you thinking? How could you turn your back on me and start sleeping with this bitch? Does this bitch have some magic potion or something? Everybody she comes into contact with wants to get down and dirty with her, including you."

Armani stood there in total awe, realizing the break up with her husband had affected her more than she could ever imagine.

Infinity's eyes roamed over Armani's body as she recalled the intimate embrace between her and Tanisha. Seeing Tanisha standing there naked and Armani's arms around her triggered a reaction. Her mind flashed to images of Tanisha and her husband in bed together.

"Armani, I'm telling you, don't bite the hand that feeds you, because everything you have is because of me, and trust and believe, I'll take it from you so fast it'll make your fuckin' head spin."

"For the hundredth time I told you, it wasn't like that and don't go throwing shit up in my face about what you've done for me because technically, you haven't done shit for free. I work for everything I get. I can understand your feelings, but you can't go around taking your anger out on everyone else. You should've left her where she was, but no, you wanted to get to know the person your husband was boning to see what she possesses that you don't."

Infinity shook her head. "No, at first I had good intentions. At least I thought I did, and then I got this weird feeling of revenge in the pit of my stomach, and I still feel the bitch needs to pay for what she did."

"I understand your anger and I understand that you're hurt, but to what lengths will you go to, to see her punished? No matter how much you do to her, it still isn't going to rid your hurt. Wounds heal in time, but the scars will always be there. I have one question for you as a friend, and please don't take it the wrong way, but your husband knew he was a married man, so why is she the one you're out to punish?"

Infinity opened her mouth to interrupt, but Armani cut her off. "I'm not justifying her role in all of this, but doesn't the problem start at home? I don't want you to get in too deep being vengeful out of anger."

"She pretended to be a friend to me. All the time she was fucking my man and making me out to be the fool," Infinity cried lightly.

"She was never your friend and you know it. Everything was based on business and you never mix business with pleasure. Everybody was out for their own personal gain, including Roscoe. A man is going to be a man regardless of what we may want. Either we have one that's going to be true to us or we learn to deal with the one we know deep down in our heart is a snake in the grass and means us no good. It's all up to us. Weren't your reasons for joining Women's Refuge to release yourself from all of this resentment and anger? I honestly thought it worked for you. You put on a good game face." Armani looked at Infinity, able to see the pain she endured from her past disappointments.

Infinity shrugged. "I guess that's what you do when you live your life with someone that wears many different masks. I adapted. My mind is made up and until I start to feel otherwise, I'm going to do what makes me feel good, and there's definitely an icebox where my heart used to be."

"And what's that? What's going to make you feel good?" Armani asked.

"To fuck Tiny up—oops I forgot you like to call the bitch Tanisha! I intend to rock that bitch's world every chance I get. I'm going to destroy her life. Fuckin' punta!"

"What good is it going to do if she doesn't know you're doing it?"

"What is this? Are you trying to play both sides of the field?" Infinity grew agitated.

"Of course not, I'm trying to make sense of all this."

"Don't worry, mami. In due time she'll know when she least expects it! Trust and believe that!" Infinity gave a curt nod.

"I guess your mind is made up then. I'm not going to stand in your way. You know we're thick as thieves." Armani didn't want Infinity to think she betrayed her.

"Now you're talking like my girl. Go see what's taking that bitch so long." Infinity rolled her eyes.

"Would that bitch be me?" Tanisha walked in on the end of Armani and Infinity's conversation.

Infinity turned and answered, "Yes, that would be you, but I didn't mean it like that."

"Oh, it's okay for you to walk in on something and take it the wrong way, but if I walk in on someone verbally assassinating my character, I'm supposed to let it roll off my back? Personally, I think people should give the respect they look for in return. What about you?" Tanisha asked.

"You're right. I never saw anybody that's so smart be so stupid," Infinity said.

"Now you're calling me stupid," Tanisha replied, bucking her eyes and poking out her chest.

"Everything you've been saying for the last three minutes isn't like that."

"What is it like then? If you have a problem with me then you need to tell me now, so we can nip this in the bud. I can go my way and you can go yours."

"It's not like that. I really like having you around. I just let my emotions get the best of me sometimes."

"Well, that makes two of us."

"I'm very territorial."

"I'm not trying to take over your territory. I hope you're not dredging up old bones?"

"No, I don't give a damn about Roscoe. I couldn't care less. It's not like he's going to mean any woman any good. He will reap what he sows."

"Yeah, we all reap the benefits of our actions, be it good or bad. All that is water under the bridge, so let's leave it there."

"I agree. Are we cool?" Infinity asked.

Tanisha smiled her agreement and gave Infinity a hug.

Armani stood back wondering how long Infinity was going to be able to keep her game face on. A very serious game of chess had begun.

Chapter Eleven
WORK HARD FOR THE MONEY

E ver since she walked in on the ass end of Armani and Infinity's conversation, Tanisha felt uncomfortable hanging around and sleeping in Infinity's house. She needed her own.

After two months of feeling like a free loader, Tanisha finally got her own apartment. Nothing too expensive, but it was home for her. The rent was $475 a month. Definitely nothing like the houses the other girls had. Two-bedrooms, one bath and a small kitchen with an eating area just big enough for her.

As Tanisha surveyed her new apartment, her cell phone rang. It was Armani asking if she wanted to go to Chocolate Castle. At first Tanisha was undecided, but then she felt that this might be just be what she needed, and in the meantime it would give her a chance to get out and have a good time.

That late evening, Tanisha stepped inside Chocolate Castle accompanied by Armani. She never thought once she stepped foot in Chocolate Castle her life would change tremendously.

Armani, already familiar with the club, escorted Tanisha over to a reserved table in the VIP section by her six foot tall, fifty-year-old Caucasian sugar daddy, Mr. Levert Langston. Mr. Langston possessed the body of a twenty-four-year-old Olympic athlete with low spiked dark brown hair. Well groomed and casually dressed to impress, he always left an after scent in his path that made women want to chase him.

As they took their seats, one of the waitresses walked over to the table wearing a thong bunny suit with fishnet pantyhose. "There's a two drink minimum, your choice," she said. Without hesitation Armani reached into her purse and ordered two double shots of Patron. Tanisha refused, motioning her hand.

"Armani, if you don't mind I'd like to purchase my drink at the bar. I'm sure that will give you time to take care of business with your sugar daddy," she whispered. Tanisha excused herself from the table with a grin and a wink. Wearing a Versace cat suit that looked painted on, she strolled across the room as if the world belonged to her. Even the glances of naked women fell on her. Taking a seat at the bar, she ordered a virgin strawberry daiquiri.

"Are you sure you don't want to live a little—maybe put a bit of spice to your life?" the bartender asked, standing there looking like Suge Knight but sounding like Tank.

The bass in his voice made Tanisha grin as she admired the bartender's appearance. "No thank you. The last time I tried to live a little, I paid for it severely with an ongoing headache and exhaustion followed by a weird feeling in the pit of my stomach."

"You appear to be a fierce woman. I know you're not scared to try something twice."

"I thought the saying was, never be afraid to try something once." She flirted back, proceeding with caution.

"So what brings a beautiful lady like you to Chocolate Castle?" He quickly removed some glasses from the bar, placing them in the small sink behind him.

"I came with a friend. Did you see one of your waiters direct us to the VIP section?"

"Yeah, I did. Can't a man try to feel a woman out first?"

"Why can't a man just be straight up when he sees something he likes."

"You could've been with LL."

"Who's LL?"

"The white dude in VIP with the woman you came in with."

"Me, with a white man? I don't think so. I don't believe in going outside my race."

"Hey, a man never knows until he asks, right? LL is a regular and he brings strong paper in for our girls just as well as his other colleagues, especially around this time of year. Excuse my French but like Jay-Z says, 'Money over bitches.'"

"I can understand that." She slowly sipped the virgin daiquiri through the straw.

The bartender stood there wearing a tight, silk white muscle shirt, black Sean John jeans and a black belt with a flamboyant silver buckle labeled SJ in cursive, observing the surroundings in the club.

"Have you ever thought about being a dancer?" he asked her.

"Are you talking to me?" Tanisha responded with a snobbish look as if she'd never done anything worse.

"Is there anybody else sitting here? I don't know why you're looking like that. Did you see how you had heads turning when you were walking over here to order your drink? Men and women."

"The thought never crossed my mind to turn and see if anyone was watching me, but if I were them I'd watch me too." She smiled.

A waitress walked over to the bar with a dozen roses and handed them to Tanisha. "A gentleman asked me to bring these over to you. He also said to tell you all your drinks for the remainder of the night are on him," she said.

"Where is he?" she asked, overwhelmed by the gesture.

"Sorry sweetie, but he paid to remain anonymous. He says he likes your style." The waitress walked away. Tanisha turned around on the barstool.

"Tell the anonymous man thank you for the roses," Tanisha called out over the music. She turned the barstool back, facing the bartender.

"I told you so."

"Told me so about what?" Tanisha couldn't stop smiling.

"You should consider working here. The men already like you. I'm sure after your audition, boss would hire you in a split second." The bartender looked her up and down.

She did need a job. She'd been looking for the past two months and nothing. Pinching off ten thousand dollars wasn't going to last long. She needed a car and had to pay to keep a roof over her head. Why not try it?

"How do you know your boss will hire me?" she asked.

"Ma, that body has serious potential. The least you'll make in one night is a grand and you don't even have to come that night if you don't want to. It's just a few simple rules to follow and the rest is a piece of cake."

"How do you know the type of dude that sent the roses wants to see me dance? He could be looking for a wife.

"Not in this club he's not. Maybe a mistress or a young tenderoni to make something stand up," the bartender replied with a smirk.

"So you wouldn't take me for a wifey?"

"I wouldn't exactly be the one you would want to ask that question." He lowered his head slightly.

"Why not?" Tanisha folded her hands and placed them on the bar.

"Because I'm strictly dickly."

"You're what?"

"Yeah, you heard me right. I'm strictly dickly."

"No, you're a down low brother is what you are, and you're a bouncer!" She looked at him with a mysterious smirk on her face.

"I'm not a down low brother. I don't exploit my business in the street, but I'm not ashamed of what I do. As for me being a bouncer, I'm still a man. I got my strength and the strength of ten more muthafuckas just like me. A brother still has to eat, don't he?" the bartender said in a deep frustrated voice.

"Calm down, I'm not discriminating against you. I was thrown by you trying to come on to me."

"I didn't try to come on to you. I was giving compliments where they were due. Being gay doesn't mean I don't have eyes to see. I can recognize a beautiful woman when I see one."

"I had a best friend die about six months ago from AIDS. He was homosexual. I miss him so much.

Sometimes I wish I could dig him up. I've never had a friend like Frenchy."

"Did you say Frenchy?" the bartender questioned.

"Yes, did you know her?"

"Did I? That was one high priced hoe! He loved all the top of the line couture clothing and could sniff out a baller from a mile away. That shit his brother pulled was real fucked up."

"How did you hear about that?"

"News travel fast, especially behind the wall. I just got outta the Feds a year ago. Talking ass Jimmy Jr. down there telling everybody business. He's still trippin' about dude boning his wife. He didn't want to tell that, but everybody knows somebody that knows something about it."

"I hate Jimmy Jr. with a passion. I'm stunned at you though; this is a small world. It's funny how we sat here and had this long conversation and don't even know one another's name."

"My name is Delicious," the bartender responded.

Shocked and tickled she responded, "You know what Cedric the Entertainer said about a man named Delicious?"

"You got jokes, huh? Maybe Cedric will find you a job as a standup comedian since you're his spokesperson."

"Delicious is my stage name. Dameon is my real name."

"That sounds more like it. Hold up. Stage name? You dance too?"

"A man has to eat, doesn't he? Now that I'm a convicted felon, I can't carry a gun anymore and I'm not trying my luck with the Feds again. This job doesn't pay as much as my previous job as a bodyguard. I guard the women to make sure the men don't do anything they aren't supposed to do to them while they're in the club. I'm gone guard your sexy body the same way when you start working."

"Who said I'm going to take the job?"

"I can see it in your eyes and hear it in your voice when you ask me all these questions."

"Anybody can ask questions. That doesn't mean they want the things they're asking the questions about." She smiled and gathered her roses. "Nice talking to you." Tanisha said and then left the bar, considering Delicious's suggestion that she dance at Chocolate Castle.

Chapter Twelve
THE AUDITION COMES FIRST

anisha headed back to VIP, but bumped into some guy she didn't see and the bouquet of roses fell from her hands. The glass vase shattered on the floor. On instant reflex the dude grabbed her to keep her from falling.

He looked at Tanisha and asked, "Are you okay?"

"No thanks to you, I'm okay," she answered.

Delicious rushed over to them. "Boss, you cool?"

"I'm cool, but as you can see the pretty lady here is upset with me. Would you see to it that she gets a fresh dozen roses? And for the next year every time she steps foot into this club her drinks are on the house," TD said. He left the bar area as quickly as he first showed up.

"I gotcha boss," Delicious replied.

"Now that you've met the boss, what do you think of him even though you were being a bit arrogant?" Delicious asked, kneeling in front of her to clean up the mess.

"It depends," Tanisha responded with her index finger on her cheek.

"On what?"

"Is he gay, too?"

Delicious smacked his lips and asked, "What does

that have to do with what you think of him? Does he look like he's gay to you?"

"Who are you to ask me a question like that? You don't look gay, but you are. Looks can be deceiving!" she lashed out, trying to get her point across.

"All bullshit aside for real. Boss isn't gay and whatever you do, don't even let him or anyone else hear you say that. You might come up missing."

"Missing? And you think I want to take a job here. Shit, what if I do something else he doesn't like?"

"Simple, you're fired. Everything is business with him. He's a ladies' man, but he always says 'Money over bitches.' TD's never found that woman whose scent stays on his dick to make him call her the next morning. They always have to call him. Then they're lucky if he cares to spend one more night with them. You saw that bling in his ear?"

"Yeah, is that supposed to mean something?"

"When he removes them, that's when he's found the woman that can get on his level."

"Like his ass is all that! I hate an arrogant ass man." Tanisha grimaced.

"He's not arrogant. Boss is just good at everything he does, including charming the panties off of beautiful women like you. All the women stay on the tip of his dick, I can tell you that. TD got that old money. He's labeled an American Gangsta and his reputation speaks for itself. Look, your girl looks like her meeting was adjourned. She's walking over this way and LL is leaving."

Tanisha turned just as Armani walked up. "Have you taken care of your business?"she asked her.

"Yes girl, that was a piece of cake. I've been giving

him the run around for a whole year now, and he still breaks me off proper. I guess conversation still rules the nation," Armani said.

"Are we going to chill here or get into something else tonight?"

"No, I need to drop you off back at your apartment. I have a few errands to run."

"What kind of errands do you have to run at this time of night?"

"Walk with me so I can speak to you in private," Armani said. She and Tanisha walked away from the bar and then sat at an empty table.

"Tanisha, I'm not trying to brush you off, but I really have business to take care of. Truth is, I can't procrastinate with LL anymore. He didn't give in this time like he usually does. He straight laid down rules. I have to comply."

"Why don't you have your own money?"

"I do, but the things I have to do to get it. . . . I'm just tired, and Infinity thinks she rules everybody she helps get on their feet."

"Infinity? Shit, I thought you two were fucking, to keep it real."

"I can't go into details, but I have to give it up to LL. Are you ready to go?"

"I think I'm going to stay here and chill with the bartender. I'll get him to take me back to my apartment. I'll call you in the morning."

"The bartender? Girl, you better bring your ass on here. I heard he's a fuckin' queer. You better be careful who you entertain!"

"Girl, you never give up, do you? First you started with Jazzy and Venom about them getting married. Now you spreading rumors and don't even have the facts. Are you homophobic or something? You better get off that high horse and stop judging other people. Here you are getting ready to go fuck your sugar daddy that I'm sure has many more women just like you, and I'm almost certain he's a married man. What does that say about you?"

Armani twisted her Coach handbag back and forth. "I'm not judging you. I wanted you to know what type of guy he is."

"I'm a big girl. I can handle myself."

"Okay. You'll call me in the morning to let me know you're okay?"

"I can do that."

"One more thing, Tanisha."

"What's that?"

"Whatever you do, don't tell Infinity I went with LL."

"Last time I looked, you were grown."

"Just don't say anything," Armani begged.

"Scouts honor. I'll call you tomorrow. Don't give Mr. Langston a heart attack," she whispered in Armani's ear. Tanisha gave her a kiss on each cheek before she exited the club.

Heading back over to the bar, she took a seat in front of her new found friend. "Delicious."

"Yeah?"

"Give me another strawberry daiquiri," she insisted. "This time make it delicious and add a little spice to it. I'm a big girl. I want to enjoy my night. I feel like the diamond princess. I'm single and on the prowl."

"Now that bitch there has a banging body," Delicious said, complimenting the rapper Trina.

"Oh yeah, so what type of scale would you put us on

from one to ten?"

"I'll give you an eight 'cause you have to step up your dressing game 'cause she got you beat."

"What the hell you expect? She's in the music industry making mad paper. Shit, she gave back the promise ring. A bitch like me would've sold it."

"You don't have to hate. Your industry is staring you in the face. All you have to do is take advantage of it."

"What industry? You?"

"No girl, the club. The kind of money you'll make here with that body, you'll be able to dress like the diamond princess. Now that's a banging ass combination! All you have to do is audition and agree to the rules. I'll guide you with everything else."

"Let me see the rules."

"Sorry baby, the audition comes first!" Delicious wiped across the bar with a white towel as he scoped out the club.

Tanisha sat there like she was contemplating her decision, but she had already made up her mind. She just didn't want to seem desperate.

"When will I be able to audition?" she asked Delicious.

"All you have to do is say the word and I'll get boss. Oh, whatever you do, don't call me Delicious around my boss. Call me Dameon."

"Your boss doesn't know either?"

"Yeah, he knows. He doesn't like to hear nobody calling me Delicious."

She laughed, pointing at him. "So boss feels the same way Cedric the Entertainer feels, huh? Most of the things the comedians be saying are true. They joke about things that happen in everyday life."

"I'm going to get boss for that audition." Delicious snapped his finger and put on his runway model walk as he turned to leave.

"Wait. Is it that simple? Where am I gone audition at?" she screamed with a nervous stomach.

"It will be on one of the smaller stages. We're going to pull the curtain around so it'll only be the four of us." Delicious took a few steps toward her.

"Wait a cotton picking minute here. The four of us will be watching you? Who are the four of us?"

"I know you're not scared to take your clothes off in front of three people when you're going to have hundreds of men and women surrounding you on a daily basis."

"I'm not scared, maybe just a little nervous."

"I tell you what. Most of the girls take about two shots of Tequila, get on that stage and give it all they got. It'll loosen up your nervousness. What about your clothes? What are you going to wear?"

"You get me those two shots of Tequila, your boss, and I will worry about the rest."

"I'll get one of the ladies to escort you to the dressing room."

Delicious went to fetch his boss and Tanisha got ready to take the stage to prove she had the potential to bring prominent customers to the club. The only thing running through her mind was being the best at whatever she did, and in time she'd get better. This was a piece of cake. Taking those two shots was going to be the hardest thing she had to do that night. After the last drink of Tequila she'd had at Armani's house the night of the party, she definitely didn't want to experience that feeling a second time, but she tried her luck anyway.

A dancer escorted her to the dressing room, holding

two shot glasses in each hand. Once inside the large brightly lit space, she set them on the table. "Drink them back to back and you'll feel confident," she advised. "The easy way to let the Tequila go down smoothly is to put salt on the back of your hand. Suck the lime, lick the salt and down the shots."

Tanisha hesitated on downing the shots. She had to get in touch with her inner self. *I'm no wuss. I've been through worse. I know I can do this.* She pumped herself up.

With salt now on the back of her right hand, she sucked the lime and almost got lock jaw. She licked the salt before downing the Tequila shots. It was time to put on a mask and wear it well. She grabbed her breast then slid her hand over her washboard abdomen, ready to make a good first impression.

Once her nerves settled, she realized she still had no outfit. She thought, *It's a good thing I wore a silver G-string underneath my cat suit to match my shoes. That's all the outfit I need. No need for a top, I'll wear my invisible bra.*

Stepping out of the cat suit, she checked her armpits to make sure the Secret deodorant she applied earlier didn't start to tell on her. Then she two fingered the little girl kept warm between her thighs and sniffed. Thank goodness, she was as fresh as Irish Spring. Tanisha took a deep breath, ready to give them a show they'd never forget! Apparently, she'd taken too long; Delicious came back to the dressing room.

"Boss is waiting and he doesn't have all day," he said to Tanisha.

"I'm coming out naked. I don't have anything to wrap around me," she answered back.

"Get one of the towels off the shelf next to the shower."

"Oh!" she said, feeling embarrassed. She grabbed the towel from the shelf and wrapped it around her body and headed out to take the stage.

Delicious stood in the doorway. "Damn, mother nature has truly blessed you."

"Delicious, what are you doing watching me? So you do like kitty cat, huh?" she joked.

He smirked. "Don't flatter yourself. I wouldn't touch you with a ten-foot pole. I waited here to see you get rid of your stage phobia."

"Yeah, that's so far behind me now. But do you think I can get one more of those shots before I go out just to knock the chills off?"

"I'll be right back. If you miss Boss tonight, you gone be assed out because he's going to take one of his girls on a seven day, six night cruise to Hawaii."

Delicious left to get that last shot and Tanisha stood there shaking her arms and legs. A few minutes later, he came rushing up to her with a shot glass. She took it to the head without any lime or salt this time. Just as her throat started to heat up from the Tequila, Delicious said, "Have you thought of a name for yourself?"

Without thinking she just said, "Shanoah."

Delicious reared his head. "Shanoah? Why Shanoah? And what does that name represent?"

With a sassy neck roll she said, "I like Shanoah. I've used that name before and it carried me a long way until I got myself caught up. But this time it's a whole different ball game. It represents the Queen of the Indian reservation. How about that!" she joked.

His right brow lowered. "Okay, whatever you say.

What song would you like the DJ to play?"

"Technology. By Fifty and Timberlake."

"You have to do a fast and slow song. What do you want the other song to be?"

"Damn, I have to go through all that? I thought you said he was going to hire me on the spot just by looking at me."

"Technically yes, but he still has to examine the merchandise. The outside in clothing may look good, but if you have stretch marks or saggy tits, that would be bad for business. The joke would be on us. This is an upscale club. Nothing but the best is allowed on stage."

"I don't need a lecture, Delicious. Play 'When a Woman's Fed Up' by R. Kelly for the slow song."

As they exited the entryway she parted her hair down the middle and braided it into two braids on each side. Delicious stopped in front of her. "Do not call me Delicious in front of TD," he reminded her.

Walking into the room filled with about ninety men and fifty women, including the dancers, chill bumps covered her body as if she'd been a cat thrown into a cage with a gang of hungry, vicious dogs. It's a good thing the stage was positioned on the right side, closest to the dressing room. She took her stance on the stage then swung the towel around her curves in a slow seductive motion. Very light on her feet she moved as if she were in a figure skating competition and every turn would determine if she'd be the one to get the gold medal that night. The music began to play. Tanisha tamed the stage and all eyes were locked on her. Even Delicious's attention was hers. She knew if she had his attention she had nothing to worry about. With much confidence she glanced over at the DJ and then TD, giving him direct eye contact. TD showed no emotion but watched her throw one leg across the other as she left the stage to caress his neat, closely shaven beard. From then on he gave every move she made his undivided attention. After mastering Fifty and Timberlake's song, Delicious walked up to her with a white towel to wipe the sweat away from her face. It was show time. Tanisha wanted so desperately to prove herself and what better theme song than "When a Woman's Fed Up!" She knew all about that and had a passion for the words in the song. Now it was her opportunity to take advantage by letting her body do the talking her heart wanted so deeply to cry out about.

Dancing in a seductive motion, she caressed her breasts, pushing them up and letting her tongue barely brush across the nipple. Forgetting all about an audience, she was into loving herself and making love to herself. The only thing missing was penetration. She caressed her entire body with both hands meeting one another in the mid-section of her back. Placing one of her Indian braids between her teeth, she turned her back to them center stage. Tanisha bent over, bringing her hands from her ankles up to her glute muscles and around her ass. One of her fingers slipped between her cheeks, catching a hold of the tiny string connected to the rest of her panties. She pulled it away from her skin and off the rest of her body. Throwing both arms into the air then letting them fall slowly until her hands rested on her neck, her body swayed back and forth from one side of the stage to the other. Watching those Beyoncé and Shakira videos really paid off. She revealed a seductive smile. Losing all control, she let her body do whatever it needed to do to get her the job. Stepping off the stage to give a table dance, she strutted over to TD like she was on the cat walk. Confidence allowed her to stand directly in front of him like a black stallion tamed to stand in position until told to move. With no reservation she rolled her belly and made her clit wink at the same time. Immediately, he pushed his chair back and excused himself. Delicious and the DJ turned to look, trying to figure out what had just happened. Delicious went after him, leaving Tanisha wondering if she'd done something distasteful. Tanisha stopped as if the music had been turned off. What had just taken place? In that instant she felt as if she was back on the block ready to sell her pussy to anyone willing to pay for it.

Chapter Thirteen
TAME THAT TONGUE

W hat could I have done that's distasteful? This is a strip club. What was he expecting? Tanisha thought.

Delicious returned. "Tanisha, go get dressed. Something came up and TD had to go handle business. He's going to hit me on the Blackberry in about fifteen minutes."

Tanisha stomped and let out a squeal. "I can't believe this, Delicious! I went through all that and he didn't have the decency to let me know if I got the job or not. Now that was a real player move." It made her feel like he had just pulled some shit Roscoe would've pulled. She stormed into the dressing room and put her clothes back on.

Totally humiliated, all she could do was take that stupid ass seat back at the bar, hoping Delicious would still take her to her apartment. She could feel the look of stupidity and humiliation ruling her face.

"Why are you looking like you just lost your best friend?" Delicious asked. If eyes could cut she would have slit his throat in two when she raised her head to respond to his question.

"How could you ask me a question like that? Maybe you're used to taking your clothes off for nothing, but where I come from there's a fee for anything you do pertaining to removing your clothing. I feel stupid and humiliated. I don't give a fuck about your boss being an American Gangsta or whatever you call him. If he doesn't have any respect for me, I don't have any respect for him. Respect is earned just in case you didn't know. Another thing, for future reference. When I do step foot back in this club if I ever do, I'll pay for my own fuckin' drinks. Now will you please take me home? After all, you influenced me to do this stupid shit."

"If I told you I would take you home that's exactly what I meant. I'm a man of my word."

"Oh, now you're a man of your word!"

"All bullshit aside. Girl, I don't know what you've been through, but I can tell it runs deep. Soon as you think your back is against the wall or the joke is on you, when it's really not, you get defensive. You need to learn how to tame that tongue."

"Yeah, yeah, yeah. It has the power of life and death in it," Tanisha added.

"Yeah, and it can build a business or tear one down as I've been told. So be quick to listen and slow to speak. I called boss. He said you were too much for him and he knows the rest of the girls are in for some serious competition because you're a bread winner for sho'."

Overjoyed, she jumped from her seat, grabbing Delicious around the neck.

"Chill out, chick. We're conducting business here," he said.

"I can't believe I got the job!" She was ecstatic. "You're not going to tell him the things I said, are you?" Tanisha held her breath waiting for him to respond.

"You don't have to worry. I won't tell him all the

slick shit you said." Delicious laughed.

"Can you promise me that?"

"No, promises are made to be broken."

"Okay, I don't mean to push. Let's talk business. When do I start?" she asked anxiously.

"There's a few things we have to go over first." Delicious fumbled through papers under the counter.

"Like what?"

"Like the rules. I'll need you to read them and if you agree to the terms, you sign and the job is yours." Delicious gave her a few sheets of paper. She began to read them one by one.

Thank you for joining Chocolate Castle.

As you know there are several clubs similar to ours in the area. However, Chocolate Castle is one of the more upscale bars and we plan to stay in business for years to some. After reading the rules and regulations set forth and you agree and wish to comply with them one hundred percent, print and sign your name and date.

Thank you for considering Chocolate Castle.
Rules:

1.Men are not allowed to touch you in an inappropriate manner.

2. Never mix business with pleasure.

3. You must be on time. If your shift is at 7:30 do not show up at 8:00 without prior notice.

4.You must work at least three nights a week, unless a doctor excuses you or some other medical condition occurs. You may switch shifts with one of the other ladies.

5. You must dance at least three rotations throughout the night. Three songs are required on main stage and one song on three of the four smaller stages.

6. Food and Beverages license along with a T.B. test is required. No exceptions. The local health department will be more than happy to assist for twenty-five dollars.

7. There will be a cover fee in the amount of seventy-five dollars per night on weekends. On weekdays you will tip out the bouncer, DJ, bartender and doorman.

8. Each song for a private dance is twenty-five dollars.

9. VIP will be seventy-five dollars plus drinks and table dances are an additional charge.

10. You will wear a thong at all times, including heels with the exception of thigh or knee high flat boots. On your third song you are to take everything off. Choose your clothing wisely, as we do aim to please here at Chocolate Castle.

11. You must be professional and carry yourself like a lady at all times.

12. If you fail to comply with these rules, you will be

fined the first and second time. If you fail to comply within a ninety-day period three times, you will then be asked to leave and cannot reapply for twelve months depending on reason for termination.

If you agree and feel you are able to comply with these rules to join our team here at Chocolate Castle, please sign.

Thank you,
Tommy Downs

*Print*_____

*Sign*_____

*Date*_____

Damn, she thought as she read over the rules. This shit seems real crazy. *All this to work in a strip joint?* But then she had to take a look around. It wasn't the average strip joint. Everything was intact and everyone was on their best behavior. It was squeaky clean and everything was well managed. For some strange reason, her gut gave her the feeling that more than clubbing was going on. One thing was for sure. If it was, the Feds would have to use a fine tooth comb to find it.

Tanisha caught herself watching TD on multiple occasions. This TD dude really had his shit together. He was the perfect business man and had such a mean swagger. TD was the type of man a woman would kill for. She wondered who his lady was, even though it was none of her business. Besides, she knew he didn't want an ex-junkie, no matter how good she performed with her clothes off. One of the rules of the club were never mix business with pleasure.

She was shaken out of her daydream by Delicious. The club was getting ready to close and he needed to make sure all the other ladies got into their vehicles safely. You never knew who was stalking who.

On the way to Tanisha's apartment, her cell phone vibrated while she and Delicious were in the middle of a deep conversation about his deceased best friend and hers. She didn't want to answer because Delicious had gotten extremely emotional about his friend and his sexual preference. He couldn't help but hear the buzzing and feel the vibration, insisting that she go ahead and answer.

The only people with her number were those cut

throat bitches, and the bad part is she didn't know who was playing who. The phone would vibrate then stop and start again. Tanisha decided to answer, wondering who was calling her at 3 a.m. that it couldn't wait until daybreak.

"Hello?" Tanisha answered, hearing someone sniffling. "Hello. Are you crying?" she asked.

"Yes," Venom answered. "I can't sleep. I've been up crying all night long."

"Where's Jazzy?"

"Working the graveyard shift."

"Call her. I'm sure she'll come home to check on you."

"That's the thing; I don't want to call her or any of the other girls."

"Why me?" Tanisha wasn't up for any tricks tonight.

"What the hell do you mean 'why you?' You're my friend, too. Besides, you already know my situation."

"Do I really? Meet me at my apartment in about twenty minutes." She couldn't turn Venom away.

"Okay, I'll see you in twenty minutes."

She hung up the phone and looked over at Delicious, hoping to continue the conversation, but that was a dead horse.

Delicious asked, "Was that the woman with LL?" He was all up in her business.

"Excuse me?" Tanisha asked.

"I'm not trying to be in your business or anything. I just wanted to know if she was okay. I'm concerned, that's all."

"Her name is Armani. No, it wasn't her. It was one of my other friends named Venom."

"Venom?" Delicious asked jerking his head in

surprised.

"Yes, Venom."

"I have a friend named Venom. That's an odd name. My girl Venom works for an escort service."

"No, that couldn't be the same person. This one is about to marry a woman, so it couldn't be her. Her fiancée wouldn't approve of that at all," Tanisha said, defending Venom's character.

"I have to agree with you on that one. Unless they have an open relationship. The woman I know doesn't date women. She's totally against bisexual relationships."

"What's the difference? She works for a call center."

"Yeah, but she only takes dates with men."

What if it is the same woman? she thought. Shit, she fucking men and her fiancée don't have a clue.

"It's funny how two people with the same name can be so different, huh? It makes you think about a lot of other things that go on in the world."

"Yeah, you're right. It really does make you think." Delicious turned up the radio.

We'll see if this is the same woman when we get to my apartment, she thought. Tanisha guided Delicious to the front of her apartment building. They sat there talking for another twenty minutes waiting for Venom to arrive. Several cars turned in, and neither of them was her.

A red convertible Mustang with black stripes down the side and tinted windows parked next to them. No one exited the car. They figured whoever was in it probably sat there talking just as they were. Tanisha grew tired of waiting on Venom. She knew Delicious had things to do besides sitting there killing time with her. Being the gentlemen he'd been since the first drink she ordered from him, he walked her safely to the door.

"Good luck working at Chocolate Castle," he said to her with a toothy grin. With that, he was off to whatever rendezvous awaited him.

Chapter Fourteen
BEST OF BOTH WORLDS

Not even five minutes after Tanisha secured her door, undressed, and headed for the shower, there was a knock at the door. She grabbed her robe, walked over and looked through the peephole, thinking Delicious had come back for something. Instead, there stood Venom with swollen red eyes, a snotty nose, and crumbled tissue in her hand.

Immediately, Tanisha removed the latches from the door to let her in. She fell dead into her arms, crying and sniffling.

"What's wrong?" Tanisha asked, closing the door with her free hand. She led Venom over to the couch. Venom laid her head in Tanisha's lap as she stroked her hair.

Now she knew this was no joke. Venom was seriously dealing with something. A few scenarios clouded her brain, but Tanisha tried her best not to think anything negative. She left Venom on the couch while retrieving a washcloth to wipe her face. By the time she returned and handed her the washcloth, she was up and ready to talk.

Wiping the tears away, Venom began to ease words

out bit by bit. She cried, "I-I-I don't know what to do. I've really messed up this time, and I don't know what to do."

Tanisha thought of the night of the party when Storm's condom burst. Did he give her an incurable disease?

Venom's sniffles and cries broke Tanisha's thoughts. "I've done many things in my life, but they never seemed to catch up with me like this. I know every dog has his day, but it isn't just about me anymore. I've brought someone else into my mess that didn't even ask to be a part of it. On top of all that, Jazzy and I are supposed to get married in three to six months. I know she loves me with all her heart, but I jumped in too fast. This life with her isn't what I want. I enjoy being with her, but it was only a fantasy I wanted to fulfill. I didn't mean for it to spiral out of control like it did. I don't want to hurt her, because I've made her so many promises that she's looking forward to."

Tanisha tried to be as objective about the situation as she possibly could, but she was dying to know what happened. Coming from her background there wasn't anything Venom could tell her that would surprise her. Tanisha responded with caution, "It's not good to make promises, but I'm sure as much as Jazzy loves you, you should be able to sit down and talk with her and tell her that marriage isn't what you want."

"It's more than not wanting to get married. It's all the lies I've told in the process. I was hurt so badly by a previous relationship, I went searching for love in all the wrong places."

Venom sniffled. "For some strange reason I prey on men. I want to punish them, or for lack of a better word, train them. Then I love to penalize them. I want to see them squirm and do whatever I want them to. I feel a certain kind of way when I'm in control. When I lose control, I feel like I've lost myself and I end up back in that position with my father's girlfriend, like she's controlling me all over again. I don't know how to shake it."

"What in the hell did your father's girlfriend do to you?" Tanisha asked as a chill ran up her spine.

"My father's girlfriend took me under her wing, gave me the world, and then snatched it right from under me when she felt it was appropriate for her to make a move. She'd lay me down and give me a pillow to cover my face so I couldn't see what she was doing and she'd tell me she had a feather. I knew what she was doing wasn't right, but I still laid there and cooperated with her. My father worshipped the ground she walked on and he could see no wrong in her and the feeling was mutual. She knew that and manipulated the situation. Me, being young, naïve and not knowing how to bring this to my father's attention, I kept quiet. Every time she said, 'I'm going to get the feather,' I knew what the protocol was." Venom started sobbing again.

Tanisha slowly shook her head, and said, "Venom what you endured as a child was not your fault. You were a helpless, naïve child. Don't beat yourself up about it."

"What's even worse is Jazzy is just as screwed up as I am. She was molested too, but her story is even more devastating than mine. That's why Jazzy desperately wants to work her way up to detective to work on cases where children have been molested or neglected in the home. She's not giving that up for anyone. She trips on me at times, but I know she loves me to death.

Everything in her life right now is going so well. And if I disappoint her she'll be devastated, but at the same time I can't make the wrong decision for myself either. I'm the one that will have to live with the decision for the rest of my life, and I don't think I can bear it."

"What is it? What could be so bad that you feel like you'll spoil her whole world?"

"I'm pregnant," Venom said almost silently. The faucet was turned on again as tears streamed quickly from Venom's eyes.

"You're what!"

"PREGNANT!"

"Are you sure?" Tanisha asked, trying see what pregnancy looked like by analyzing Venom's body.

"Yes, I'm sure. I took a home pregnancy test. As a matter of fact, I took three different kinds. They all were positive." Venom's hands shook so badly Tanisha was barely able to hold them. Tanisha had her own theory of who the father could be, but she didn't know Venom well enough to be sure. People only told what they wanted you to know.

"Who's the father?" Tanisha asked, knowing Venom was going to say Storm. She paused for a few minutes with her head down and wiped her face with the washcloth.

Ignoring Tanisha's question, Venom said, "I have a migraine headache out of this world. Do you have anything I can take for it?" She pressed her fingers to her temples.

Tanisha was pissed because she wanted to know if Storm was the daddy, and this bitch was beating around the fucking bush. She excused herself from the room to get some aspirin from the medicine cabinet. There were only two left in the bottle. Thank God.

A minute later, she returned to the living room and sat down.

"Venom, I asked you who's the father? You never answered. Do you know who it is?" She passed Venom a glass of tap water and two aspirin.

"Hell yeah, I know who the father is. What kinda question is that?"

"It's a logical question, especially being in the state of mind you're in. I'm trying to figure out why you're getting yourself so worked up because you're pregnant. Do you know how many women in this world wish they could have children that will never be able to? Do you?" Tanisha yelled. "I'm one of those women! Being on drugs and getting raped, catching a disease I'd never heard of before made me sterile. I don't even have a womb to carry one in. So you need to stop your pity party right now! I don't want to hear you weeping about something good in your life."

Venom gulped the water along with the aspirin and slammed the glass on the table. She walked over to the door and gripped the doorknob, glaring back at Tanisha. "You know something. I came over here looking for a friend to confide in. Instead of me being able to do that you're making it all about you. It's not about you tonight, bitch." She tapped her chest with a slightly curved index finger. "I'm not the reason you chose to smoke crack! I'm not the reason you can't have children! You should've taken that up with the person who caused it. I was looking for somebody to listen to me about what I'm going through at this very moment. I see that you're not that person, so I'm leaving. I'd rather go talk to a stranger on the fuckin' streets!" With that, Venom stormed out of the apartment.

Taking in her every word, Tanisha instantly felt remorse. No, it wasn't about her and the least she could do was be there for Venom because she didn't have anybody to talk to.

Tanisha raced out of the apartment and down the hall. She caught up with Venom and grabbed her arm. "Please don't go! I'm sorry for overstepping my boundaries and for making the situation about me and my past. I get very emotional and sensitive when baby conversations come up. I know I'll never be able to have one. I promise you if you stay I won't make it about me. I promise. Stay here tonight. I'll sit, listen, and talk to you for as long as you need me." Tanisha held out both arms to comfort her. Declining the offer, Venom headed back into the apartment. Tanisha followed and closed the door behind her. Venom dropped her purse on the table and fell down on her knees, crying out more.

Tanisha lowered herself to the floor next to her. Venom bawled as mucus poured from her nose and threatened to seep into her mouth. Tanisha took the cloth from her hands and wiped her face.

"No, I don't know," Venom cried.

"No, you don't know what?" Tanisha asked as she stroked her hair.

"No, I don't know who's the father of this baby," she screamed.

Tanisha was almost certain the father was Storm. She guessed Venom must have been having unprotected sex with other men. Tanisha felt like she was walking on eggshells with her. She didn't want to say anything to make Venom shut down.

"Do you have any idea who it could be? If so, we

could narrow it down," she asked in a gentle voice.

"Yeah, I have three men to choose from." Venom sniffled.

"Is Storm one of them?"

"Yes!"

"Who are the other two?"

"A man named Levert Langston, and the other man's name is Morgan Mims. The only problem is that those two are married. I don't know if they'll even take a DNA test."

Two crazy things crossed Tanisha's mind for real now. She knew the world wasn't so big that there were two Levert Langstons roaming their small town and preying on young women. Unless there was a Jr. and a Sr. Could it really be the same Levert Langston from the club that Armani is dating? she pondered.

"Tanisha." Venom tapped her shoulder. "Where were you?"

"I'm sorry, I was thinking about something," she replied. "No need to worry about them volunteering to do a paternity test. It's simple, the way they do paternity test these days. I'm sure we can get it done without them even knowing."

"How is that?" Venom asked, eager to find out.

"Girl, technology is a muthafucka these days. Use your big head for thinking more often. A little research is all we have to do."

"What kind of research?"

"Research on how we can determine paternity without the father. Don't you watch all those cop TV shows like Law and Order and CSI where they take hair and saliva to determine DNA?"

"I prefer to watch The Wire and Desperate

Housewives." Venom smiled.

"Is that a smile I see on that pretty face? I haven't seen an inch of a smile all night. Excuse me, I meant all morning!" she joked.

That was the first breakthrough she'd seen since Venom walked through the door.

"If we are able to determine paternity without the men knowing, what difference is it going to make? You still have to tell Jazzy. That's the person you asked to marry. You do remember her, don't you?"

"That's the problem. I don't know how or if I'll be able to tell her."

Tanisha frowned. "You have to go home and in a few months your stomach will show."

"What if I decide to abort the baby?" Venom asked.

Tanisha wondered if she was saying this out of desperation and was totally against it. "Is that something you really want to do?"

"Not really, I just don't want to make a fool out of myself. I've bragged so much about not doing men. Now this shit has some back to bite me."

"Regardless of all that, the way I see it is if you do decide to abort the baby because you're worried about someone else's feelings, you'll be terribly sorry in the end. The baby growing inside of you didn't ask to be conceived. That's a life inside of you. Do you realize that? You've already made yourself look like a fool. It may not be out for the naked eye of others to see, but you'll know, and that's just like being in the closet. The bad thing about this is the only one that's going to suffer in the end is you. How did this happen? Do you have unprotected sex with every man you lay down with?"

"It's a long story that I don't care to discuss at the

moment," Venom said.

Venom's pregnancy was a touchy subject and the morning was still young, considering all that was going on. Tanisha stood and went to look out the front window of her apartment. While surveying the parking lot, she realized Venom's car wasn't there.

"Venom, if you don't mind me asking. How did you get here? I don't see your car outside," Tanisha asked.

"My car may not be out there, but the car I drove is out there."

"What car?"

"The red Mustang."

"That Mustang pulled up when I was sitting out there with my friend that gave me a ride home."

"Would that friend's name be Dameon?"

"Yeah, his name is Dameon. How do you know him?" Tanisha turned to look back at Venom.

"We work together."

"At Chocolate Castle?" she guessed. All she had to do was put two and two together from the earlier conversation she had with Delicious.

"No, we work for the same call center."

"Why didn't you say anything while he was out there?" Tanisha joined Venom on the sofa.

"I didn't want him to see me looking like this. My business isn't everybody's business. Dameon doesn't know that I date women."

"Why are you hiding your relationship with Jazzy if you're not ashamed of what you're doing?"

"I'm not ashamed. I just want the best of both worlds. I bet you want to know why I chose to work for a call center, too. Don't you?" Venom asked sarcastically.

"You took the words right out of my mouth." Tanisha

stared into her eyes.

"It's not your average call center. It's much more to it than sex talk and going out to eat as a companion. I chose it because of the money. I don't want to live in poverty."

"Nobody wants to live in poverty, Venom."

With dry eyes Venom stated, "I want to be able to go in stores and buy whatever I want, and I want to be able to bring something to the table when Jazzy and I get married."

"Oh, so we're back on that again?"

"Enough about me. What were you doing with Dameon?"

"I met him at Chocolate Castle tonight and he influenced me to get a job there. I've searched high and low with no luck until tonight."

"Was this your first time going to Chocolate Castle?"

"Yeah, I went with Armani," she responded before thinking. Armani asked her not to tell any of the girls.

"Armani? What the hell was she doing there?" Venom asked, looking bewildered.

"Don't ask me any questions and I won't tell you no lies." Tanisha quickly tried to cut the conversation about Armani short.

Venom stared at Tanisha as if more information was available. To no avail. Tanisha wasn't about to give up any more details than she already had.

Chapter Fifteen
RECOGNIZE GAME

Since Venom couldn't get anything out of her about Armani, she focused the topic back on Tanisha. "Tell me how Dameon got you to work at Chocolate Castle, out of all places." Venom asked.

"He said I could make lots of money." Tanisha gave a slight shrug.

"You know you have to do an audition, right?"

"You're late. I've already done it."

"Yeah. So you've met the boss then? Ain't TD finer than a muthafucka, girl?" Venom licked her lips and nudged Tanisha's arm.

"Yeah, but he's kinda scary at the same time, too. You never know what he's thinking. The expression on his face never changes."

"I don't give a damn about his expression. He's fine as shit and he's got that old paper. Girl, do you hear me? Your girl loves him to death."

"Who?" Tanisha asked, lowering her eyebrows.

"Infinity. Oh yeah, baby. If it's any man she wants to be with, she has her eyes feasted on him," Venom said, dramatically moving her neck from side to side.

"Really!" Tanisha smiled.

"Talk is, she does business with him or for him. I'm not sure. That's just a rumor I heard."

"So you're passing rumors about your friend now?"

"Damn, don't get so defensive about another bitch. Everybody passes rumors once in their life. How do you think word gets around? There's always some truth to them. . . . Hmmph!" she said, snapping her fingers. "I told you that you were loyal. She'll have you on a leash before you know it."

"Yeah, some rumors do have truth to them, but you're a damn lie about me being on a leash." She leaped up and stared angrily at Venom.

"Did you ever ask Infinity about the rumors?" Tanisha asked since Infinity had told her she wasn't ready for a relationship right now.

"Hell no, girl. I'm not getting into that girl's business like that. I'm in enough hot water of my own. I'll tell you what. She's not living like she's working a nine to five. Not even a job paying a hundred thousand a year without taking out taxes could cover her lavish living." Venom turned her lips up.

"I didn't hear anything about him and drugs. I only heard he was a heavy gambler."

"Well, damn girl. They don't have to say anything about drugs and TD in the same sentence. When they refer to him as an American Gangsta, that's enough! Don't you watch TV? They have a series that comes on once a week on Thursday night. That's all it talks about, old gangstas and their life in the drug game. Stop being so naïve. I can't believe you've been on the street and you still can't recognize game," Venom replied.

"It's not that I don't recognize game; I didn't think like that because I was distracted by other things."

"Being distracted by other things can get you killed, too, if you're not paying attention to your surroundings.

Being in the streets isn't the only place where you have to pay attention to game," Venom retorted.

"From now on, I will pay more attention. The last thing I want to do is get caught slipping."

Venom and Tanisha talked at length about everything under the sun, from relationships to how many men they'd been intimate with. Venom's number was unbelievable and she'd never smoked crack. Tanisha thought she had got down and dirty with men, but Venom left her in the dust. She assumed it was why she took to her so well instead of the other girls. Then she began to get extremely open when she told Tanisha she had a sex addiction and just wanted to get down and dirty with any and everybody she came in contact with, male and female. Tanisha thought back to when Venom came into the shower on her. Maybe she wanted her, too.

The sun began to shine through the window. Venom's eyes were bloodshot from crying and Tanisha was tired as hell, yawning and trying hard to keep her eyes and ears open for Venom.

Morning came and there was a knock at the door. The first thought that came to Tanisha's mind was it's one of the other girls. Venom lay there sound asleep. Tanisha looked over at Venom, not wanting to wake her so early. She definitely didn't want the other girls to know she was there. Quietly, she walked over and peeped out the peephole. A man dressed in a brown UPS uniform held a big box neatly wrapped with a big red bow on it. Her first thought was, He must really have the wrong door, unless Infinity sent her something.

Curious, Tanisha opened the door. "May I help you?" she asked softly.

"Are you the owner of this apartment?" the gentlemen

asked.

"Yes, I am. How may I help you?"

He extended his arms to hand her the wrapped box. "This is for you," he responded.

"For me? Are you sure?" She hesitated taking the package.

"If you're the owner of this apartment, I'm sure. If you're not, then we have a problem. But by the looks of it and the way the guy described you, he was dead on point."

What guy? she thought as she opened the door just enough for him to slide it inside of the door. He started to walk away without her signing anything until she stopped him. "Hey, wait. Do I have to sign anything?" she asked.

He stopped in his tracks and turned to face her. "Why would you have to sign anything?"

"Don't you work for UPS?"

"Yes ma'am, but this delivery didn't come from the company I work for."

Now she was puzzled. "Well, where did it come from?"

"I was making a delivery in the area and a man walked up to me and offered me money to deliver the box. He said he wanted to surprise you. He gave me your apartment number and described you to me. I didn't see any harm, so I decided to do it for the two hundred dollars he offered me."

"What did he look like?"

"I can't remember. He was a black man though."

The gentleman began to walk off as she still tried to question him. "Do you know how many black men there are in the world? Give me more info," she begged. The man walked away with his hand thrown up in the air, refusing to tell her anything else.

Tanisha cursed and slammed the door. Shit, what if it had been a bomb? Would he have delivered that too? She was pissed.

Her inquisitiveness dissolved her anger pretty quickly. She was eager to know what was wrapped in the box. This was the second time in two days she'd been surprised by someone. She didn't know if she should have been happy or what. It could have been a secret admirer or a stalker. At this point it didn't matter.

Tearing into the package, she was overwhelmed to find a sixty-inch plasma flat screen. She couldn't believe it. She had to wake Venom up.

She hurried over to Venom and shook her. "Venom, Venom, wake up!"

"Huh!" She jumped out of her sleep alarmed and confused. She slowly scanned the quarters and slid her dress strap back up on her shoulder. Is there something wrong? What time is it?" she responded in a deep throaty tone.

"Girl, fuck the time. You are not going to believe what just happened."

"Try me. I know it better be good the way you scared the hell out me when you woke me up."

"Girl, look at this!" Tanisha pointed to the TV leaning up against the wall. "A guy from UPS just delivered it and the weird part about it was, the person that asked him to deliver it didn't go to UPS; he met him in the parking lot and gave him two hundred dollars. The guy gave a clear description of me and my apartment number."

"Damn girl, who did you fuck last night?"

"Why did I have to fuck somebody to get something nice? It's not always about giving up the pussy. At least I see that now."

"Well, that's you. I love to fuck. I can't live without it."

"No, you're a nymphomaniac."

"Tell me something I don't know, and I've taken every group session I could find for addicts of all kinds to get help. All the classes in the world are not going to help me."

"If you knew this, why would you try to commit to marriage? "Do you think that would be fair to the person you're involved with? You say they love you for you, but in all realization they don't know who they're really sleeping with?"

"Maybe I won't get married." Venom lay on the floor looking up into the ceiling and wagging her legs side to side. "When I get to be an old lady, I'll start fucking niggas twenty years younger than me!" She laughed, then popped Tanisha on the leg.

Tanisha shook her head in disgust.

"I'm just kidding, girl. You thought I was serious, didn't you?"

"These days I don't know if you're joking or not. I see you have your sense of humor back, but you better fuck safely so you can live to be an old lady. Or you won't be fucking nobody."

"Look who's talking."

"I know I've had my share of men. It's better to be careful when you get a second chance. Now I take the necessary precautions. After my friend Frenchy died, that was an eye opener for me."

"I feel you, girl, but back to this plasma. Who do you think sent it?" Venom asked, straight cutting her conversation.

"I have no clue." Tanisha shrugged.

"Let's just pray he's not a stalker. One thing's for sure, he has to really like you."

"I have to admit, it's kinda exciting to have a secret admirer." She grinned.

"Yeah, it is. Girl, I'm happy for you."

"Enough about me and this mystery man. I'm sure he'll soon show his face because he's not giving gifts for free. What about you? What are you going to do about the baby?"

"I have plenty of time to decide. When I figure it all out you'll be the first to know. Meanwhile, keep it between me and you."

"You don't have to worry about me like I told you before. Now can I get an installment?"

"What installment?"

"I thought I was gone get another ten grand."

"You're serious?" Venom asked.

"No girl, I'm just kidding, but I do need a favor."

"Anything, if I can do it."

"I need a car to get back and forth to work. Will you take me to a few used car dealerships. I've got twenty-five hundred to spend on a little bucket to get me from point A to B."

"I can do that. Let me run down to my car to get my overnight bag. I need to take a shower." She slowly stood from the floor and stretched.

"Do you go everywhere with an overnight bag?" Tanisha asked, confused about her lifestyle. "Where does Jazzy think you are when you're out all the time?"

"That's the good part. She works the graveyard shift mostly, so I don't have to worry. I just press *72 and transfer the house phone to my cell like I never left home."

"You got it together, don't you? I hope it doesn't blow up in your face."

Chapter Sixteen
TAKING CARE OF BUSINESS

V enom and Tanisha went to five different used car dealerships before finding a reasonable dealer that wasn't trying to sell her a lemon and overcharge her for it.

From the highway road Venom saw a sexy young brother showing a young couple a used Maxima. Tanisha could tell by the look in Venom's eyes and the way her conversation stopped that her clit jumped at first sight. She's such a ho, Tanisha thought.

They pulled into the car lot, exited the Mustang and while Tanisha looked around, Venom interrupted the salesman's conversation with the young couple. After talking to him for a few minutes she found Tanisha looking in the window of a used Ford Taurus.

"Which car do you want?" she asked her. "The dealership belongs to dude's father and I promise you can get whatever car you want for fifteen hundred."

"Really?" Tanisha asked with hopeful eyes. She didn't have anything to lose and didn't want to cut the other people out of getting the car they wanted, but she really wanted the Maxima. It was the nicest and newest looking car out there.

"Yes, really. Be right back," Venom said.

Tanisha observed while Venom jumped into action.

She switched her way back over to the salesman and whispered in his ear; the salesman blushed. From Tanisha's view, Venom was working him good. The car dealer looked like he wanted to purr as Venom stroked his back. He walked over to the couple he was previously showing the Maxima and concocted a story because the couple left looking disappointed. When he announced that he was closing for the day, Tanisha knew Venom had some freaky shit up her sleeve.

"Gimme the fifteen hundred and point out the car you want," Venom told her.

Tanisha gave her the money and pointed to the Maxima. "Okay, now go sit in the car and wait until I'm done."

Twenty minutes had passed and Tanisha thought Venom was never going to come out of that building. She nodded off, woke up and Venom still hadn't returned. Just as she was about to go check on her, Venom came walking out the door smiling and directing her to come inside.

"It took you long enough. Girl, you ain't shit."

"You need to sign the papers and pay a twenty-five dollar title and tag fee."

"You really are something else," Tanisha said with her hand on her hip.

"Girl, fuck that shit. I saw something I liked, so I went for it. You wanted the car, didn't you? So don't give me no lip. I'll tell you all about it in the car. People buying plasma and shit, the nigga should've bought your ass a car. Let's get these papers signed so we can bounce," Venom whispered.

Tanisha didn't have any room to argue with her. She

wanted the car.

After Tanisha looked over the paperwork she noticed the amount of the car was still showing $4,500. But the salesman also had a receipt ready after she signed the papers and got her set of keys. He also asked if she'd like to leave the car to get a tune up and oil change. Tanisha agreed and decided she and Venom would go and eat while the car was being serviced.

They went to Red Lobster for lunch.

As soon as their appetizers were brought to the table, Tanisha was bursting with curiosity. "Girl, I tried not to ask you any details, and you're just sitting there getting off on me wanting to know."

Venom sat across the table from her looking like she was on cloud nine. "I'm not trippin' off you wanting to know. I'm just enjoying my pussy still throbbing, girl. OMG! I wish I could put your hand inside of me so you can feel what I'm feeling. My clitoris is so sensitive right now. All I have to do is squeeze my legs together and I'll start cummin' all over again. You feel me, girl?"

"I can't even believe you had sex with him in that office."

"Girl, fucking in places like that is when it's good. It's like you're stealing it. Dick is sooo good when it's not yours. I can't help it, girl."

"Did you use a condom?"

"Yeah, but I should've had him take it off, then I could have put the baby on him." Tanisha gave her a 'you need to stop it' look.

"Girl, lighten up a little. Where's your sense of humor?" Venom tilted her head.

"Stop playing so much. Just tell me what happened." Tanisha grabbed a cheddar bay biscuit.

"Girl, I just walked up and asked him how long it's been since he's had a good wet pussy that kisses his dick and sucks it at the same time? Soon as I whispered that in his ear, I stuck my tongue in his ear and blew on it. The bulge in his pants grew and I knew I had him. That nigga weak as water. He asked me what I wanted because he knew I wanted something. I told him I wanted the Maxima. He asked was I gone pay up front. I told him I stay ready. That's when he closed shop and we took care of business. I had to show him what to do with all that dick he got."

Smiling and sitting up straight she asked, "What else happened? I told you I want all the details."

"Are you sure? You might want him to fuck you after I tell you about this good young dick I just had." Venom's face was lit up like a Christmas tree.

"Girl, stop fucking around and tell me, damn."

"When I went in his office he locked the door and threw everything off his desk on the floor. He picked me up and sat me on the desk. Girl, before I knew it my pussy was already wet. He gently pushed me down on the desk. I pulled my skirt up and he moved my panties to the side and unzipped his pants, letting the python escape through the hole in his boxers. He took his hand and rubbed it across my clit, fascinated at the size of it. Fat and juicy . . . Shoot, Jazzy sucks on it every chance she gets."

Frowning, Tanisha announced, "Too much information. Can you finish telling me the story?"

"Okay, okay. He stroked the shaft of his penis while watching me stroke my clit. Juices ran from my vagina down between my butt cheeks. I scooted back so he could get a good view. He pulled out a condom and put it on his penis. Instead of fucking me, he got down on his knees and lightly beat his tongue against my clit. Then he pushed one of his fingers inside me, searching for my g-spot. I moaned and groaned. The more I moaned the more excited he got. Men love it when you make noise. Girl, my pussy was so wet. I know he was dying to dive inside to fuck me good. The more he caressed my clit with his tongue, the harder his dick got. My tongue traced my lips every time I threw my pussy back into his face. Then that unexplainable feeling started coming into my body. I rode his face like a cowgirl. The feeling got more intense. I grinded his mouth like a big dick was inside me. I couldn't help myself. I wanted to keep holding his head, but my clit got so sensitive my instant reaction was to back away, knowing I wanted to stay right underneath his tongue and those sexy lips. I tried to squirm away, but he grabbed me around the waist so I couldn't get loose. All I could say was, 'That's enough, that's enough, please stop. I came already.' But he kept eating my pussy, saying he was gone get his money's worth. I didn't know what I got myself into, girl."

Tanisha's eyes widened as she reflected on a similar escapade with Roscoe at the Sheraton hotel.

"Girl, then he moved his head from between my legs, still gripping me around the waist with one arm and stroking his penis from the bottom of the shaft to the tip of the head with the other hand. Girl, for the first five minutes he kept his head down watching his flesh enter mine. When the head went in, I almost had a panic attack. I could've let him fall asleep inside me, wake up, and start hitting it all over again. It felt so good, girl. If he would have stuck his dick in the ground, all the dirt would separate! He turned me over on my stomach and the side of my face was pressed against the desk. He started slow rolling inside of me and talking to me simultaneously." Venom danced in her seat.

"What was he saying, girl? You can't stop there." Tanisha wanted to hear more.

"I wasn't gone stop. I was just thinking hard about it. Damn, he was good. As I'm telling you the story, I swear it seems like it's happening all over again. Girl, with my face pressed up against the desk, I could feel slob running out my mouth and I didn't care. I looked back and he had one hand pressing the lower part of my back, and the other one on his hip slowly grinding inside me, ricocheting from one wet wall to another. His conversation and thrusts was turning me on more and more. I moaned louder so he could keep talking. With each moan, he'd say, 'Owwwww shitttt, this pussy good. I can't hold out no longer.' He was at his peak.

"I begged him not to cum and stay inside me. He said, 'I'm trying, but this pussy good. Shit!' Sweat poured from his face. Then he screamed, 'Shit, shit, it's cummin'.' With his jaws locked tight and eyes almost closed, he pulled me all the way back to the edge of the desk with the heel of my shoes placed firmly on the floor, and my legs spread apart. He penetrated me harder and faster from that point, gripping me around each hip to keep his balance and me in position. I was throwing it back to him like he bought it for the duration. He moaned really loud. I could feel the throbbing sensation inside of me like something was gonna explode. Trying to keep his mind focused so he wouldn't get soft, he wanted to lay inside me. I told him no, I had to leave. He pulled out, turned me over and kissed my clit. He put two fingers inside me once more, then looked at me and shook his head as he sucked his two fingers."

"You didn't even wash yourself." Tanisha frowned.

"I almost forgot; that's the funny part. He gave me a bottle of Aquafina water. Girl, and some wet wipes. Now that was funny as hell. I couldn't even say nothing."

"I guessed right. A nasty fucker! Then he gone hand me a pen to sign some papers," Tanisha griped.

"You should've come to watch. You know I don't mind!" Venom smiled wickedly.

Tanisha felt the stares of other customers aimed at them. "You should see the way the people behind us are looking. It's obvious they can hear you."

Venom turned, glaring at the other customers. "Damn, everybody's looking like they've never had great sex before and for those of you that haven't, maybe you need to try it. Great sex is what always keeps your man or woman from wandering the streets looking for somebody else to give them what they aren't getting at home."

"Venom! Turn your ass back around. Please," Tanisha begged. Venom went on asking other customers if they were a couple or were they out cheating on the people they went home to every night. The people didn't respond but sat there staring as Venom made a fool out of herself. Like, who is this crazy bitch looking at? Venom's cell phone started ringing. She glanced at it and almost went into panic mode.

"It's Jazzy. Shit! I don't even know what to say." The phone rang about seven times. Venom looked at Tanisha as if she'd already pressed the talk button. "Be quiet!" she said.

"Hey baby!" she answered. Tanisha couldn't hear what Jazzy was saying, but she did know Venom was lying her ass off.

"No, I ordered some food from Red Lobster and I'm about to pick it up. No, you don't have to meet me. I want to eat at home. . . . Just tell me what you want and I'll bring it with me. Why do you always want me to repeat something back to you? Yes, I can remember." Venom laughed and repeated Jazzy's order. "Okay, you said a Caesar salad, three pounds of crab legs, a shrimp trio with double fried shrimp and one order of shrimp scampi. I told you I'd remember." Venom must have forgotten one thing, but she cleaned it up pretty quickly. "Don't worry about no dessert, you not gone have room for it when I'm finished with you. I'm all the dessert you gone need." That was the end of that conversation.

Before Venom hung up the phone, she blew Jazzy a kiss like she hadn't just finished having sex with somebody else.

"I know what that means," Tanisha said to Venom."You've gotta go check in with momma."

She rolled her eyes, pouted and said "Tiny, I need to drop you back off at the dealership to pick up your car. I gotta go. I'll tell the waitress to get the food ready to go while I place an order for Jazzy."

"That's fine, but could you do me a favor and don't call me Tiny anymore. Call me Tanisha!"

"No problem, Tanisha!" Venom rolled her neck.

Chapter Seventeen
DOING HER OWN THANG

For Tanisha, it had been an extremely long afternoon. Venom dropped her off back at the dealership to pick up her car. She had a few more papers to sign before leaving with the vehicle. "Excuse me, do you mind if I ask you a question about your girl?" the salesman asked Tanisha.

"It depends on what you wanna know?" Tanisha looked up from signing the papers, then looked back down.

"What's her name?" he asked.

"Whatever she told you her name was." Tanisha smiled as her signature began to dry on the dotted lines.

"She never told me." He eyed Tanisha.

"Well, I can't help you." Tanisha giggled as she passed him the papers. She couldn't believe they fucked and he didn't even know her name.

Wannabe slick muthafucka really tried to play me stupid, Tanisha thought. Still, she couldn't give him any information because she didn't know if Venom wanted him on her jock like that. He played stupid and so did she. Tanisha took his information and told him she'd be sure Venom got it. How the fuck you sell a car and don't know who you selling it to? she thought. Damn, you gotta be careful fucking these nasty ass niggas. They'll do anything for a piece of ass.

She got in her car just in the nick of time. Tanisha almost forgot she needed her driver's license and TB test for the club. Tonight was going to be her first night officially working. Damn, I have to get some fresh gear, too, so I can be the hottest thing working the pole! She wanted all the men to sit there and imagine being inside of her and only her. She had to get as much money out of them as quickly as possible because nothing lasts forever. She loved the thought of having her own shit. The way she saw it, it was every woman for herself. Tanisha knew it was going to be some serious cut throat bitches lurking around. If this was what she had to do to get shit, then she had to have a plan. Every bitch gotta crawl before she walks, she thought. But she wouldn't have minded going from crawling to running!

A shrill ring killed her thoughts.

"Where the hell is my phone? I know I hear it ringing," she said aloud. After searching the front seat, she placed her hand on the phone on the side of the seat near the seatbelt.

"Hello?" she finally answered.

"Girl, what you doing? I've been trying to get in touch with you," Infinity said.

"That's funny you say that. This is the first time my phone has rung all day." This bitch really trying to play me and I'm starting to see just what Venom meant. But I'm gone give the bitch enough rope to hang herself. If she fucks around and brings out the old me, that's her ass for real. Fake ass hoe!

"Girl, I'm on my way to the Health Department," Tanisha said.

"Who you been fucking?" Infinity responded, trying

to be funny.

Tanisha started to get slick with the bitch and say "If I got it, you got it, as much as your husband slept in this pussy." But she kept cool though, as always.

"Why is it every time somebody go to the Health Department people like yourself automatically assume the negative? If you must know, I have to get a TB test for my new job."

"New job?" Infinity asked in an obviously disappointed voice.

"At Chocolate Castle."

"Chocolate Castle?"

"Yes, Chocolate Castle. Is there a problem with it?"

"No, you just caught me off guard."

"Why? You didn't think I had sense enough to try to fend for myself?"

"No, that's not it at all. I was calling you to get on with me. You could make more money than you do in that stupid ass club. You don't have to take your clothes off. Didn't you tell me you were tired of taking your clothes off? What's the difference in what you're doing now and what you've been wanting to put behind you?"

"There's a big difference. I'm not fucking for it. I'm entertaining and I don't see anything wrong with it."

"Okay, you're grown. You make your own decisions. I hope it doesn't blow up in your face."

"If it does, which it won't, I'm a big girl. I can handle myself."

Infinity turned the entire conversation around, but Tanisha cut her off every chance she got.

"So how are you getting around?" Infinity asked.

"Oh, I didn't tell you. I have my own car now. It's used, but it's mine," Tanisha said, dying for Infinity to ask her how she got it.

"Did somebody give you one?" Infinity asked.

"To be honest with you, I was so desperate to get a car, I went back to my old ways for just twenty minutes."

"What you mean 'back to your old ways?'"

"You know . . ." Tanisha derived this crazy story about selling her pussy in exchange for a car from some random guy she'd met at the gas station. The last thing she told Infinity was, "You taught me to shave my pussy for it to be pleasing to the eyes. Girl, that's the best thing you could have done."

Infinity went silent and Tanisha was shocked that she still held the phone through the entire story. She didn't know if Infinity believed her or not, but that was the only explanation she was getting out of her. Tanisha's granny taught her to tell people only what she wanted them to know. Especially if she didn't know if they had her back one hundred percent.

"Infinity, you there?" Tanisha asked, giggling to herself.

"I'm here, girl. You're wild. Are you serious? Did you do that for real?" Tanisha could tell by Infinity's voice that she didn't like what she told her, but in turn she played on Infinity's intelligence like she often tried to do to her.

"You think I'm lying. I got the car and the title to prove it. . . . SHIT!"

"What? What's wrong?"

"I almost ran dead into the car in front of me. I'm gone have to call you back before I wreck some shit." Tanisha's cocky attitude told her she didn't need Infinity any more. She was doing her own thang from now on.

"Okay, but you can't call me back. I'm out of the

States. I decided to take a vacation with a friend."

"Wait a minute. Is this friend a guy?"

"Why would you ask me that?"

"Because you told me it was going to be a while before you date again."

"I gotta go. I'll talk to you in six days. Bye."

"Wait!"

Infinity hung up the phone leaving her in suspense.

Now Tanisha knew two plus two equaled four. And she could be wrong, but her instincts were telling her that Infinity wasn't alone on her trip. Delicious said his boss was taking his girl on a seven day cruise and Venom said Infinity and TD were connected in some kind of way. She didn't know if she had something here or not, but she wasn't gonna let it take up too much space in her brain, especially when it didn't benefit her.

Whatever!

Chapter Eighteen
ONE CAN NEVER BE TOO CAREFUL.

Fifteen minutes later, Tanisha walked into the Health Department and was surprised to see a familiar face. She never guessed this person would be sitting in the Health Department. Should I go over and show my face or act like I don't see her? she wondered.

Tanisha decided to go take care of her business first and if she was still there, then she'd go over to see if there was anything she could do.

Twenty-five minutes later, she was all done and the lady was still sitting in the same spot. If Tanisha hadn't looked closely, she wouldn't even have known it was her sitting there reading a newspaper. Like it was nothing, she walked over and tapped her on the shoulder. The woman was startled and gasped. Tanisha could tell she wasn't too jaunty to see her. A black ring marred her eye and the swelling in the middle of her face made her look like Rocky after a boxing match.

"What are you doing here?" Tanisha grabbed the bottom of her chin to get a good look at her face. "Who did this to you?" she asked with concern.

Armani gently pushed her hand away as tears filled her eyes and threatened to fall.

Tanisha and Armani detoured to the nearest restroom, walking down the long hallway covered with white tiled floors. Armani's head rested on Tanisha's shoulder and Tanisha wrapped her arm around Armani's back, comforting her.

When they entered the restroom, Armani leaned against the wall and stared into the mirror. She smiled, but it wasn't the usual happy-go-lucky smile. It was more of an 'I can't believe this happened to me' smile.

"After the monster wined and dined me, we retired for the night in an elegant suite filled with roses where he had a hot bath already waiting on me. I was very well pleased. While I was in the hot tub, he began washing my back and caressing my breasts at the same time. I just held my head back and enjoyed the pampering. He laid a rug at my feet for me to exit the hot tub so he could dry every inch of my body. All I had to do was stand there.

"He placed a robe around me and took me onto the veranda. The stars in the sky were so beautiful. He rocked me back and forth with him holding me close from behind. From that very moment, I felt like I was beginning to fall in love all over again after I thought it would never be possible. I took it so hard when my husband, Cliff left me for a younger woman. But anyway, I was so relaxed that he could do anything to me and I'd easily let it happen."

"Wow Armani, that sounds beautiful," Tanisha said solemnly.

"Never did I think I was in for the shock of my life. Once we were in the bedroom, he pushed me down to the bed still fully dressed in his suit, climbed on top of me and pushed his tongue down my throat. He tied my arms to the bedpost and that's where the night took a turn for

136

the worse." Tears flowed freely down Armani's face. Tanisha grabbed more tissue for herself and Armani. Armani took the tissue and tried to smile.

"He placed his hand around my jaws. The more he kissed me, the more aggressive he got. I asked him to stop. He laughed even louder. I told him it wasn't funny.

"He unleashed his belt buckle and released his filthy, uncircumcised dick from his pants and rubbed it across my lips. I cried because I was afraid. I fought with my legs, but it only made him more angry. He ripped the spread from the bed and pulled the sheets from underneath me and tied my legs down. He shoved his dick in my mouth and said, "Suck it, bitch!" As I was sucking his dick, he told me I better not let one tooth touch it or he'd kill me. I was gagging; he pushed deeper into my mouth as if he had his dick inside somebody's pussy. When he finished jacking off on my face, he rubbed the sperm with his fingers and shoved them in my mouth.

"In an instant he turned into a total maniac. He slapped me and punched me in my ribs. I thought he was going to kill me. That first hit swelled my face instantly. He called me a nasty, filthy, dirty bitch. A diseased, infested ass whore. He said his wife filed for divorce because he contracted a disease from me and gave it to her. But I never even slept with him unprotected. How in the hell did I give his sorry uncircumcised ass a disease?" she whined. "I wouldn't dare let him stick that in me without a condom. I think he needed somebody to blame and he chose me. Finally he untied me and just left me there. I was so overwhelmed and terrified, and when morning came I exited out the back entrance of the hotel."

"Did you call the police?" Tanisha questioned, but Armani ignored her.

"Girl, I know I didn't give him no damn disease, but I felt it necessary to come get checked so I could be sure." Armani tried to fix her hair in the mirror.

Tanisha stood with her arms folded, angry at Armani's attacker. "So you've told me the story, but you never mentioned who did it. Who did this to you?"

"Who was the last person you left me with?" Armani asked, avoiding Tanisha's eyes.

"Are you talking about back at the club?" Tanisha asked.

"Yes, and I can't stand to mention his name."

"Levert Langston? The clean cut white guy?"

Armani nodded yes. She dried her tears with a wet paper towel.

"I hope the police are looking for his ass, so they can smoke him like a cheap cigar." Armani gave her a shallow look.

"I know damn well that look doesn't mean you gone let his buster ass get away with this shit? Have you taken a good look in the mirror?" She pushed Armani close up to the mirror.

Armani lowered her head then turned to Tanisha.

"Okay, Tina Turner, or do you wanna be Anna Mae Bullock? Take your pick. Look how long she put up with Ike's abuse trying to save face," Tanisha said, hoping she was convincing enough that Armani would press charges against Levert Langston.

In a pleading voice similar to a five-year-old little girl, Armani begged, "Tanisha, please, let's keep this strictly between you and me."

"I won't tell this to a soul. If anybody finds out,

you'll be the one to tell them. Now let's go get these tests run, so you can find out the results. I'm gone spend the remainder of the day with you. That is, if you want company."

"I thought tonight was gone be my first night at work, but I can't get the results back from my TB test for forty-eight hours. I'm a free spirit until then."

Armani gave a grateful smile through her sore cheeks. "I would love for you to spend the rest of the day and night with me if you don't have other engagements."

"Even if I did, I would put them all aside for you because right now I can see that you really need a friend."

Armani hugged Tanisha. They returned to the waiting area and waited for the nurse. When Armani was called to the triage area, she asked the nurse to test her for every disease under the sun, including HIV. Tanisha decided to get tested also. One can never be too careful.

Seven days later, both Armani and Tanisha's test came back negative.

Tanisha stayed with Armani for the entire seven days, comforting her and trying to get the swelling on her face to go down. She enjoyed staying in Armani's home. She probably would've stayed just on GP if she'd asked, but Tanisha was sincere about everything she'd done for Armani while she was there. She hadn't thought twice about her job, which was a stupid move to begin with because she wasn't going to be the one to take care of her if Tanisha got thrown out on her ass. There's nothing like having your own. Even if it's a hut with the bedroom and bathroom all in one. She couldn't take that for granted.

While checking her voice mail, she counted ten messages left by Delicious. She hadn't bothered to answer the phone, dodging him because she didn't know what to say. Her phone rang and it was Delicious. She sat there staring at the phone. She let it ring until he got the answering machine. Tanisha was so relieved when she checked that last message. She didn't think she'd be as happy to check her messages all week. She listened to Delicious' voice. "Tanisha, I know you received all my messages. This is my last one. Boss is gone be at the club tonight. I can cover for you for all the days you've already missed. If you don't make it tonight you won't have a job at Chocolate Castle. I really thought you wanted the job after all the shit you talked. Call me."

As soon as she finished listening to his voice, she built up the nerve to call him. She was nervous to hear what he had to say, but at least she knew she still had a job, so it didn't matter.

Delicious answered without giving her a chance to say anything. "Girl, I know you heard all my messages on your answering machine and you've been dodging me. This is not the way you handle business. I know this is a strip club, but you're supposed to treat it just like a regular job and respect it. You didn't have the decency to call me to give notice." Delicious sounded disappointed.

"I've been—" Just when Tanisha wanted to lie, Delicious cut her off.

"Don't say nothing. Let me finish. I know after you take a TB test it only takes forty-eight hours to get the results back. What's your excuse? Don't come at me with no bullshit."

"I don't know what's been wrong with my phone. I probably didn't have a signal," she lied.

"If you didn't have a signal, how did you get my message this time?" Delicious wasn't biting.

"Shit, you tell me. I heard it ringing; voice mail

picked up before I could get it. That's why I called you right back."

"No, you called me right back because I told you, you still had your job and this was your last chance. Are you comin' in tonight or what? We're really gone need you because one of the girls called in sick. There's going to be plenty of ballers tonight with big money and they go bananas for women. They're like virgins all over again every time they come in."

"I promise you I'll be there."

"Don't make me no promise. Your word is fine with me. By the way, you gone have to learn to trust somebody. I'm not the enemy."

"I know you're not. Thanks a lot for everything."

"Tanisha, one more thing. Don't give me no more bullshit about not having a signal on that phone." Delicious said his peace and hung up the phone.

Tanisha could tell he didn't like the way she handled things. He appeared to be a pretty straight up guy. Maybe now he'd have to second guess everything she said. That old saying came into her mind: When you lose someone's trust in you, you'll have to jump hurdles to get it back, if ever.

Tanisha knocked on Armani's room door to check in on her before she left.

"Come in!" Armani was laid up in her large king-size bed covered with blue satin sheets and the comforter to match, watching Lifetime.

"I came to see how you were resting," Tanisha said.

"You've been taking care of me for the past week. You need your rest," Armani replied.

"Speaking of getting rest. If I don't go to work tonight, I'll be getting lots of rest. Without a home to rest in."

"Yes, you never told me where you're working at."

"At Chocolate Castle."

"Were you ashamed to tell me that?"

"Of course not. You had your own problems to worry about. My job wasn't important at the time."

"Oh okay, I was about to say don't ever do anything you're ashamed of doing. It's not a good feeling."

"You're talking like you're doing something you're ashamed of."

"It's not that I'm ashamed. I don't feel it's the right thing for me to be doing."

"Well, why do it?" Tanisha wondered what Armani was talking about.

"I don't have a choice at this point in my life. I'm in over my head trying to maintain my household and my lifestyle, which can't be managed by a regular job. On top of all that, when I got into all this, I gave Infinity my word that she could call on me at any time. Besides, when I started throwing hints that I didn't want to do it anymore she started tripping and throwing up all the things she'd done for me trying to make me feel guilty. I'm tired and I'm scared, but I don't want to keep on doing what makes her happy. That was my reason for messing around with Levert. I thought he was my way out. I thought he wanted me to be his wife by the way he treated me, and all the while he told me that he and his wife were on bad terms and how he wished it could only be me and him. I guess I got a little caught up when I was vulnerable. I believed everything he told me. It's not bad for a girl to dream, is it?"

Armani was full of hurt and pain. One could never tell by looks unless Armani told her story. She really had a lot of unresolved issues she needed to deal with. Infinity, her so-called friend, fed off her weakness. That bitch didn't mean anybody any good. Tanisha knew firsthand what it felt like to have your weakness held against you.

"What time do you have to be at work?" Armani asked.

"Tonight, I'm going in kinda early. You know Delicious? The one that got me the job? You know, the one you said is a queer. He said one of the girls was sick. Besides, I wanna get a feel of the dance floor before the place starts to get crowded. I'll call you to check on you when I get to work."

When Tanisha grabbed the knob, Armani sat up in the bed.

"I really don't want you to go. Can you just stay here with me for another hour or so?" she asked, and Tanisha couldn't refuse.

"Another hour, I can do that." She sat on the couch three-feet from the bed.

"Where are you going?" Armani pulled the covers back, inviting her into the bed.

"No, I'm okay over here."

"But I want you close to me." Not thinking anything of it, Tanisha kicked off her shoes and climbed into the big bed with her. Armani pulled the covers up and turned her back to Tanisha, continuing to watch Lifetime. She had to have seen the movie before. Every time a part came on that she liked, she'd say, "This is my favorite part." Tears filled her eyes as her emotions got the best of her. Just before the end, Armani flicked the channel complaining that she'd already seen that show before. Tanisha couldn't understand that because she was so into the movie at first.

"What are you looking for on the TV? All the crying you were just doing. I thought you were deep into the movie."

"I just like that part. I want to see something I've never seen before."

"Like what?"

"I don't know. I'll find something in a minute." Armani continued flipping the channel, then finally stopped on Playboy. She sucked her teeth and rolled her eyes in disgust at first, but she kept the TV on the channel. Then she nibbled at the tip of her thumb, gazing into the TV.

"Look, Tanisha," she said as if she'd never seen porn before. Her feet eased closer to Tanisha's feet. Then Armani turned over and put her arms around her, looking into her eyes.

Is this the woman that said she's strictly dickly? Tanisha thought.

Armani placed her lips on Tanisha's lips, then proceeded to stick her tongue in her mouth. Tanisha pushed her away and quickly turned her head.

"I know you've been through something, but this isn't the way to get rid of your problem. If we were to do this and tomorrow is another day, the same wounds you have today are going to be there until they heal themselves. Only time heals wounds. I've been there and done that."

Armani cried, but still tried to force Tanisha into having sex with her. When she saw the sincerity in Tanisha's eyes she became angry, and yelled, "Bitch, I hope you don't think you're all that. You're still a ho! I see why you got treated the way you did. Get the fuck out my house and don't come back!" She turned to her side, snatched the covers over her head, and flipped through the channels with the remote control.

The pleasure is all mine, Tanisha thought. She didn't want to be involved in a bisexual relationship. Not even for a moment. Tanisha was glad she followed her first mind to take her ass to work. That was some shit a man would do when he wasn't given the pussy. Kick the woman's ass to the curb.

Chapter Nineteen
CRAZY LOVE

D amn girl, what are you doing? You don't even hear people walking in your house," Infinity asked Armani after letting herself in. "You look like you've seen a ghost. What the hell happened to your eye?" Infinity was disturbed at seeing Armani's face.

"It's a long story, and I don't feel like getting into it."

"You better get into it. I wanna know what happened to your face?"

"I was leaving Joe's Underground," Armani lied.

"Joe's Underground? You know you're too classy for that shitty ass place," Infinity commented with an attitude.

"Are you going to let me finish? A girl needs to try something different sometimes. . . . Damn!"

"Go ahead," Infinity said, mumbling her sarcasm underneath her breath. Joe's Underground? What the hell? I bet she sees now what new grungy, low class places will do for her ass. I can't believe she took her ass down there. She gone get enough yet.

"As I was saying, I was leaving Joe's Underground and this guy that offered to buy me drinks all night ended up following me outside. And yes, I let him buy my drinks and I conversed with him for quite a while. Anyway, he followed me outside the club all the way to my car and thought I was going to sleep with him. When I told him no, he hit me, threw me up against the car and tore my panties and forced his finger inside me. He covered my mouth with his other hand, but I bit his finger and kneed him in the dick. I got inside my car, locked the doors and sped off. I couldn't believe he did that. What guy would do that? My heart was racing a hundred miles an hour. There was nobody in sight the entire time this was going on," Armani explained with a straight face in hopes of Infinity believing her untruthful story.

"Did you call the police?"

"No, I didn't. What was I going to tell them? I don't even know the guy."

"That's beside the point. You could've at least called Jazzy. She could've given you some advice."

"Jazzy, out of all people. Be serious here. I'm not her favorite person these days." Armani kept one hand on her forehead and the other on her hip.

"You should still call her. I'm sure she has some friends on the force willing to help out."

"I said no. Why can't you respect that?" Armani screamed at the top of her lungs, almost spitting in Infinity's face.

Infinity didn't pry any longer. Reluctantly, she changed the conversation. "Did you take care of business while I was gone?" she asked in a strong tone.

"You know I did. I'm getting kind of spooked, too."

"There you go with that spooked shit again." Infinity ran her hands through her head and massaged her temples.

"I could go to jail and I don't want to go to jail."

"Girl, yo' ass not gone go to jail."

"How do you know? You never take anything seriously, do you?"

"You always have a second option. You can move into an apartment and get a regular nine to five," Infinity said.

"Are you threatening me?" Armani walked toward Infinity and looked her up and down.

"No, that's a promise. You know I promised this man we would come through for him whenever he needed us."

"That's the problem. You made a promise, but I do all the work. So if I quit, you're going to lose your man because that's all you care about. Then you're walking around here like you're Queen Elizabeth or somebody. I thought you didn't want no man after Roscoe? I thought you were giving yourself time to heal. I guess that's where we all have a lot in common. Those group sessions didn't do any good. Soon as we left group, we all went back to our everyday lives." She shook her head and chuckled.

"I don't wanna hear shit about no group session. That was only a bunch of nosey bitches sitting around to hear everybody's problems. Nosey muthafuckas! Hell no, it didn't do nothing for me." She slung her keys. "I have to live in the real world outside of those fuckin' group sessions. What the fuck did they do for you? Nothing. That shit so in the past for me, and nobody tells me how to run my fuckin' life. I do what I wanna do. And this is business. I don't mix business with pleasure."

"You're right, you do what you want to do, but don't you ever speak to me in that tone again." Armani pointed at Infinity, her eyes boring a hole through her. Infinity raised both eyebrows, a tad bit surprised to hear this field mouse trying to become King of the Jungle.

"And oh yeah. About this not mixing business and pleasure. If that statement is true, why are you letting TD control you? You're allowing him to keep your relationship a secret. To me, it seems like he's using you, or a better word for it, manipulating you to do whatever, whenever."

"You don't know what kind of work I put in. Nor do you know anything about what type of relationship we have. I see why TD tells me to keep my friends out of my personal business." Infinity didn't want Armani to know how much she cared for TD, but she was so transparent.

"Why is that?"

"As if you don't know." Infinity folded her arms. "Y'all want what I have."

"And what is that? To be on the rebound? He would tell you that, and you don't recognize game when you hear it. At least I did learn something from my sorry, cheating ass ex-husband, Cliff. It seems as though you didn't learn anything from your experience." Armani walked toward the mirror to check out her face.

"I know one thing's for sure, TD does recognize and appreciates a good woman when he sees one."

"And that good woman would be you?" Armani pointed assumingly at Infinity.

"Who else?"

"The way I see it, you're the woman he can depend on to do his dirty work. He gives you a little dick every now and then to keep you happy, and the rest of his leisure is spent with another woman."

"I can't believe you're saying this to me." Infinity paced the floor in circles.

"I don't want to argue with you, Infinity. You're my

friend and I love you. We can't let a man come between us." She grabbed both of her hands.

Infinity pulled back slightly.

"I love you too, girl. I promise this isn't gone go on much longer. I'm gone be the girl to get those earrings out of his ears. I can feel it in my bones!" Infinity smiled. "I think it's meant for me to fall in love again."

"I think you love the challenge." Armani turned the conversation, not wanting to spoil Infinity's dream. "Girl, you love an aggressive man. I don't know why, but I'm happy for you if this is what you want. I hope everything goes the way you want it to without costing you anything."

"Costing me anything like what?" Infinity tilted her head and leaned back.

"Heartache and pain is the worst thing you could have to pay besides your life. You've been a woman scorned and so have I, so we both know what it feels like to some degree or another."

"You're right, but if we never take a chance how will we ever know who's the right man for us?" Infinity replied.

"I can't answer that question, but we do tend to attract men that aren't good for us. I refuse to wear my heart on my sleeve again," Armani said. She searched the dresser for a comb.

"I'm gone go out on a limb for this one. You just promise me you gone be my friend no matter what." Infinity's face was full of joy as she clenched Armani's shoulders.

Armani hugged Infinity and said, "I'll always be here to catch you when you fall. If it's God's will for him to be the man in your life, who am I to argue with that?"

Quickly changing the mood and getting to business Armani asked, "Are you ready to count the money?"

"Yeah, we can do that. How much did you exchange?"

"Seven hundred and fifty thousand. The other two hundred fifty thousand I'll exchange next week. My friend at the bank went on vacation."

Armani unzipped the suitcase, started counting the money, and let Infinity blab off at the mouth still wanting to know who she was doing her transactions with. Armani was already spooked. She'd been in and out of banks trading smaller bills for larger bills for almost a year. The money would be easier to carry on and off the aircraft without the police getting suspicious.

Armani and Infinity sat there counting money for hours. After they were done, Infinity still wasn't satisfied that she hadn't exchanged the other two hundred fifty thousand. Still, Infinity went out to her car, bringing back a large duffle bag full of more money, insisting Armani get that changed too as soon as possible. Armani couldn't believe her eyes, nor could she believe the nerve of Infinity after the long conversation they'd just had. Armani didn't argue with her, but she caught diarrhea instantly from the nervousness in her stomach and went running straight for the bathroom. She'd never seen so much money in her life where she could put her hands on it.

Infinity rushed over to the bathroom door to ask Armani if she was okay.

"Yes, I'm okay," Armani responded, not wanting Infinity to know exactly how nervous she was. "I think it was the milk I drank for breakfast this morning. I'm lactose intolerant and I tried to sneak a glass of milk in,"

Armani lied.

Infinity heard Armani's stomach exploding and then came the awful smell seeping underneath the door. The smell was so severe, Infinity started to gag. "Damn Armani, I'ma leave you to that." Infinity left for another room.

Thirty minutes passed before Armani exited the bathroom.

"Where are your clothes?" Infinity asked a butt naked Armani when she entered the bedroom.

"Didn't you hear the shower running? Besides, I can't use the restroom with my clothes on," Armani replied.

Infinity laughed until her stomach started hurting. "You mean to tell me you have to take all your clothes off to use the restroom?"

"Yes, I'm more comfortable like that, and I like the light off."

"I guess everybody likes what they like!"

"I guess they do!" Armani said, referring to Infinity liking TD.

Armani sat on the couch in her bedroom lotioning her body. Infinity came over to her with four stacks of money tied together and threw it on the couch next to her. "This is for you."

"How much is it?" Armani asked, smoothing lotion over her legs.

"It's forty thousand dollars. When you finish the rest, I'll give you sixty thousand," Infinity stated.

Armani's eyes gaped open. "You're being very generous this time."

"You had it coming. TD just had a lot he needed to get established first. He says after two more rounds he's going to retire. Do you think you can hang for two more rounds?"

"I can do that as long as you're sure it's only two more rounds. You won't have any complaints from me."

"Just two more rounds, that's it, I promise. How about we do something wild and exciting tonight?" Infinity asked.

"Like what?"

"Like go to Chocolate Castle and get our drink on."

"You mean go to Chocolate Castle to watch TD!" You just spent a whole week with him. Damn girl, give the man a chance to miss you!"

"Please, go with me," Infinity begged.

"Look at my face. You want me to go there looking like this?"

Infinity pulled her large lens Chanel shades from her purse. "Here. Wear these and nobody will ever be able to tell the difference." Armani was reluctant to go because she didn't want to run into LL. On top of that, she had to tell Infinity that Tanisha worked there before she found out on her own and started to think Armani had betrayed her. She knew Infinity wasn't going to take the news of Tanisha working at Chocolate Castle around TD very well.

"You know Tanisha works there now. Tonight is going to be her first night on stage since her audition." Armani rushed it out.

"TD did tell you he hired her, right?" Armani asked.

"No, he didn't. It must have slipped his mind," Infinity lied. TD never shared his business at the club with her. "Ain't that a bitch. A junkie on the stage performing in front of all those rich, irresistible men."

"Do I hear a hater? The girl don't even do drugs anymore."

"That's beside the point. She used to . . . Once a junkie, always a junkie."

"That's not necessarily true, and her appearance sure shows differently. Tanisha is a knock out now. Any man would be pleased to have her on his arm. I saw her with my own eyes."

"Maybe your eyes were playing tricks on you. You're always taking her side."

"You're the one that brought her around us. She didn't ask you for your help."

"Well, I guess it's time for a moment of truth. That bitch is gone pay for sleeping with my husband. I don't care what her excuse was. Crack head or not, I don't give a fuck. Yeah, I went along with it, but it's killing me to my bones. I hate that bitch's guts with a passion. I hope you didn't think I was kidding about what I told you about her before."

"I knew you were serious. Why this hatred still, when you claim to be falling in love with another man?"

"It doesn't matter."

"I think she senses that something isn't right with you."

"That ho done smoked so much crack it's fried her brain. She don't sense shit!"

"If you say so. Tanisha's not that same weak woman your husband took advantage of." Damn, this bitch is still madly in love with Roscoe, Armani thought.

"Infinity, stop it. Let's not argue. Friends are supposed to be able to talk about anything."

"Friends are going to disagree and have their own opinions, too. So don't give me no shit," Infinity responded.

"I'm going to get dressed. You need to go home and

do the same. I'll meet you at the club around eleven o'clock and don't take those shades with you," Armani shouted from inside her large walk-in closet.

Infinity threw the shades on Armani's couch, singing TLC's "What About Your Friends" as she headed out the door.

* * * * *

On Infinity's way home, her cell was ringing off the hook from the moment she got into her Range Rover. She smiled, anxious for a call from TD. The caller ID showed it wasn't him.

Infinity answered, "Hello?"

The operator responded. "This is a prepaid call from a Federal Prison. You have a call from . . . JJ. You will not be charged for this call. Hang up to decline the call or press five to accept the call. Press seven if you wish to block calls from this facility." Infinity pressed five to accept. JJ immediately began to get on her case.

"Damn, girl. I've been calling you all week. Is this how you treat yo' brother after all I've done for you?" JJ said, referring to the keys of coke and money he gave her when he robbed Roscoe.

"You didn't do shit for me. All you did was give me what belonged to me."

"Stop trippin'. None of the money belonged to you. You were a do-girl just like that bitch, Tiny. Roscoe didn't give a fuck about you. All he cared about was getting ahead in the game, no matter whose toes he had to step on to get in, including yours. Damn girl, wake up. Yeah, I robbed him, but it was personal. And I gave you the money and the work to look out. I could never thank Mom and Dad enough for adopting me. You're my only family and that's what I believe in. Family comes first with me. But I see what people in prison mean when they say if you go to prison, people in the free world consider you dead until they have to walk in your shoes."

Infinity let everything he said go in one ear and out the other.

"So, you said all that to say what? You need some money? I got you in the morning."

"I don't want it in the morning. I want it tonight," JJ insisted angrily. "Man, I gotta go to commissary tomorrow. Shit, what a nigga gotta do? Beg? It don't take you long to swing by Western Union. It'll only take you fifteen minutes to get the money." JJ was desperate.

Just to shut him up, Infinity lied and agreed to go to Western Union on the way home. That still wasn't enough for JJ. It seemed like he wanted to start an argument. He was pissed that he'd given her every cent to his name, and she wasn't sticking by him like he thought she would.

"You know news travels fast in prison, right?"

"That's what they say even though they don't have their facts straight," Infinity responded, hoping JJ's fifteen minutes would soon be up.

"The streets talk, you know. I hear you going out with TD. Before you start to deny it, just know he's worse than that fuckin' nigga, Roscoe. He manipulates people to get what he wants. He takes young bitches under his wing by showering them with expensive gifts and showing them the good life, and when he's all done with them groupie bitches, he throws them to the next nigga in line waiting to hit the pussy. You ain't learned shit from that nigga, Roscoe? I'm telling you sis, dude is bad news. . . ."

"Hello! Hello!" Infinity shouted into the phone. No response. JJ's fifteen minutes ended. Infinity passed the

Western Union without a second thought. She had bigger fish to fry and JJ wasn't on the 'to do' list for the night.

Pulling into her driveway, Infinity cut the engine of her car, leaving the music down low thinking about everything Armani and JJ had to say about TD. Her mind raced back and forth. No matter what came to mind, it all ended back at the same thing. This was the first time in a long time she'd come close to being in love again, but deep down she still had crazy love for Roscoe. But her love for him didn't outweigh the heartache and pain he caused her. She'd set her mind and heart on TD, determined to be the one to get those diamonds out of his ears so she could take him off the market. She sat there contemplating. All kinda thoughts raced through her head like a busy California highway. Everybody is hating. They don't want to see me happy. I can't believe my own brother is saying the shit he's saying about TD. It doesn't matter. I know how TD treats me when we're together. Fuck all of them. I refuse to let them fuck up a good thing for me because their lives are so fucked up.

Infinity didn't want to face the reality that there could be some truth to what Armani and JJ had to say. She definitely had a mind of her own and it was made up.

She felt Armani was always talking down on TD because she didn't have a man of her own. Armani thought every man was going to turn out just like that sorry ass ex-husband of hers, Cliff. And all JJ cared about was blowing money in the Fed. She knew it didn't take that much money to survive in prison. That nigga was crazy. What the hell could he buy? Shit, JJ don't wanna see me with nobody. He ruined my fuckin' marriage getting all in my personal life. My parents should've left his ass where he was: in the play pen with all those other bastard children waiting to get adopted. Damn, I hate his ass sometimes!

Infinity finished collecting her thoughts, still determined to win over TD's heart no matter what anybody had to say. She secured her Range Rover, shook off all negative thoughts and headed in her house to get ready to meet Armani at Chocolate Castle.

Chapter Twenty
CHOCOLATE CASTLE

Armani arrived at the jam packed club in her Lexus Coupe. She noticed Infinity's candy apple red Range Rover parked in the parking lot. She proceeded out the door wearing Chanel shades, an all black Dolce & Gabbana sleeveless dress that clung to her body, a clutch purse and a pair of Jimmy Choo heels. Her hair was pulled to the side in one ponytail stopping above the elbow and five karat diamond tear drops were hanging from her ear lobes.

Armani was as clean as a new car and hoping for the night to turn out spectacular. Her only worry was bumping into Mr. Levert Langston. Just in case she did, she was cocked and ready to retaliate.

Entering the club, Armani tried her hardest to zero in on every angle, north, south, east and west, making sure Levert Langston was nowhere in sight. After mingling a little, Armani received a tap on the shoulder. She paused, pulling her purse close to her breasts. Afraid to turn around for a second, she took a deep breath, turned and there stood Infinity with two drinks in her hand. Infinity smiled.

"Damn girl, you're acting like you've seen a ghost or

something."

Armani retaliated harshly. "Hell no, I haven't seen a ghost. You're always saying that when you sneak up on me. I don't like it when you sneak up on me. I'd prefer you not do it ever again."

Infinity took two steps back and glanced at Armani, unable to see the look in her eyes because of the shades covering them. "Excuse me, but I thought we came out to have a nice time. If I did something wrong, I apologize." Infinity's attitude took a turn for the better. She was expecting to see TD, and she wouldn't dare let him see her step out of character. She didn't want him to see the bitch she could really be.

Armani reigned in her racing emotions. "No, forgive me, you didn't do anything wrong. We did come here to have a nice time and I'm not going to be the one to spoil it." Armani smiled, still paranoid.

Infinity handed Armani a drink with a naughty look on her face. Armani took it from her hand, gulped it down and insisted on another to get rid of her nervousness.

"Now this is the way to get the night started off right," Infinity said, taking a look around the club and pouring her drink down her throat at once.

She went back to the bar and ordered two more drinks. Infinity was stunned when Armani took both drinks and downed one then the other. She put the empty glasses back in Infinity's hand. Infinity had never seen Armani act this way before.

They went over to the bar and ordered more drinks. Infinity leaned over the bar to get Delicious's attention.

"Hey, if you don't mind, can you bring the drinks over to our table personally?" Infinity asked out of fear and a guilty conscience, as she remembered what she'd done to Tanisha during the male review party. Delicious responded in a way she never would've expected. "I'm sorry, but there's no special treatment around here. If you don't want the waiters to serve you, you'll have to get up and get it yourself."

Infinity was hurt deeply on the inside by Delicious's reply and felt like daggers had penetrated her heart. She was expecting special attention that she wasn't going to get. She was overstepping her boundaries and knew that TD wouldn't approve. He was private when it came to his personal life, but she wanted women to think TD was her property.

"Oh, that looks like Tanisha," Armani said, knowing damn well the woman who walked past looked nothing like Tanisha. "Oh, that's not even her." She pretended she didn't hear what Delicious said to Infinity, trying to not make her feel worse than she already did. "What did the bartender say?"

"Nothing." Infinity escorted Armani to their table in the VIP section. After the fourth drink, Armani was feeling light on her feet. They both sat there observing the women dancing around them, enjoying the atmosphere. In that very moment, they both fantasized about what it would be like to trade places with the dancers for one night. They wanted to know how it felt to have multiple men hovering over them all at once and throwing dollar bills to see them prance their bodies back and forth across the stage. One didn't want the other to know how much she admired the women that were able to go out and do what they desired to do. They were too afraid.

Armani couldn't sit in one spot any longer. Infinity

waited patiently to see TD show his face in the club.

Armani paced the floor, anxious to see Tanisha take the stage. She wanted to see if Tanisha had what it took to dance in Chocolate Castle. Armani roamed the floors of the club, and crashed head on into TD. To prevent her from falling, he grabbed her with one arm around the waist and pulled her to him with her breasts pressed firmly against his chest. He smiled into her eyes without a word. Armani was startled and she blushed. It took her a moment to realize those eyes belonged to TD. Infinity caught a glimpse of that, locking her eyes on them without one blink. TD whispered into Armani's ear, still holding her around the waist, so he wouldn't have to scream over the music. "What's a lovely lady like yourself doing letting alcohol get the best of her?" TD could smell the liquor on Armani's breath. "It's not ladylike and you're making a fool of yourself. I'd suggest you not have anything else to drink tonight," he expressed in a deep, sexy tone.

Armani was so embarrassed she didn't know what to think or say. She agreed by nodding. He released her.

Infinity sat from afar wishing she possessed bionic ears, desperate to know what they were talking about and why he had his arms wrapped around Armani's waist.

Armani found her way over to the bar and ordered a cup of virgin coffee, black with no sugar and no cream. Armani sat at the bar for quite a while, twirling her chair from left to right while watching the girls perform on stage.

When that last song was over, the DJ announced another dancer to come on stage. Armani gave her undivided attention. It wasn't Tanisha. Armani turned back around finding Mr. Langston sitting on the bar stool staring her in the face. She was terrified, but she wouldn't dare let him know it. She knew he wasn't going to do anything to harm her physically in the club around the bouncers, nor did he want to embarrass himself in front of his colleagues that were plastered all over the club.

Mr. Langston grabbed Armani by the arm without notice and forced her into an abandoned corner to interrogate her. She went quietly, not wanting to cause a scene.

"You disease infected bitch! Look at you. Prowling around, looking for another life to destroy!" he shouted at Armani. Spit sprayed from Levert's mouth. Armani attempted to turn away. "Look at me!" Levert grabbed her chin, turning her face to his. "You're a dirty, black, nasty bitch. A dirty, black bitch. Do you hear me?"

Armani responded, "I wasn't a dirty, black, nasty bitch when you were paying to lick my pussy every chance you got."

"Shut up, bitch! And if I say you're a nasty, black bitch, you're a nasty, filthy, black bitch. I hate you. Bitch, I should have killed you in that hotel room and left your body there to rot."

Armani let Mr. Langston talk, while reaching in her purse for ammunition. "All this assassinating my character is going to cease tonight. I'm sick of your shit. I'm sick of it! Do you hear me?" Armani's fear vanished into thin air.

Levert snatched the purse away from Armani and rummaged through it in search of a weapon. He found two tubes of lipstick, a set of car keys, three magnum condoms that his uncircumcised dick surely couldn't fit, a sample bottle of Victoria's Secret body spray, a major credit card, her driver's license and a piece of paper neatly folded.

"Excuse me. Is there a problem over here?" Delicious asked out of concern for Armani. He was three times the size of Levert Langston.

"There's no problem." Levert grabbed Armani around the waist and kissed her on the cheek, assuring Delicious everything was fine. "Is there?" Levert asked Armani with a smile, hoping she wouldn't reveal the excruciating facts of their conversation.

"There's no problem," Armani replied with a smile, desperately wanting to tell Delicious what was going on.

Delicious returned to the bar after Armani confirmed her safety. Mr. Langston was confused, wondering what Armani was searching for in the purse. Levert gave the purse back and started at Armani again about destroying his life. Armani reached in her purse, pulling out the piece of paper showing she was negative for all sexually transmitted diseases, including HIV and AIDS. Unfolding the document, she handed it to Mr. Langston proving he couldn't have contracted any kind of disease from her. Mr. Langston took the paper and read it twice in decimated disappointment. Balling the paper up, he shoved it into Armani's chest and walked away filled with embarrassment for accusing the wrong woman of giving him a disease. He exited the building wondering where he'd contracted the disease from. Could my wife have given it to me? he thought.

Armani was more relieved than anything since he could no longer accuse her. She stood in the corner making sure her clothing was intact. Armani escaped to the ladies room to freshen up.

As she returned to the table, she found Infinity approaching her. Infinity was dying to know what

Armani and TD were talking about, but she wouldn't dare let Armani know she was that insecure of her relationship with TD.

"Who was that white guy you were talking to over in the corner? He's hot!" Infinity asked.

Armani felt her entire body go stiff. She didn't know Infinity had been watching her and Levert. She wondered how much Infinity saw.

"Just a guy telling me how much he admired my beauty and how he wanted to come over to meet me personally," Armani lied.

"All right, you know what happened last time someone admired your beauty at Joe's Underground. You better be careful with these strangers," Infinity said.

"If I don't talk to strangers, I'll never meet anybody. So I guess I'm damned if I do and damned if I don't, huh?"

Infinity and Armani were so deep in conversation they hadn't realized they had a visitor standing there. TD cleared his throat. As soon as Infinity turned around, a puppy love look glistened in her eyes. There stood the man she'd been waiting on all night. He kissed Infinity on one cheek then the other and motioned her to take a seat.

He sat next to her and crossed his legs. Armani sat on the opposite side of TD. His eyes x-rayed the entire club from every angle. He barely acknowledged Infinity sitting there beside him.

Some well dressed distinguished men walked over to TD and shook his hand letting him know they preferred to come to his club. TD stood.

"Gentlemen, I'm in this business for the long haul, and I aim to please. If you gentlemen have any ideas that you want to run by me to better accommodate your visit, I'm always open to making enhancements in the club."

The gentlemen thanked him for his hospitality and walked away enjoying the night with two beautiful women on their side. Infinity placed her hand on TD's lap, getting quite comfortable. TD turned to her with rage in his eyes. "Here and now is business for me and if you ever disrespect me like that again in public, I'll break your fingers myself," TD calmly said into Infinity's ear. He looked up, wearing a smile.

Infinity was thrown by his reaction. TD gently placed Infinity's hand back on her lap, removed himself from the table, and left her with a smile and a kiss on the cheek.

Four steps away from the table, TD turned back to look at Armani and said, "I'm happy to see you decided to take me up on my offer." He walked away, hands stuffed in his neatly pressed beige linen pants suit pockets, leaving a lingering fragrance behind.

Infinity couldn't understand why TD acted the way he did. She wasn't used to that kind of treatment from him. But she'd never been in public with him unless it was out of town. All she could come up with was he wanted to show out because Armani was sitting there.

Chapter Twenty-One
COMPLETE DENIAL

T he music mellowed out, and the DJ announced the next dancer to the stage.

"Ladies and gentlemen, may I have your attention. This next lovely lady that's about to tame the stage as she puts it, says she's the Queen of the Indian Reservation. Now even the Egyptian Queen Cleopatra can't touch her. The Queen says she seduces and stimulates the mind with the movement from her body and teases the eyes with her physical. Be careful approaching the Queen, she might hypnotize you. Please welcome the newest talent at Chocolate Castle, Queen of the Indian Reservation, Shanoah."

Tanisha came out on the stage strutting like Naomi Campbell with a vengeance.

Men crowded the stage from one end to the other. Tanisha wore two thick Indian braids. She sparkled from head to toe, starting with the swirling diamonds around her braids, to the diamond choker around her neck to her matching sequined bikini. The bra only covered her nipples and the panties only covered her clit with a spaghetti string lining the crease of her ass. Men applauded in unison. Their mouths dropped open in awe. Her beauty had taken them by surprise. She stood in a class all of her own. Her personal style and confidence was apparent. Frenchy would be proud. Tanisha took a hold of the pole and worked that muthafucka like she was born to do it. Seductively, she glided all the way to the top and slid down backward writhing her body like a snake. Even though she was entertaining by taking her clothes off for money, she worked her body like a classy lady on stage, demanding respect and all eyes on her. She danced through two songs. Then her favorite song began to play: "When a Woman's Fed Up" by R. Kelly. It was time to reveal the birthday suit that had matured so beautifully. She swayed back and forth to center stage, so the men could get a better view. Seducing them with every movement, she turned her back, rocking her derriere as she removed her bra. The twins were let loose. She bent down, grabbed her ankles and slowly lowered her body into a split. Benjamin Franklin's rained onto the stage. As she rose, she looked between her legs and spotted TD front and center, staring at her every movement. It was hard, but she kept her composure and leveled herself. She bent back, rocking her hips. She snatched her panty from between her legs and twirled them around her head like a cowgirl. While biting one side of her bottom lip she slow rolled her belly. Staring into the crowded club of men and few women through hazel contacts, she batted her eyes several times and circled her lips with her tongue, leaving them wet and luscious. Tanisha felt like she was on top of the world. Even the nervousness of TD being there had vanished.

Just as the song was coming to an end, Delicious approached the stage as Tanisha made her exit. "Hey Tanisha!" he said, getting her attention. "A guy came over to the bar and left two thousand dollars. The guy wants you to do that last song one more time."

There's no way she was going to refuse. "Who is he?" she insisted on knowing. Who was this mystery man that kept popping up everywhere she went? Tanisha assumed he was the same guy—her secret admirer famous for leaving generous gifts.

Delicious left the side of the stage without giving her an answer and signaled the DJ to play that same song again.

Infinity and Armani came closer to center stage. Everywhere TD's eyes shifted, Armani noticed Infinity's eyes followed. She could tell by the shifting body language and sudden red tinge to her skin that Infinity was furious at the attention TD was showing Tanisha. She'd bet money Tanisha was every crack head in the book to her. TD's eyes were fixated on Tanisha's body. Even if he didn't want her and even if he wasn't the mystery man, Tanisha was still an attractive woman with a sexy body and TD was a man who was not blind. He enjoyed what he saw.

Armani's eyes shifted from Infinity to TD's then toward Tanisha controlling the stage like it was her home away from home. In the middle of the song, she walked across the stage on her hands and knees like a tamed, harmless jaguar showing all the definition in her body as she purred like a kitten. She flipped over on her back like a cat getting her tummy rubbed and held her legs in the air with her ass facing the audience. Waving her legs back and forth like a princess in a pageant she bounced her ass cheeks up and down in a seductive motion like two basketballs, dribbling one behind the other. She lifted her head and looked through her legs and caught the perfect photographic picture of TD sitting in the same position as he was when she first saw him. All eyes were still on her.

Smile, you're on candid camera, she thought, looking at him with a smile and wondering if he could be the mystery man sending her all these unexpected gifts.

Infinity glimpsed the eye contact Tanisha gave TD. Tanisha bet it tore that bitch up, asshole to appetite with envy. Armani stood on the sideline, observing.

Her four songs were over, and she gathered her things from the stage. Delicious stood at the bottom of the stage to give her a helping hand down the stairs. He was always a gentleman to her, making her feel like a true princess. Being the Queen of the Indian Reservation was her alter ego; she was on cloud nine and filled with excitement. Tanisha felt like she'd conquered the world on that stage. She felt beautiful again, after all she'd been through. A small accomplishment was better than none at all. She went back stage to freshen up and get dressed.

Once she walked into the dressing room, Infinity appeared out of nowhere, standing in front of her wearing the look of hatred and envy in her eyes. Tanisha knew exactly why Infinity was in the dressing room making a scene. She was insecure and thought Tanisha was going to make a move on TD.

"I know what you are trying to do. A leopard never changes his spots, does he?" Infinity blocked her way.

Insecure bitch, Tanisha thought. "What do you mean by that?" Tanisha asked like she didn't already know.

"You slept with my husband and now you are trying to get my boyfriend, too. I knew I should have never trusted you. Crack head bitch!" She got up in Tanisha's face almost kissing her.

Tanisha didn't back down. "Hold up one

muthafuckin' minute here. You knew the situation with me and Roscoe. I thought we put all that behind us." Tanisha played on her intelligence. As if she didn't know Infinity had a thing for TD that was making her chaotic.

"You may have put it behind you, and I thought I could put it behind me, too, but I was wrong. Especially when I see you doing it again out of spite." Her jealousy was full blown.

"Wait a minute! That's where you're wrong, bitch. I'm not doing shit out of spite. This is a place of business. I came to do my job, and anything I'm called to do, I'm gone do it to the best of my ability. If you can't keep a grip on the person you're trying to stake claims on, then that's your business," she stated, leaving Infinity standing there unable to digest her words. The bitch could've choked and died, and Tanisha wouldn't have given a fuck. Tanisha put on a tank top and pulled on a pair of skin tight jeans. I can't believe this bitch would try to check me about a nigga that don't belong to her. The bitch told me she wasn't ready for a relationship. I'm glad I got an earful from this bitch tonight. Everything Venom told me about the bitch was the truth. This bitch had an ulterior motive from day one. This bitch is deadly. But I'll be damned if I'm going to let this bitch fuck up a good thing for me. Fuck this hoe! And ten more bitches just like her. The bitch's pussy must not be any good. Insecure ass hoe!

In a raging tantrum, Infinity rushed Tanisha and hit her in the back of the head. Tanisha stumbled forward a little.

"Hell no you didn't, bitch!" Tanisha grabbed the back of her head and turned to face Infinity. Her instant reflexes forced her to retaliate. Tanisha charged Infinity, throwing her to the floor.

All the ladies in the dressing room were standing around chanting as they watched Tanisha on top of Infinity punching her in the face, and beating her like she'd stole something. The ladies were reluctant to stop the fight. They were too busy trying to see who would win. None of the ladies cared for Infinity. She always came in the club thinking she was better than everybody else. Tanisha, on the other hand, was the new kid on the block raking in all the money. That bothered the girls, too, but they figured she was new pussy and that soon would come to an end. Infinity, on the other hand, they wanted that bitch's head on a silver platter.

Delicious heard the excessive screaming and shouting. He rushed into the dressing room shouting to the top of his lungs, "Back the fuck up!"

TD followed Delicious's every move. His arms were folded in a calm and collected demeanor as always. Delicious pulled Tanisha off Infinity. TD helped Infinity up from the floor. Infinity's pearl white, Vera Wang summer strapless dress was covered in blood from her busted bottom lip. Delicious took Tanisha out of the dressing room through the back so she could exit the building. He didn't want people in the club to know what transpired in the dressing room.

"What the hell happened here?" TD asked, giving Infinity a wet wash cloth one of the dancers brought over to him. TD stared at her. Infinity couldn't get two words out. TD didn't want to hear it.

"Look at you. You always let me down. Just when I think you're the one, you always let me down. There is no excuse for you to be in this dressing room. You're starting fights with my dancers. I don't know what to expect out of you next."

"But you don't know her like I know her." Hoping TD would feel sorry for her, Infinity slouched herself down in a chair crying, sniffling and breathing hard as if she couldn't catch her breath. TD stood there shaking his head, rubbing and stroking the bottom of his chin in disappointment. He grabbed Infinity's chin, holding her face up to look at him.

"You're a loose cannon. Don't make me have to get rid of you. Women are supposed to be seen, not heard. Always remember, attitude can make or break a business. Before I let you destroy anything I worked hard for, I'll kill you. You're a weak link in my organization. I sensed it from the beginning. I still went against my better judgment to give you a chance. I thought you had potential, but you think with the wrong head."

"The bitch started it!" Infinity spoke through clenched teeth.

"Most of all, I need to fault myself for mixing business with pleasure. I should've kept this good dick to myself. Damn, a man give up a little dick and you women automatically get emotionally attached. You better not fuck up what I got going, and you know what I'm talking about. Do you hear me? Are we clear?" Sweat popped up on TD's nose.

"Yes, I understand," Infinity cried.

TD kissed Infinity on both cheeks and left her sitting there with something to think about.

Clearly, he was telling her it could never be. The more he rejected Infinity, the more she loved him. With mascara running down her cheeks and eyeliner smeared around her eyes, Infinity cried her eyes out. That was the least of Infinity's problems; she was more embarrassed than anything. Her pride was shot to hell. She'd just made a complete idiot out of herself.

Infinity never thought Tanisha would hit her back. She never thought she had an ass whipping coming. TD was disgusted with her. Infinity struck out twice in one night. On top of that, she wore a serious ass whipping that the women were going to talk about for months to come.

Armani got wind of what happened and went to Infinity's rescue. She walked in the dressing room calling out Infinity's name and never getting an answer. She only heard a fading cry and sniffling through the commotion of the dancers walking back and forth, changing their clothes and getting ready to perform.

One of the dancers stopped Armani and asked in a soft voice, "Are you looking for the girl that was just into it with Shanoah?" She stood there twirling her hair in a red lace thong, bare-breasted and wearing red high heels and popping gum.

"Yes, where is she? Is she still here?" Armani was in a hurry to find Infinity.

The dancer pointed toward the bathroom stall. "She's in there."

"Thank you," Armani responded, rushing over to the restroom stall. Tapping on the door Armani asked, "Infinity, are you in there?"

"Open the door, baby. Everything is going to be fine. Let me help you," Armani insisted.

The last time Armani saw Infinity like this was when she told her she divorced Roscoe. Infinity didn't know how to let go. She'd grown attached like a fetus to a womb. Roscoe was her life. Even though she said she was over him, it still took some time getting used to the fact of living life without him.

The situation with TD was different, but so similar when it came to her feelings. Infinity hated losing at anything, and she didn't like not being able to have control. In her marriage she could act as if she was in control because Roscoe allowed her to do so because of all the deceit he brought to the marriage.

Infinity stood to remove the latch from the stall door. Bending back down to the floor Infinity cried out, "I just want him to love me, that's all."

"I'm your friend and I wouldn't tell you anything wrong," Armani replied, taking the tissue from Infinity's hand, trying to wipe off the running mascara.

"Baby, look at me," Armani said to Infinity in a soft voice. "You can't make somebody love you. They have to love you because they feel it in their heart. You already knew in your heart that he didn't love you. You know it's only business. But it isn't about that right now, is it? It's about you feeling like another woman has taken something that belongs to you. Talk to me! You have to let it out."

"It's not just another woman and she didn't take anything from me. It's that stanking, crack head whore, Tanisha, that you tend to love so much. The bitch ain't your friend. The bitch dirty like that, crack or no crack, like I've told you before. Maybe she wishes she had everything that I have. I know now TD loves me, but she's trying to block him from seeing it. Just like the rest of these stanking bitches in this nasty ass club."

"Infinity, what are you saying, sweetheart?" Armani asked her. How in the hell can I help my confused friend? She doesn't even realize she's in complete denial.

Chapter Twenty-Two
SECRET RENDEZVOUS

On her drive home, Tanisha was devastated. She parked her car in front of the apartment building, switched the light on at the top of the rearview mirror and stared at her face. She couldn't believe what happened. She didn't even know if she paid attention to all the traffic lights on the way. God had to have been with her in order for her to get home safely. She still hadn't digested all of this. It's funny how things changed within the blink of an eye.

Tanisha didn't feel bad about kicking Infinity's ass; she was asking for it. There was no way she was gonna let the bitch get away with putting her hands on her a second time. Infinity may have gotten away with that shit in the hospital, but she'd be damned if she was going to get away with that shit now. That bitch really tried her, and she was keeping it real with her. Tanisha would've been a better friend to her than all of those snake bitches she dealt with. She couldn't believe she did that shit over a nigga that probably didn't want her ass to begin with. Tanisha thought she should fuck TD just to show that bitch who got the comeback pussy.

Damn, my face is scratched the fuck up, she thought as she touched the raised marks on her face. This shit is gone need some serious cocoa butter, but in the meantime I'll just have to use some concealer to hide the scratches. There's no way in hell I'm gone miss any days at work because of this shit. "Damn, I may not have a job," Tanisha said as she stared into the mirror. She didn't know what TD would have to say about this. "Fuck! This bitch probably cost me my job!" Tanisha clutched the steering wheel of her car, disgusted with herself.

She really stepped outside of her character tonight. "Fuck that! TD has to understand that it wasn't my fault. I didn't start it. What am I going to do? I need my job. Things are just starting to look up for me," she reasoned.

She got out of her car, locked the doors and headed to her apartment. All she wanted was a good hot shower and a good night's rest. She figured she could worry about what she was going to say to TD tomorrow.

As soon as she entered her apartment, she began to undress. She turned the shower on as hot as she could stand it and stepped in. Tanisha washed her body from top to bottom, flinching at the few tender spots from the brawl with Infinity. But it was nothing she couldn't handle. She'd had worse aches when she was leading the life of a dope fiend. She'd acquired a high tolerance for pain. But the bruises weren't going to do her any justice at work. Damn that bitch. She fucking with my money! Tanisha thought.

After thirty minutes of letting the hot shower beat against her body, she left the bathroom dripping wet. Barely toweling off, she decided to let the remaining moisture on her body air dry. She could parade around her house in her birthday suit. There's nothing like having your own. Nobody can tell you when to clean, eat, sleep or shit!

She sashayed down the hallway and into her living room. "Ahhhhh," she screamed and ran to the bedroom, grabbed a towel and wrapped it around her body. She examined the room for her cell phone, contemplating calling the police. A man was sitting there like he owned the place and didn't budge. Actually, he smiled at her.

Still frightened she asked, "How did you get into my apartment? What are you doing here?"

"No need for the screaming. Calm down. You didn't lock the door behind you. I knocked several times. I didn't get an answer. I knew you were here because your car was out front, so I let myself in. I thought something was wrong after I turned the knob to find the door wasn't locked, until I heard the water running from your bathroom. I took it upon myself to wait until you came out. I hope you don't mind. You're as beautiful as ever. Come over here and sit by me. We have a lot of catching up to do. I bet you didn't think you'd see me this soon, did you?" He patted his hand on the couch, beckoning her over to him.

"Let me go get dressed first." She headed down the hallway.

"No need to get dressed. It's not like I've never seen you naked before. Come over here," he insisted.

Tanisha trembled all over. Her heart raced faster with every step. She was so afraid. But he was right on her nakedness not being a first nor second for him. He sat there calm and collected staring at her. Once she calmed down, she realized he wasn't going to cause her any harm.

"How did you find out where I lived?" she asked.

"No need for questions, I'm here now. I brought wine. It's not the most expensive, but I was hoping you'd have a few glasses with me."

"Okay, I'll go get the glasses," she said, wanting an excuse to leave the room. She didn't know what he wanted or how he found out where she lived, nor how long he was planning on staying.

"No need to get up and get glasses." I brought those too." He pulled glasses from each of his jacket pockets and poured her a glass of wine, then himself.

"What is it that you want to talk to me about?" she asked. He sat there, charming as ever. She felt somewhat ecstatic that he was in her presence, but she didn't want to seem overly excited to have him there. She decided to follow his lead.

"Right now I don't want to talk. I'm thinking about the first time I met you. You don't mind if I think while I admire your beauty, do you?" She shivered as chill bumps dotted her bare skin.

"I really need to get on some clothes. It's getting a little chilly in here," she said, shuddering.

"I'm sorry. Excuse me for not being a gentleman." He removed his jacket then his top shirt and passed it to her. His muscular physique was looking deliciously hot.

"Here, take my shirt. I don't want you out of my sight for one second more than you have to be," he insisted.

He was buff as shit. Oh my God! What am I thinking? He has to get out of here!

"Drink your wine." He gestured toward her glass with a nod of his head. "Let's make a toast." He pulled her hand in mid air and circled his arm around hers. "To new beginnings." He smiled. His beautiful white teeth were sparkling.

She went along with the toast, not knowing what the hell he meant by new beginnings. Tanisha took one, then two sips of the wine. The next thing she knew he refilled her glass. The warmth of his shirt covering her body made her feel comfortable. They began to talk about things they had in common, then said things to make one another laugh. She was even able to finish some of his sentences. She didn't know what she was doing, but it felt right. It felt good. She had already had a long day at work. He wasn't doing her any harm, so she decided to let him stay and keep her company. She didn't think he would leave if she told him to.

They finished the entire bottle of wine. In a few hours, daybreak would soon be creeping up on them.

"Do you mind if I stay here for the night? There's no way I can drive in my condition." He played on her and she knew it. Tanisha wanted so badly to say no, but something inside her wanted to say 'hell yeah' as she surveyed his body with her eyes. "I promise I won't do anything that you don't want me to do. If you give me a blanket I'll sleep right here on the floor," he said politely.

She could tell he wouldn't take no for an answer. What if I put him out and he gets in a wreck from drinking and driving? No I can't do that because what if the shoe was on the other foot . . . She searched for reasons to let herself give in.

"Okay, you can stay. You have to be out early because I'm going to church tomorrow morning." She went to get a comforter for him to sleep on the floor. She could feel his eyes feasting on her from behind. The top part of her ass protruded from the back of the shirt and the other half was barely covered.

"Thank you." He removed his shoes, took the comforter and spread it on the living room floor. "Do you mind sitting with me for a little longer?" he asked, patting his hand on the floor next to him. "Just for a few minutes," he insisted. As she looked into his eyes, she already knew this was where she wanted to be.

"I thought you'd never ask." She took a seat next to him.

"You're a beautiful woman. I've always thought that since the first time I laid eyes on you. That's why I wanted you around." He stroked her face gently on one side then the other as he peered into her eyes, telling her how beautiful she was over and over. "I can't believe you haven't been scooped up yet, but I see you're doing well all by yourself. It's good for a woman to stand on her own two feet. It makes her appreciate the finer things in life.

"You know what? C'mere." He pulled her to him before she could resist. Before she knew it, Tanisha was sitting on his lap, lip to lip, eye to eye and body to body. He enveloped her bottom lip with his.

"When this dick get good to you, call him Mr. Sweet Dick. If you don't, he'll get jealous and start howling like a wolf." He smiled. He didn't give her a chance to tell him no. Tanisha didn't want to let the word no even think about escaping her lips. She wanted him. She needed to be touched. It had been so long.

His hand disappeared underneath the shirt, sifting through the few hairs on her pussy to find her clit. "I love hairy pussy. Let your hair grow back," he said. She knew she shouldn't have listened to Infinity, and shaved her pussy. Bitch! He stroked her clit twice, then flipped her backwards with her pussy lips kissing the sexy lips on his face. Her body tensed up; she pretended to resist, refusing to show him she wanted him as badly as she did. Tanisha wanted him to bury his face deep between her thighs.

"Wait, do you have a condom?" she moaned softly.

He answered, "Yes."

Gently, he kissed her pussy lips then pushed his tongue inside her hole. She moaned uncontrollably. He removed his tongue and laid her flat on her back, propping her legs up. The gentle touch of his hands was soothing to her body. It felt like they had touched her soul. He lay flat on his belly between her legs. "Relax baby." He caressed her breasts with his tongue, one after the other and down her torso to her throbbing wet pussy. He spread her lips open and gently stroked her clit with his tongue. Her body stiffened with pure pleasure as he tongue fucked her clit. She relaxed when he'd ease up. Her legs trembled, her stomach tightened. All the moisture in her mouth disappeared. She tightly gripped his head, stilling him. She was about to cum. The first wave came, leaving her jerking as she erupted.

"Mr. Sweet Tongue," she moaned three times. Tanisha attempted to push his head away, yet she wanted him to stay put at the same time. Her clit was too sensitive. The shit felt good! He aggressively continued at it. She wanted him, but he was too much to handle. Two kisses on the pussy, and he removed his head from between her legs. He knew he had accomplished his goal. Dripping wet, her pussy juices continued to flow.

"Are you ready for Mr. Sweet Dick?" He dropped his pants.

Mr. Sweet Dick stared at Tanisha, his dick hard as a brick. She placed her hand around the head as pre-cum seeped through. She wanted to take Mr. Sweet Dick in her mouth and deep throat him, but it was too soon to bring out her secret weapon.

He removed her hand and began stroking it himself as

he stood in her face. He rubbed Mr. Sweet Dick across her lips and kneeled down to the floor. He pushed her down on her back and raised one leg in the air. Her pussy inhaled and exhaled as he watched moisture flow down from her pussy and between her ass crack. He positioned himself underneath her with her leg resting on his shoulder and teased her pussy with the head of his dick. Finally, he entered her with a small thrust. She wanted all of him inside her. Three stokes of the head, she took him around the waist and pulled him deep inside her. She couldn't control herself, and he was loving it.

After some time had passed, the camel hump appeared in his back. He took her around the neck, eased his tongue into her mouth and they began to tongue wrestle. The more they tongue fucked the wetter her pussy got and the harder his dick beat the pussy up. "Mr. Sweet Dick. Oh my goodness, Mr. Sweet Dick," she moaned, still tongue fucking him. "Get this pussy, Mr. Sweet Dick." She stuck her tongue in his ear and then ran her tongue over his neck.

She could feel his body grow rigid. He slowly painted the walls of her pussy as if he were Picasso and she was his masterpiece. He rolled her over on top of him and she placed her hands on his chest. He palmed her ass and spread her cheeks apart. She straddled him fiercely, reaching her hand between her legs and gripping the shaft of his dick with her pussy. His legs tightened as hers did during her climax. She removed her hand and took as much of him inside her that could fit. She could feel him in the mid-section of her stomach.

My goodness! This is a nice, big dick, she thought. His dick fit her pussy like a glove. It's hard to find good dick in the world today! My goodness! She could feel his dick tickling her g-spot. Her knees buckled. He sat up and wrapped his arms around her back, Indian style. The two were glued to each other. Tanisha was on cloud nine. She wanted to fuck the life out of him if that were possible.

"Ummmm, umm, mmmm! Oh my goodness. Good pussy, good pussy," he moaned, gripping her body tighter. He pressed her down on his dick as he grinded in her pussy.

"Ahhhhh, shit!" he screamed and bit her on the shoulder, reaching his climax. They both were happily exhausted and fell asleep, cuddled into each other's arms.

Morning came. Tanisha laid there with her eyes closed thinking about the magic Mr. Sweet Dick and she made. The way they fucked was so good. She rolled a little as if she were still asleep, trying to get close to him, but she couldn't feel him anywhere. She opened her eyes and Mr. Sweet Dick was nowhere in sight. Gone without a trace.

She sat up and wrapped the comforter around her. Why didn't he wake her up? she thought, feeling vexed. She wanted a repeat of sexual ecstasy. She wanted to fuck! He left her with a throbbing pussy.

As she examined the room, there was an envelope left on the floor beside her. She picked it up and opened it. Two thousand dollars and a note was enclosed. Did he just treat her like a whore? Tanisha thought before reading the contents of the letter.

Good morning Ms. Good Pussy:

I had a nice time last night. Mr. Sweet Dick was well pleased with the inside of your peach as well as the taste of the juice. I can still taste your pussy on my tongue. Smile!

I left you a little something. I'll be back to see you

soon. In the meantime, let's keep this between you and me.

Love,

Mr. Sweet Dick.

P.S. Don't share that pussy with nobody. If you do, I'll be very disappointed.

She tore the note into tiny pieces and trashed it. Just like that, Mr. Sweet Dick was gone, and she didn't know when they would have another secret rendezvous.

Knock, knock.

"Who is it?" Tanisha called out. "Who could this be knocking at my door this time of morning?" She looked out the peep hole. There was nobody there. That was strange.

Against her better judgment she opened the door and barely peeked out. No one was in sight. As she began to close the door she looked down. A DVD called Sliding Door with a note taped to it lay at her feet. She picked it up, locked her door then removed the note and began to read it.

I thought this would be a good movie for you to watch. It teaches you about life. Mainly, it gives you a chance to see how two different things can happen to the same person and have a different outcome. Make sure you pay close attention to the movie. You wouldn't want to miss it. So get your popcorn before the movie starts.

Enjoy!

Now her mind started to wonder. At first she thought Mr. Sweet Dick sent it, but the handwriting was different. Then she thought about the other guy who had been sending her gifts. She couldn't possibly send a plasma television or a complete living room set back, because she had no one to send them to. Plus, Tanisha enjoyed each and every one of them. She figured soon he'd show his face.

Tanisha had to get ready for church. She needed God to shed some light on her. The movie would have to wait.

Chapter Twenty-Three
THROUGH THICK AND THIN

nock, knock.

Armani knocked on the bathroom door.

"Yes," Infinity said softly, covering the receiver of her phone.

"You know we have to get ready for church," Armani said, fastening her bra.

"Yes, I know. I'll be out in a bit."

"Are you okay?" Armani asked. She wondered if Infinity was still dwelling on the fight she and Tanisha had last night or had she let it go. Then again she knew in her heart of hearts Infinity never let anything go because she couldn't stand to lose.

"Yes, I'm fine. I'm not a child. Give me a break." She rolled her eyes and stuck out her tongue behind the closed door.

Armani sighed and stormed away from the bathroom door.

"Hello. You still there, Sam?" Infinity whispered into her cell phone. Many nights since the blow up with Roscoe and Tanisha, Infinity had endured sleepless nights and fought so hard to find true forgiveness in her heart, but she couldn't muster up enough strength to control her emotions.

"Yeah, I'm here. What up?" Sam replied in a deep, scratchy voice.

"Did you take care of that?" Infinity asked desperately.

When all the girls were sound asleep, Infinity slipped out of the house. She took Armani's car and went to James Brown Boulevard and Ninth Streets to find Sam, a well-known crack fiend who would do anything for a few dollars. Infinity was so confident Sam would do her dirty work because he'd come through for her several times in the past.

"Yeah, yeah I took care of that," Sam said.

"Good!" Infinity smiled. "You did make sure she got it before you left, right?" Infinity asked.

"Yeah, I made sure she got it. I knocked on the door and hid. I watched until she opened the door. I saw her pick up the DVD and take it inside," Sam assured her.

"Okay Sam, thanks. Don't be stealing out your momma's house either! I know you'll sell the stank of shit if you could." Infinity joked.

"Speaking of selling something, I got some DVDs myself. Help a nigga and take 'em off my hands."

"I gotta go, papi. I'll look you up next time I need you." Infinity hung up the phone.

She sat on the toilet. Now the bitch got the movie. That bitch is gone fall the fuck out when she watches it. What better movie to watch than one you're acting in yourself. Talk about payback is a mutha'. Next time that bitch think about me she'll know I mean what I say when I say don't fuck with me. I'm gone make millions of copies and sell them to anybody that want to buy them. Yeah, it's more than one way to skin a bitch. Fuck skinning a cat! Infinity had set her plan in motion.

"Damn, Infinity, are you dying in there?" Armani banged twice on the bathroom door, bringing Infinity out of her devious thoughts.

"Girl, I'm comin' now." She slung the door open. "Damn girl, two more pounds and I won't be able to fit your clothes anymore." Infinity admired Armani's dress on her body as she looked in the mirror. Armani was the size of a toothpick, but had the curves every woman dreamed of. "I don't know why you wanna go to church anyway." Infinity glared at Armani's reflection. Armani stood behind her making sure every hair on her head was in place. "You ain't been going."

"People tend to go astray for a moment. We've been going through so much lately. We need God's presence right now," Armani declared.

"You're right. I can't argue with that. Where's Venom and Jazzy?" Infinity asked.

"They're in the family room waiting on us. They were here for you last night. It's good to see that you're doing better. Last night you were a nervous wreck," Armani spoke with caution. She didn't want to speak of the ass whipping Infinity wore and upset her.

"Tell me again why you called them bitches last night anyway?" Infinity asked, peering into Armani's eyes. Infinity could've kept the fight with Tanisha to herself; she would have never told any of them.

"I didn't know what to do for you. The last time you were like this, we all found comfort in each other," Armani replied.

"Well, I didn't need them. It was already embarrassing enough with all those bitches watching me at the club." A tear dropped from Infinity's eye. She quickly blotted it with a handkerchief from her bosom.

"Fuck those bitches at the club!" Armani stated. "They're the last thing you need to be worried about. You need to focus on yourself. Jazzy and Venom are your friends. Friends are supposed to be there for you through thick and thin," Armani declared.

"I need to focus on me and TD. I know I embarrassed him last night. I could tell by the way he looked at me. I should've never let that bitch take me out of my character. It doesn't matter. I'm gone do whatever it takes to make it up to him."

Armani watched her rave on and on about TD. She couldn't understand why Infinity still wanted this man after the way he treated her in the club.

"Okay, whatever you want to do, but let's go to church and see what message God has for us today. Another thing, don't mistreat Jazzy and Venom. They were here for you."

"Don't mistreat Jazzy and Venom," Infinity mocked Armani. "That sounds weird comin' from you." Infinity laughed.

"Actually, I've had a change of heart. If they want to get married, I'll be there for them. You know I love them girls. Everybody has their own opinion about certain things. I had mine about gay marriage. I now know to keep my opinions to myself."

"Yeah, good idea. Keep your opinions to yourself," Infinity agreed.

"Anyway." Armani dismissed Infinity's last statement with a wave of the hand. "One more thing."

"One more thing," Infinity mocked. She smiled as she smoothed on her lipstick.

"On the way back we have to stop by Chocolate

Castle so you can pick up your car. I couldn't find anyone to drive it home for me last night."

Armani headed toward the door. Infinity trailed behind Armani. "What if that bitch did something to my truck?" Infinity pretended to be worried.

"I don't think Tanisha would do that."

"You don't think the bitch would do a lot of things. It seems to me that you're always siding with that bitch over me. That crack head bitch got some dirt or something on you?"

"Infinity!"

"Hello no! She doesn't have any dirt on me," Armani lied. She thought about the incident at the health department and when she tried to seduce Tanisha and Tanisha rejected her. She was ashamed, and prayed that skeleton never came out the closet.

Venom and Jazzy were in the family room. They'd been there all night and all they heard for consecutive hours was crying from Infinity, who refused to talk to anyone. She was so full of pain. The last thing she wanted was for Venom and Jazzy to see her like that.

"Damn, what's taking them so long?" Jazzy asked Venom, getting agitated and running short on patience. She wished she would've stayed home.

"Give them a few more minutes. I'm sure they'll be out soon." Venom tried to keep Jazzy calm.

"You know I have to work tonight," Jazzy said.

"You have to work the midnight shift again tonight?" Venom asked as if she were upset.

"Yeah, I thought I told you." Jazzy kissed Venom passionately on the lips.

I'm going to work too, little does she know, Venom thought.

"No, you didn't." Venom returned the kiss. "I thought we were gone have some time to ourselves tonight," Venom replied. Venom was ready to get into her usual sexual encounters, without Jazzy.

"Y'all girls ready to get this over with?" Infinity entered the family room like last night never happened. She sparkled from head to toe. The concealer covered every scratch on her face. Her skin was flawless, but she still wore a pair of designer shades. The thought of knowing the bruises were still there made her a bit uncomfortable.

"Good morning, ladies." Armani entered the room directly behind Infinity. "Thank you so much for coming over last night. I really appreciate it. I hope you guys made yourself comfortable, as always."

"No problem. What are friends for? Oh yeah, and we ate you out of house and home," Venom joked.

Infinity didn't want to hear anything they had to say about last night. She totally ignored their conversation.

"Are you ladies ready?" Armani asked. She caught Infinity's reaction to them joking about eating the food the night before. They had thirty minutes before church would begin. Without a word, everyone grabbed their purses and headed for the front door.

"My goodness, Venom. You sure have put on some weight," Armani said, trailing the girls down the corridor toward the front door.

"I really haven't had too much to do lately. Jazzy works all the time. I stay home and there's nothing to do but eat and watch TV.

Venom's breast were enlarging, her hips were spreading, and her skin was glowing. The pregnancy was taking over her being. Headed into her second trimester, she began wearing clothes that were larger than usual.

Venom being pregnant was the last thing on Jazzy's mind. "Everybody can't stay a size one-two or three-four like you, Armani," Jazzy lashed out. Jazzy thought Armani was being arrogant because she'd always been so judgmental in the past.

"Can we please not argue this morning? I wasn't being funny. Look at her. She has gained weight. Hell, if you didn't work so much you'd notice her more," Armani spat.

"Okay bitch, I've had enough of your smart ass mouth. For the last time. Stay out my fuckin' business. Homophobic, bitch!" Jazzy spazzed out. She turned to Venom. "I knew I should've stayed my black ass at home. If I come over this bitch's house again, something big gone jump outta her." Jazzy was pissed.

No, something big is going to jump out of me, Venom thought of the unborn child in her womb.

"I'm not going to be too many more of your bitches. Especially, not in my own home," Armani replied in a soft proper tone that only pissed Jazzy off more.

"Hey, hey, hey. Y'all need to stop this shit right now," Venom interjected.

"That's that bitch!" Jazzy pointed to Armani.

Venom stood between the two of them and turned to Jazzy.

"Apologize right now," she demanded.

"Apologize! Why am I always the one to apologize to her?" Jazzy placed her hands on her hips and rolled her eyes.

"Because you're wrong. I have gained five pounds." Venom gazed into Jazzy's eyes.

"Baby, I'm sorry. I didn't notice you gained any

weight." Jazzy examined her body. "Baby, do you think I've been neglecting you for my job?" Jazzy's eyebrows wrinkled and she stretched out her arms to hug Venom. Jazzy realized Armani had been right. She had been thinking more about her job and making detective than putting time into her relationship.

Venom prevented Jazzy's arms from locking around her. "All that shit is irrelevant right now. You need to apologize to Armani. Damn, that tongue gone get your ass in trouble one day, with that smart ass mouth!"

Jazzy barely sighed as she approached Armani. "I apologize. Will you accept my apology?" Jazzy hated that she had made a fool out of herself once again. What she hated even more was apologizing to Armani, but she was wrong this time and an apology was in order. Inside, Jazzy always felt that Venom sided with Armani. She was deeply hurt and didn't want it to show.

"Yes, I accept your apology." Armani smiled.

All the girls headed out the door, clean from head to toe. A cellular phone began to ring. All the girls looked at one another. No one was expecting a call, yet they all reached in their purses for their phones. Infinity flipped her phone open. "Hello?" she answered,

"I need to see you. Here at Denny's on Washington Road. We can have breakfast," TD insisted in a deep, masculine tone. Infinity took a few steps away from the girls and lowered her voice.

"I can't come right now. I'm on my way to church." Infinity cared more about going to meet TD than if she had to go to her dead mother's funeral. Her smile almost swallowed the phone she kept pressed to her face.

"I'll tell you what. Just as soon as you get out of church make sure you call me. When is church over?"

"I'll be out around one o'clock. I'll call you on your cell as soon as I get out," Infinity whispered, hoping church would be over soon so she could get to TD. She wanted so desperately for him to want her the way she wanted him.

"Make sure you do that. I have something important to talk with you about," he said, hanging up without Infinity getting another word in.

Infinity wondered what TD wanted to talk about. She wondered if he was still upset about last night. Dismissing her worries, all she really cared about was being in his presence. If he was in hell burning to death, that's where she wanted to be. Infinity stood gazing into the blue sky above her. It was a bright, sunny and beautiful day outside. TD's call made her day even brighter. All her worries were over.

"Excuse me," Armani said, tapping Infinity's shoulder and bringing her back to reality. Infinity was still smiling. She wasn't about to let anybody spoil her day. She acted as if God himself had called her.

"Are you ready? Or are we just going to stand here so you can watch the sun set, too?" Armani asked, being sarcastic. They were minutes from getting to church late.

"Okay, I know you wanna know. That was TD on the phone. He wants to see me after church." Infinity drifted to the passenger side of Armani's 745 Beamer she'd won from her divorce settlement.

The nerve of her, I can't believe she's still going to see him. Is she stupid or what? Damn he must have roots on her, Armani thought as she entered the car and started the engine. Jazzy and Venom were already sitting in the backseat.

Everybody was silent. Armani popped in Marvin

Sapp's CD and played "Never Would've Made It." All the girls were in their own world, miles away as the song penetrated their hearts and souls.

"Why are you on Laney Walker Boulevard? What church are we going to?" Infinity asked, in a hurry for church to start and be over. She was ready to drop them bitches and burn the road up getting to TD.

"We're going to Good Hope Baptist Church down on East Cedar Street today, ladies. I'm in the mood for some soul singing and some good preaching. Pastor Hatney is awesome. Any objection from anyone?" Armani glanced over at Infinity, and then in the rearview mirror at Venom and Jazzy. Not a word escaped from anyone's lips.

Chapter Twenty-Four
THE WORKS OF THE FLESH

T he ladies parked and got out the car. Each one of them was focused on the other, trying to make sure everything was intact. They understood it was Sunday service, but they still wanted to be the center of attention. They never gave a second thought to the saying, 'Come as you are.' All they knew was 'dress to impress.'

Everything was everything as Venom would put it, meaning everybody was clean and nothing was out of place.

The three ladies walked ahead of Infinity into the church. Just as Infinity was entering the doors she glanced to the right and there stood Tanisha. Her stomach churned instantly. If Infinity's eyes could kill through her designer shades, Tanisha would've dropped dead right then and there.

Infinity swiftly turned her head and proceeded into the church. She was very uncomfortable knowing her world appeared to be upside down every time she came in contact with her.

The usher passed a program to Infinity and she waltzed down the aisle searching for the pew where Armani, Jazzy, and Venom were seated.

Armani noticed the disturbed look on Infinity's face. She leaned slightly and whispered, "What's wrong with you?"

"There's nothing wrong with me. Why do you ask that?" Infinity whispered back, hating that Armani could read her so well.

"Your entire demeanor changed. When we got out of the car you were fine." Armani thought it had something to do with TD. "You even have a wrinkle in the middle of your forehead. I know what that means."

"Stop watching me so hard. There's nothing wrong. My stomach's queasy, that's all."

As Tanisha walked by, Armani's eyes bucked and it was as if a light bulb flashed in her head. She now knew exactly what the problem was.

"I bet your stomach is queasy," Armani said sarcastically. "You saw her before you entered the church, didn't you?" Infinity didn't respond. "Today is the Lord's day and there will be no fighting or arguing. Do you hear me?" Armani asked in a low, but serious tone through clenched teeth.

"Girl, it's not that serious. I told you my stomach was upset. This is my first time seeing her."

"Yeah, right," Armani mumbled as she positioned herself forward.

Jazzy also spotted Tanisha and gave a slight shove of the elbow to get Venom's attention from reading the program. Venom's heart was smiling; she was excited to see Tanisha, but didn't want the other girls to know. She smiled as Tanisha took a seat on the pew in front of them.

Infinity couldn't keep her eyes off Tanisha. She hated her with every fiber of her being. She wanted to hurt her in the worse way possible. If she could kill her and get away with it, then so be that too.

The pastor had everybody stand for prayer. The church was packed to capacity. During prayer, hands waved in thanks to the Lord. All that was heard was "Yes Lord" and "Amen" as the pastor's voice penetrated the ears of everyone in the congregation. Some believed, some didn't, some came to praise and some came because being in church on Sunday made them look good. When prayer was over, everyone took their seats.

"Today I had my sermon planned out, but the Lord has led me in a different direction and I have to let His will be done today," Pastor Hatney stated as he had the choir begin service in song.

The choir stood to their feet and began to sing Hezekiah Walker's "I Need You to Survive."

"Stand to your feet, church. Turn to your neighbor and give them a hug. Tell them you won't harm them with the words from your mouth," Pastor Hatney chimed in as the choir continued to sing. Submissively, the church did as the Pastor asked. The church was full of joy and praise throughout the song.

"Oh yes, today is the day that the Lord has made; let us rejoice and be glad in it," the pastor stated.

The Intercessory Prayer was recited. Praise and worship was done, scriptures were read, the choir sang again and the announcements came last. The baskets for tithes and offerings was passed around. Infinity went into her purse and dropped a wad of cash into the basket. Jazzy glanced at her and wondered if Infinity thought that would pay for all of her sins.

When the time came for the sermon, the pastor opened his Bible, turned to Galatians 5:19-21 and asked the congregation to join him. They read about the works of the flesh and how if they are practiced, the Kingdom of God would not be inherited.

After the pastor finished reading the verses, the bass of his voiced boomed throughout the church when he said, "Is there anyone in this congregation that doesn't want to inherit the Kingdom of God?"

"No, no, no," the congregation shouted in unison.

"Very well then, I didn't think so." He wiped sweat from his brow with his handkerchief. Then he read about the fruits of the spirit from Galatians 5:22-26.

The pastor concluded his sermon. Every word touched Armani's heart and tears streamed down her face. Her makeup was ruined; she didn't think twice about it.

An uneasy feeling conjured up in Jazzy's body and she knew she had to do something with her lifestyle or bust hell wide open when her day came to meet her higher power.

Infinity eyed her watch every five minutes, ready to get the hell out of there to meet TD.

Venom thought more about her unborn baby than anything else.

* * * * *

Tanisha took in everything the pastor said. She wanted bygones to be bygones. She didn't want any more animosity, no more fighting. Life is too short, Tanisha thought as the words from the pastor manifested in her heart.

It was time to open the door for all sinners to come to the Lord, repent and be forgiven of their sins.

The choir stood to their feet just as the rest of the congregation did. The pastor called out to anyone that wanted to be forgiven of their sins and walk with the Lord to come to the front center of the church. The choir softly hummed a tune. People began to head toward the altar. Tanisha's tears were unstoppable. She had no control over what she was feeling.

She eased by the people on the pew. "Excuse me, excuse me," she said as she made her way to the center of the podium. Tanisha trembled with fear, but knew this was what she needed. She had to do it. It was time for a turning point in her life. Tanisha knew she had to crawl before she walked, but she was willing to take that first step. Nothing in her life would change overnight.

* * * * *

Tears streamed steadily down Armani's face. Her body tensed up, but she felt her feet moving, her body followed suit. Go, go, it's the right thing to do, she thought as she turned to look back at her friends. But something inside her told her to keep her head straight, facing the pastor. She wasn't doing it for them, she was doing it for herself. When the time came to stand in front of God on judgment day she knew that nobody would be able to answer for her, but her.

* * * * *

Tanisha looked over and was surprised to see Armani and three other people standing next to her. She was ecstatic. Her heart immediately filled with joy. She and Armani exchanged smiles. Tanisha took two steps over to Armani. She could feel her temperature rising, and the palms of her hands were beginning to sweat. The pastor proceeded to pray as he asked the church to stand.

* * * * *

Negative thoughts toward Tanisha danced in Infinity's head. Where does that bitch think she's going? That dope fiend bitch is turning the church into a circus. They look like clowns up there. They know they're going to go right back out and fuck up as soon as church is over. Why would they try to think about it?

Infinity was furious and couldn't see through her own obsession of wanting revenge on Tanisha. She didn't know that Tanisha and Armani both really wanted this transformation to take place in their lives. They both wanted peace.

The people seeking God's forgiveness repeated the sinner's prayer.

Once service was over, it's capacity started to minimize by the second. "Please hurry and drop me to my car," Infinity insisted as she stared out the car window twirling her hair.

"Let's go have lunch first," Armani suggested with a smile, ignoring Infinity's attitude.

"Hell no. Take me to my car now." Infinity turned and glared at Armani.

"It's fine, Armani," Venom chimed in. She knew Jazzy was ready to get home anyway.

"Okay, maybe next Sunday," Armani said.

"Yeah, next Sunday," Venom responded.

Jazzy didn't breathe a word because she knew her mouth always got her into trouble.

Infinity sat silently shaking her leg and hoping Armani would put the pedal to the metal and get her to her car pronto. She was dying to get to TD to find out what he wanted.

Reaching Infinity's car, the girls stared at the sign

with the sexy lady plastered on top of the building wearing a bikini and eating a chocolate bar. Chocolate Castle looked like it had been deserted. The parking lot was empty. There was no music booming, nor any lights flashing around its sign. Only one other car was in the parking lot besides Infinity's SUV. The cops had already placed a ten day tow tag on it.

Infinity exited the car without a thank you or a good-bye to the rest of the girls. Venom took the front seat. They didn't feed into Infinity's attitude, but they were sick and tired of her mistreating them and thinking she was always better than they were.

Jazzy exhaled when Infinity exited the car and thought, Bitch! It's good she got her ass kicked. She knew not to utter those words from her lips. That would only piss Venom off and she didn't want to do that.

"Are you ladies sure you don't want to go and have lunch?" Armani asked Jazzy and Venom.

"We're sure, you can just take us back to your house so we can get our things and the car. We have a busy day planned, and Jazzy has to go to work."

"Okay, I guess I'll just go home and watch a Lifetime movie and order some food." Armani sighed, knowing she'd be home alone for the remainder of the day.

"Now that sounds like a winner, but I'm not into that Lifetime movie shit. Oops, my bad. I forgot you just got saved!" Venom joked with Armani.

"Don't be funny, Venom. I felt like it was time for me to try something different in life. I was a housewife for all those years of being married to Cliff. You see what good that did me. I don't even have a husband anymore, and I was lost and making bad decisions. My whole world revolved around him. We were going to start a family,"

Armani said.

Jazzy and Venom had heard the story many times before. Venom sighed loudly and Jazzy glanced at her watch.

"It's just really complicated," Armani said.

"Girl, you gotta get over that old shit. All that stuff is in the past. You can't keep living in the past. You have to live for now. Don't let one bad apple spoil the whole bunch. You're beautiful and intelligent. There's a man that God has for you, and I'm sure if you'd be patient he'll come to you." Jazzy voiced her opinion with a sincere heart. Armani peered through the rearview mirror at Jazzy. She couldn't believe Jazzy said something to her without being sarcastic. Armani felt the sincerity in Jazzy's words.

"Thanks for the encouragement, Jazzy," Armani replied.

Venom was shocked to the point that it made her have to look back at Jazzy.

Chapter Twenty-Five
UNFINISHED BUSINESS

I nfinity didn't sit inside her car a full ten seconds before Armani pulled off.

Immediately she pulled her cellular phone from her purse and dialed TD's number. He answered on the first ring. "Meet me at the Radisson on the river walk. Room 222." He hung up without giving her a chance to respond. Infinity looked at her phone as her brows touched, putting a wrinkle in the middle of her forehead.

Within twenty minutes she arrived at the hotel. Nervous but anxious, she knocked on the door.

Waiting on TD to open the door, she received an unexpected kiss. TD's lips were glued to her neck and his hard penis was pressed against her ass. She loved every minute of it. Infinity could never understand why he was Casanova in the dark and Mr. Suit in the day. The guy that was all work and no play. She adjusted to his lifestyle so she could fit into his world, no matter how much it hurt her. Infinity was relentless and determined that he would one day change for her.

TD reached around Infinity and stuck the key in the door. Once inside the room, he closed the door behind him and turned her around and tongued her like he'd never tongued her before. They both tore one another's clothes off without a word spoken of the night before.

TD lifted her in the air. She latched on to his waist by locking her legs around his back. He gently slid inside her. With each thrust, Infinity moaned with pleasure. He walked over to the bed with his dick buried deep inside her, lying her flat down on the bed. With the camel hump still in his back, he long-dicked her, caressing her breasts and tonguing her down in unison. Infinity was enjoying it while it lasted. She didn't know what had gotten into TD. She knew he always loved her pussy and felt that's what kept him coming back, but after what happened last night in Chocolate Castle, she was a bit confused. She wondered why he hadn't mentioned the night before. Why wasn't he angry? He was not a predictable man and he was strictly about business. Pleasure always came last. Although she was curious, she didn't mumble a word about the night before.

With one gentle roll in the bed, Infinity was on top of TD. He continued to caress her breasts. She slowly gyrated her hips with TD buried deep inside her. "This dick is good, baby?" TD moaned as he circled his tongue inside her ear.

"Yes, yes, it's good," Infinity responded in pleasurable ecstasy. Her legs were shaking. "TD, oooh, TD," she moaned.

"Call me Mr. Sweet Dick, baby. Call me Mr. Sweet Dick," he pleaded, gripping her waist tightly and pulling her down on his dick.

"Mr. Sweet Dick. This dick is good, Mr. Sweet Dick. Deeper, deeper," Infinity begged, although she was in control. She rode his dick at an accelerated speed as if it was the last piece of dick she'd ever get.

In the middle of Infinity reaching her climax, TD threw her to the bed and buried his head between her thighs and stroked his tongue across her clit. Infinity squirmed to get away from the pulsating sensation that consumed her body. TD gripped her legs, preventing her from getting away as he continued flicking his tongue across her clit. Nowhere to run, and no more squirming, Infinity lay there moaning in pleasurable pain. Reaching her climax once more, she screamed hysterically. Her clit was so sensitive, but the feeling was oh so good. TD released her, stroked his dick a few times as he positioned himself on his knees between her thighs. "You wanna suck Mr. Sweet Dick for me, baby?" he asked seductively. Infinity positioned herself on her elbows and looked into his eyes.

"Yes," she answered.

A few more strokes of the dick and TD changed his mind. He flipped her and forced himself inside her again. As he long-dicked her, he said, "This is the last me you gone get a taste of this dick. You better remember it like a saint remembers a scripture. You fucked me over last night." He fucked her harder as he gazed into her eyes. Sweat from his forehead dripped onto her face. "Shit, this pussy good," he moaned as he continued to fuck her harder. "I knew you were bad for business when I found out you let your emotions control your actions . . . Aw shit, this pussy good!" He slow fucked her, sliding from wall to wall as he ranted about her impulsive, irrational behavior.

Infinity lay there in shock by his words, but his dick felt good to her. She hoped he was only speaking out of anger and would soon forget what happened last night. She knew everything he was saying was the truth. She did let her emotions get the best of her, and she let it show in the worse way. She was embarrassed at the way she acted, but she couldn't help it. She couldn't take it back and what was done was done. Her desire of wanting to be loved and having her man to herself had consumed her. Roscoe had created a monster. The wounds of pain, hurt and resentment she had toward him never had an opportunity to heal. She'd gone from man to man looking for Mr. Right. TD was the closest she'd gotten to a man that possessed the things she loved about Roscoe (good dick, charm, passion in bed and control). In her heart she knew if Roscoe got his act together she'd go running back to him in a split second. But the embarrassment of it all is that he would kill her slowly. His drug habit and the memory of her catching him in bed with another man. His homosexuality prevented her from finding and reconciling with the man she considered her soul mate.

Infinity stroked TD's back as she moaned louder, pretending she hadn't heard anything he was saying. She loved the way he fucked her and wished to be in his arms for all of eternity. She wished no one else existed in the world besides the two of them.

"Boohoo shit, this pussy wet and hot just like I like it." TD's ass began jumping like a jack rabbit. He felt what seemed to be five thousand volts of sexual pleasure pulsating through his body. Every vein in his body protruded through his skin. The level of sexual ecstasy he received was intensifying. His body began to jerk back and forth. Feverishly, he released his nut in her pussy.

Sanity entered his brain, and instantly TD pulled out of Infinity. Fuck! I didn't mean to do that, he thought. He gripped the head of his dick as he lay beside her on his back and gave a silent prayer. My God, please don't let this bitch get pregnant. The last thing I need is a seed by this woman.

Infinity was only good for business and fucking, but never as the mother of his seed, or wifey material. His mom always told him, "If you're man enough to get a woman pregnant, be man enough to stick around."

Infinity rolled over and begin to stroke TD's chest. She gave a silent prayer of her own. My God, please let me be pregnant. That's all I ask. If it's so, I promise to straighten up my act and do right. I promise.

TD grew disgusted at the thought of her possibly being pregnant by him as he lay with his hands folded behind his head. "Move, go take a shower!" he shouted at Infinity. The bass in his voice scared her. She immediately headed for the shower. TD was repulsed at the thought of getting her pregnant. He couldn't stop thinking about it. She was a jealous bitch and he couldn't stomach the thought of being connected to her for eighteen years. He knew he fucked up. Grabbing the remote, he flicked on the TV and caught the latest news on the sports channel.

Infinity let the water from the shower caress her body as she fervently hoped that TD had fertilized one of her eggs. Her heart was filled with joy. She disregarded everything he had said. She believed he was only speaking out of anger. She knew there was no way they could have had such mind-blowing sex and he didn't want anything to do with her. A typical, angry man, she thought as she washed her body and caressed her breasts. She contemplated what he'd say when she got out the shower, so she practiced on a convincing argument that would lead him to forgive her for the fight with Tanisha.

Exiting the shower with a towel wrapped around her body, Infinity modeled a smile that said Cover Girl. As she reentered the room she discovered TD was gone without a trace, not even a note was left. She dashed for her cell phone and dialed his number. No answer, only voice mail. After the fifth call and no answer she decided to leave a message. "Hi, papi. I've called you five times. Why did you leave without letting me know? Call me when you get this message." Infinity convinced herself that he had to rush out to handle business, but she knew in her heart of hearts he got what he came for and he'd call her when he needed her again.

Heartbroken and confused, Infinity flopped across the bed and tears began to fall down her face.

Her cell phone rang. She answered immediately as if she'd never been crying, "Hello? TD?" She plastered a smile on her face that not even the world coming to an end could take away.

"Hey, mami. Sorry mami. It's been so long since I've heard your beautiful voice. I've been missing you like crazy," the man on the other line spoke gently into the phone.

"I don't have time to play any games. Who is this?" she shouted angrily into the phone. It wasn't TD.

"This is the man that gives you the sweetest love. How could you ever forget me? We have unfinished business."

"Roscoe!" she yelled as she recognized his voice.

"Yes baby, it's me. I'll see you around."

Chapter Twenty-Six
HELL TO PAY

D amn! My cell phone is ringing, Tanisha thought. She could hear it, but didn't know where the hell it was. Finally, after fumbling through her purse and almost running into the car in front of her, she realized the phone was in the console. She grabbed it and glanced at a number she didn't recognize. Immediately, she answered, "Hello?"

"Hi there, Miss Lady." She also didn't recognize the voice.

"Who is this?" Tanisha asked calmly.

"You don't recognize my voice? When we last spoke I was telling you how sorry I was for everything I did to you."

"Roscoe!" she yelled. "Where did you get my number from?" She sat up straight as a board with a disgusted look on her face.

"Does it matter? I hear you and my wife are hanging out these days."

"You do mean ex-wife, don't you?"

"Is that what she told you?" He laughed, letting her know Infinity had not only lied to her, but to her friends as well. They were still married.

Lying bitch! she thought. "What reason would she

have to lie?"

"Maybe she was still feenin' for this dick that she loves so much. You do know a little about that, don't you?"

"Ha, ha, and I thought you were going to be this changed man when you apologized at the rehab center."

"Yeah, I thought the same thing, but you know how it is when a nigga ready to get loose from those crackers. I talked to Infinity. We supposed to get with each other a little later. Maybe after I finish with her, I can get some of that super head you got. Damn, my dick getting hard just thinking about it. You remember how you used to slob on this dick, don't you!"

"Look, I'm not that woman anymore, and I don't have time for your bullshit."

"I can't tell. Talk around town about you and these twins on this sex movie say that you're doing everything you used to do and then some."

"What fuckin' movie?" Tanisha asked, wrinkling her eyebrows. This must be a test. Is this what happens when a bitch decides to turn her life over and give it to God? The devil seems to be coming at me full force.

"The DVD—that's the hottest thing selling around here right now. I can't wait to go cop me one."

"I know Frenchy is turning over in her grave right now," she spoke softly, trying to remain calm.

"How you know what a dead muthafucka doing? People kill me when they say that shit."

"You know what, I'm hanging up now. I don't have time for your shit. I don't know who the fuck gave you my number, but you need to lose it with yo' gay ass. Fuckin' nigga. You a nasty muthafucka." She didn't have anything against gays, but Tanisha wanted Roscoe to feel as low as she could possibly make him feel.

Agitated, she hung up her phone and prayed to God for forgiveness. Tanisha had just got saved and already she had to repent. She knew it was too good to be true when Roscoe apologized, telling her how much of a changed man he was. Damn, where the hell did he come from? And Infinity, that lying bitch! Something about this shit ain't right. I gotta find out what fuckin' DVD he's talking about.

About ten minutes later, Tanisha reached her apartment and Delicious was parked out front in his 745 Beamer. "What's up, Delicious? You look delicious today!" She was admiring the car, not Delicious himself. She approached the car. He had the window rolled down with one of his arms hanging out the window.

"I called you several times. What's up with that? I thought you bailed out on me."

"I was on the other line with someone I hadn't talked to in a minute. My bad. What's up though?" Tanisha asked.

"Let a nigga take you out for lunch."

"I thought you were strictly dickly!" she joked with him. He had a mean swagger and she knew he could get much pussy if he wanted it, but that was definitely out of the question.

"Don't flatter yourself, baby girl. Ain't nothing changed but the time. I'm still Delicious and you'll never get a taste of this." His arrogance was taking over.

"Damn, I wish Frenchy was alive. He'd love you." Tanisha smiled.

"He wouldn't love me. No disrespect, but Frenchy wasn't my type. He was too sweet for me. I like 'em hard core and in the closet. Once they get a taste of Delicious they don't never go anywhere else. You see this Beamer I'm sporting, don't you? It's compliments of what Delicious has to offer," he said arrogantly.

"You mean to tell me one of your down low brothers bought this?"

"Yeah." He laid a kiss on the steering wheel, proud of what he'd accomplished, sleeping around with down low brothers. To him, having a BMW was one of his most profound accomplishments.

"I thought TD bought it for you."

"That's what you get for thinking. Boss don't do everything for me, just like he's not going to do everything for you. You gotta get some things done on your own."

Tanisha leaned over into the luxury vehicle and admired the peanut butter leather seats. She glanced at his DVD player. "Hey, you mind if I watch a DVD while we're riding?" she asked.

"No, I don't mind."

"All right. Let me go inside and grab it and put on something a little more comfortable."

Tanisha went inside and changed. Then she stuffed the DVD in her purse and headed back out the door.

Delicious leaned over and opened the car door. He was a real gentleman at all times when it came to women, even though he was a homo-thug type of guy. She didn't know who raised him, but they did a damn good job of it. She hopped in the car. "Where are we going?" Tanisha asked.

"Nowhere special. McDonalds. To the drive through."

"What?" Tanisha gave him a look that told him she knew he was telling a damn lie.

"I'm just kidding, girl. We're going to the Rib Shack to eat some ribs. You do eat pork, don't you?"

"The whole pig, if it's available." They both laughed in unison. She decided not to pop the DVD in because the Rib Shack wasn't that far from her apartment once they hit the expressway and especially with Delicious driving. He didn't know how to go light on the accelerator. She learned that the first time he gave her a ride.

They reached the Rib Shack and placed their orders.

"You know those private parties I told you about?" Delicious asked her.

"Yeah, your freak parties you do from that call center you told me about," Tanisha replied.

"Whatever you wanna call it." Slightly rolling his eyes, he pouted his lips.

"What about it?" she asked, knowing there was something behind it.

"There's this big party going on and they want male and female dancers there.

"You dance?" she asked with raised brows.

"I do a little of everything."

She poked out her lips. "Something about this shit don't sound right. Are you sure they just want dancers?"

"Well, you know how it goes. If they want you to do anything else, that's on you. Give it a try and see if you like it. They're paying big bucks." Delicious rubbed his fingers together trying to convince her.

"So there's going to be gay muthafuckas there, too?"

"What the hell you mean? So you being judgmental now?"

"No, no. I didn't mean it like that. I'm just saying. If they're gay men, what I need to go for?"

"It's gone be straight and gays. We're gonna be inside

a mansion on two separate sides. The girl Venom I told you about is gone be there, too." When Delicious said that Tanisha thought if she didn't want to go, she damn 'sho wanted to go now.

"Sure, I'll go. I don't have nothing else to do, and a little more money in my pocket not gone hurt anything. Does TD know about this?"

"C'mon now. It's not good to let your right hand know what your left hand is doing all the time. I do the job boss needs me to do, then I do my own thing."

"Okay, I can understand that. So when is this party taking place?"

The waiter came over asking if they needed anything. "More tea, please?" Delicious responded. The waiter refilled the glass and left their table.

"It's taking place around ten tonight, but we gonna need to get there before the crowd. You make sure you're ready."

"Who's gonna take over for you at the club tonight?"

"What's tonight?"

"What do you mean?"

"Woman, today is Sunday. Chocolate Castle is closed."

"Damn 'sho is. I don't know what I was thinking."

"I don't know either, but it's party time tonight, baby girl. Time to get that money and make sure fantasies come alive."

"I don't know what you mean, but I ain't giving up no pussy. I ain't wit' that shit. I had my days of giving up the pussy."

"I bet you have." Delicious smirked.

They finished their meals, Delicious paid and they headed for the vehicle.

"Put the DVD in," Delicious insisted.

"Shit! I don't know how to work it," Tanisha said.

Delicious started up the car and put in the DVD. He hit play and relaxed back in the seat.

"Damn!" Delicious shouted. The DVD started and Tanisha was too busy eyeing the dude next to them at the red light pushing a snow white convertible Bentley. He resembled a rapper, but she couldn't recall his name. The traffic light turned green and he sped off as he gave her a wink.

"OMG!" Delicious yelled.

"What you shouting for, Delicious? Damn, did you see that fine ass brother pushing that Bentley?"

"Tanisha look!" He pointed at the screen. "I thought you said you wasn't giving up no pussy no more," he said. His eyes were glued to the screen, admiring the naked men.

"Shit! What the fuck!" she screamed in embarrassment. There Tanisha was, letting two men fuck her like she was some prostitute off the streets. She couldn't believe her eyes. How the fuck did this happen? Who would do this to me? Then a light bulb flashed in her head. Infinity! That bitch!

"Delicious, take this bullshit out. Right fucking now!" she yelled to the top of her lungs, pressing every button she could to stop the DVD from playing. "I can't believe this shit! What the fuck, man? You see this shit?" She frowned, pissed than a muthafucka.

He moved her hand away. "Shit, I'm enjoying this shit," Delicious replied with his eyes still on the screen. He stopped the Beamer in the middle of the street. Cars behind them honked their horns.

"Take it out now, Delicious!" Her voice cracked as

tears finally swelled and fell down her face.

"Girl, ain't no use in yo' ass crying now. You damn sure wasn't crying while you were getting all that dick shoved in yo' ass!" Delicious slowly removed the DVD.

"SHUT THE FUCK UP! You don't understand. When I think everything is coming together for me, here goes some more shit on top of old shit. Take me home, right now!" she screamed.

Delicious stared at Tanisha, finally understanding the hurt reflecting in her eyes. Silence lingered between the two as he drove her home.

He slid in an Isley Brother's CD, and thumbed to track 5, "Living for the Love of You." Tanisha tried to hum the tune to the song. Her heart danced in her chest, aching with pain.

Thoughts stampeded through her brain, both good and bad. That bitch Infinity was still feenin' for revenge just like Tanisha used to be feenin' for that crack. Damn, I can't believe I let this bitch play me this close. Bitch! I can think of a million ways to handle that bitch, but I'm gone leave it alone. I was nothing but nice to that bitch and she was playing me from the beginning. Fuck! I can't believe this shit. On top of that, Roscoe calling, digging up old bones. That's the muthafucka that should've been dead, not Frenchy. Damn Frenchy, I wish you were here with me right now. All them bitches with Infinity probably shady as hell as far as I'm concerned. When I find out who the bitch is behind this shit it's going to be hell to pay.

"Tanisha! Tanisha! I know you hear me talking to you!" Delicious repeated until he got her undivided attention. She'd drifted off into her own world.

She slowly turned her head toward him and ran her

hand across her face. "My bad, Delicious. I'm just so disgusted with myself. The devil is very busy in my life right now."

He stroked her hair with his right hand, keeping his left on the steering wheel. "Woman, don't get yourself too upset. It's done now. The question is, what are you gonna do about it? It looked like you was game for what was going down. It don't look like no rape or anything."

"Naw, it wasn't a rape. It's just the fact that it's recorded without my consent. I know that bitch Infinity was behind this shit. I can feel it in my gut."

"Why she hate you so much?"

"Because I used to be on crack and her faggot ass husband loved this good head and this good pussy I was giving him," she blurted before realizing what she was saying.

"Husband? I don't think boss know nothing about that," Delicious responded.

"Yeah, husband! Then on top of that, the nigga had nerve to call me today to stir up some shit. I know it's gone be some trouble. I don't have time for this shift in my life right now." Her tears wouldn't stop falling. "I know I need to get my shit together."

"Woman, don't worry. I got you. Ain't shit gone happen to you while you with me. I got strict orders on that."

"From who? Your boss? He wants to protect his investment?"

"Naw, it's another good friend of mine that wants to be left unknown. You don't think you have all that expensive ass shit in that apartment for nothing, do you?"

"Huh! So you know where the shit come from, huh?"

"Something like that." She could tell Delicious had

given up too much information. Tanisha was damn curious to know if it was TD and if Delicious was lying to her. Damn, if Mr. Sweet Dick finds out about this DVD, it's gone fuck up all my plans. Shit, what the hell am I gone do? I know this has to be the DVD Roscoe was talking about. Shit, I can't even focus for thinking about this damn movie and whose all seen the shit. This is some fucked up shit. Damn!

"Hey there. Hey. Hello." Delicious waved his hand in her face to get her attention. "You gotta stop it, woman. You gone have a nervous breakdown. Look, home sweet home. I hope you don't change your mind about the party tonight."

"I'll call you." Tanisha snatched the DVD and rushed out of the car without giving Delicious a chance to say anything. She had to call somebody and see what the hell was going on.

As she stuck her key into the door and opened it, a shadow of something loomed against the wall, but she couldn't tell exactly what it was. She flicked on the light and roses of all colors were displayed throughout the apartment. Mr. Sweet Dick's name was written all over it.

"Fuck that. I can't think about no roses right now." She paused in her steps. "Wait a minute. How the fuck did he get in my apartment?" Tanisha glanced around. "Shit! Fuck that too right now." She dialed Venom's number on her cell.

"Hello?" she answered on the first ring.

"Bitch, I tried to be nice to y'all bitches. I got saved today and now y'all bitches bringing out my old ways. Bitch, if you don't get over to my apartment right now it's gone be some hell to pay. You hear me, bitch?" She hung up the phone.

"I gotta pay these bitches back if it's the last thing I do. I gotta get to the bottom of this shit and Armani's ass is next. I can't wait to talk to that bitch! I'm going from the bottom up," Tanisha yelled.

Chapter Twenty-Seven
NO LOYALTY

hirty minutes later, a knock sounded at Tanisha's door. She slung the door open and slapped the shit out of Venom before giving her a chance to say anything.

She put her hand up to her face and gently rubbed her stinging cheek. "Damn bitch! What the fuck you slap me for? The only bitch allowed to do some shit like that to me is a bitch I'm fucking. Are you getting ready to give me some pussy or something? If not, I'ma beat yo ass."

"Not in your wildest dreams, hoe!"

"Well, you better get to muthafuckin' talkin' 'cause I'm seconds from being on your ass," Venom shouted as she slammed the door.

Tanisha pressed play on the DVD player and slouched down on the couch without saying a word. Venom sat next to her, straight faced. Tanisha turned to her. Her eyes were bloodshot and swollen. "Did you know about this?" she asked with a shivering bottom lip.

"Yes . . . and no."

"What the fuck you mean 'yes and no?' What kind of answer is that?" Tanisha glared at her.

Venom sighed before speaking. "Well, I knew they drugged you with ecstasy." She met Tanisha's gaze, then looked down at the floor.

"They did what? Who the fuck are they? I know I slept with the guys, but some of the things I saw on the DVD I don't remember. Now I know why I don't remember. The bitches drugged me! I can't believe this shit." She folded her arms across her chest and quickly tapped her foot against the floor.

"Infinity and Armani, right?" Tanisha finally said.

"Armani was against it, but Infinity insisted she do it. And everything Infinity says, Armani goes along with it. Even when she knows it's not the right thing to do. I'm so sorry this happened to you, but I tried to tell you about Infinity, but you didn't want to listen. You swore she was the best thing for you. There's no loyalty when it comes to her. You crossed her and all she wants is revenge. I can't believe you didn't see it coming. When Jazzy got wind of them drugging you, she was pissed."

"You mean to tell me everybody knew and not one of y'all bitches told me?"

"Hey. You were Infinity's people, not ours. She brought you around." Venom threw her hand up in the air as if saying 'Hold up bitch.'

"Is there any loyalty with any of y'all bitches? I bet y'all bitches cut each other's throat. All y'all bitches name should be Judas."

"Hey, I do my own dirt. I don't have time to get into nobody else's shit," she said, clapping her hands and swaying from one side to the other.

"You damn 'sho right about that. What about that baby you got stuck up your ass? What you gone do about that?" Tanisha gazed at Venom's belly.

Venom's eyes bucked but she focused and said, "Baby, that's the last thing you need to be worried about. You need to be worried about this damn DVD before everybody and they momma see it. That's what you need to do."

Speechless, Tanisha stared at Venom. She was dazed and nothing Venom said to her registered. Tanisha was pissed and wanted to get to the bottom of this shit.

She went into the kitchen to fix herself something to drink so she could take two aspirin to soothe the aching headache that suddenly appeared. Her mind was full of vengeful thinking.

"Do you have some OJ in there?" Venom asked. Tanisha didn't respond. Venom went into the kitchen and poured herself a glass of orange juice. Immediately, after taking the first sip, Venom rushed to pray to the porcelain god. Tanisha guessed the baby she was carrying didn't like orange juice. She could hear her vomiting all the way in the kitchen.

A cell phone began ringing. Tanisha went into the living room to answer it, but instead Venom's cell phone was lit up and vibrating on the couch. Tanisha peeked at the caller ID screen and the same number Roscoe called her from earlier flashed on her screen along with the name Love. Curiosity got the best of her and she answered it.

"Hello?" she whispered.

"What up, Vee? Why you sound like you whispering?" he said.

"I just woke up. What's up with you?" Tanisha said, pretending to be Venom.

"Not much. A nigga just wanted to call and check on my girl and my baby to see how y'all doing. I know you gone let a nigga do that."

"What?" Tanisha answered impulsively, almost giving herself away.

"You heard me. A nigga called to check on his girl and his baby. How y'all doing?"

"We're fine. Where are you?" she whispered.

"C'mon, baby. You must be still sleeping. I'm still at the rehab where you dropped me off. I had a good time at the hotel, even though it was only an hour. I got one more weekend up in this muthufucka and I don't have to worry about no passes and shit no more. I can lay up and get that pussy all day and all night." He let off a loud chuckle.

I can't believe my muthafuckin' ears, Tanisha thought. Venom and Roscoe? Now this was some grimey ass shit. Now I know where this nigga got my number from. Either she gave it to him or he got it out of her phone.

"So baby, you sure they gonna let you out for good in a week?" Tanisha whispered as she picked for information.

"I'm positive. When you pick me up bring me an eight ball. That same shit you brought me the last time. And make sure you have all my clothes and shit you promised me. Okay baby?"

Damn, the bitch bring dope to the nigga, too, Tanisha thought.

"Okay, baby. I'll make sure I have everything you need and some. Call me back a little later. Me and the baby need some rest. Okay, baby?"

"Aw'right baby, no problem," he replied, seeming to be such a gentleman, but his ass was the scum of the fucking earth. Quickly, she shut the phone off and laid it back on the couch.

These bitches are something else. Damn, I must be living in a movie or some shit. Where in the hell did these bitches come from! Where the fuck do they do this shit at?

Two minutes after hanging up the phone, Venom came into the living room with a cold cloth pressed against her face. Tanisha wanted to see how things were going to play out with Venom, Jazzy, and this baby situation. Oh, and now Roscoe.

Venom slouched down on the couch with her head thrown back and the cloth now pressed to her forehead. "So Vee, have you figured out who your baby daddy is yet?" Tanisha asked, calling her the pet name Roscoe had given her.

Venom glanced at her strangely, clueless to Tanisha's motive. She sat up and removed the cloth from her forehead. "What did you just call me?" she asked.

"I called you Vee."

"You've never call me that. Only one person calls me Vee."

"Oh yeah!" She grinned.

"Yeah," Venom mocked, steaming with anger and bewilderment.

"Who is that? Jazzy?"

"No, someone else I'm involved with," she said hastily and crossed her legs, one over the other.

"Would that person be Roscoe? Infinity's husband?" Tanisha didn't have time to play cat and mouse any longer.

"Hell no! I don't even know Infinity's husband. I've never seen him in my life. I just heard all the stories she used to tell us about him. Why the fuck would you say something like that any fuckin' way?"

Tanisha looked left and then right, as if someone else was in the living room. "So you gonna sit here in my face and lie like you don't know him, and lie like that baby you're carrying isn't his?"

"That's exactly what the fuck I'm saying. I don't fuckin' know him. Now quit fuckin' askin' me that shit. I might fuck a lot of niggas, but I'm not no cut throat ass bitch like that!" Venom rolled her eyes.

"Okay, what if I told you I answered your phone when you were in the bathroom and I pretended to be you."

"Okay, and? I still don't know him."

"Girl, stop your shit. I talked to him. He thought I was you and he asked me about the baby and all. He even told me he was at the rehab center. Bitch, I know who I was talking to."

"Oh, the dude from the rehab center! His name isn't Roscoe. His name is Rodney," she said. Tanisha could tell by the way it rolled off her tongue that he'd pulled another scam on another stupid bitch. She was the stupid bitch the last time.

"His name is Roscoe. I know who the fuck I was talking to. He lied to you. That was Infinity's husband on that phone. I know the nigga's voice when I hear it. Besides that, he called me earlier from the same number. That's what made me answer it," Tanisha said, getting agitated. She knew what the fuck she was talking about and the bitch still sat in her face and continued to lie or lied without knowing.

"I don't give a fuck who you thought it was. I'm telling you his name is Rodney. You need to stop prying in my business and worry about the DVD floating around town with your ass cocked up in the air. That's what the fuck you need to do," she spat venom back at Tanisha. She took two steps toward her.

"Oh, so it's like that, bitch? But when yo' ass get in a fuckin' bind, you bring yo' skank ass to my door. Bitch, you really got some nerve." She shoved Venom. "Bitch, get the fuck out of my house!" She pointed to her front door. "Go home and worry about how you gone hide that baby that's stuck up in your ass that belongs to your friend's husband. That's what the fuck you do, hoe."

Hotter than cayenne pepper, Tanisha bolted to the door and slung it open.

"Fine bitch!" Venom slowly proceeded toward the door. Tears began to form in her eyes as her chest began to heave. With her hand placed on her hip, Tanisha pretended not to give a fuck if Venom cried blood. As she approached the threshold, she turned back and put her hand on the door, and then closed it as she proceeded to plead her case.

"Tee, I swear on my unborn baby I don't know Roscoe. Maybe Rodney sounds like him or something. I don't know what the hell is going on here. I'm already going through so much; the last thing I need is to be fucked up with Roscoe. And besides, everything I've heard about that nigga, I definitely don't want to be fucked up with him."

Tanisha put her arms around her. "Girl, I believe you when you say the nigga on the phone was Rodney, but I'm here to tell you the nigga on the phone was really Roscoe. I don't know how he pulled this shit off, but girl, he got yo' ass caught.

"How you meet this nigga?" she asked, dying to know where in the hell this mystery relationship sparked from.

Venom sniffled a few times and wiped tears away from her face. "I was at the gas station off fifty-six across from the driver's license place next to Apple Valley. He came up to my car and took the pump out of my hand and began to pump my gas. He filled up my tank and went inside to pay for it. He was looking good as a muthafucka. Well groomed, well manicured and fine as hell. Not a hair on his head was out of place and you know I love dick. He turned me the fuck on. I couldn't help myself. Anyway, after he paid for the gas I sat there in my car and waited for him to come out and one thing led to another. He told me a little about himself and I told him a little about me. Most of the things that I told him were lies, and now, from what you're telling me, I guess that makes both of us even.

"He told me he'd just gotten out of jail for possession of cocaine with intent to distribute. He also said that he had to stay at the rehab center for nine months—"

"Did you fuck him the same day?" Tanisha interrupted.

"I-I," she stuttered, "well yeah, I fucked him that day."

"Damn bitch, he paid for the gas and you gave him the pussy."

"Damn, bitch, he gave you a piece of crack and you gave up the head, and some pussy!" She hit Tanisha with a low blow to get her off her back.

"Yeah, you got me with that one, but I'm not that girl anymore. I was under the influence of drugs. What's your problem? You probably gave up the head too, hoe," she lashed back.

"Yeah, I did. And you know what my problem is? It's not like I tried to hide that from you. Shit, if he would've never touched me I would've never fucked him. Hell, I was sitting there minding my own gotdamn' business and pumping my own gas. The nigga got a good dick on him and some fiya ass head. The sad part is that I think I'm in love wit' the nigga. Girl, the nigga just do something to me."

"Let me call his cell phone," Venom said, picking up her cell. She dialed his number but got no answer.

"Girl, sometimes he has the phone on vibrate because he's not supposed to have it in there and I have to wait for him to call me back."

"Well, when he does, I'm going to prove to you that it's Roscoe and not Rodney. When he calls you back don't tell him that I'm coming with you 'cause he might make an excuse not to come."

Venom attempted to make another call, but got no answer.

"Girl, I felt the same way about the nigga at one time, but I'm telling you that nigga is bad news. That nigga's like a virus. He keep spreading and spreading. You don't need to be fucked up with that nigga. I'm telling you, girl. On top of that, the nigga fuck other niggas."

"Whhhhhaaattt?" Venom's eyes almost bulged out of her head and she almost choked.

"Yeah, he fuck niggas, too. Infinity and I caught him in the Days Inn on Washington Road getting high and fucking around with niggas right before we put his brother Frenchy to rest." Tanisha could tell Venom was disturbed by the things she said. Disappointment and shame showered her face.

"Getting high and fucking niggas?" she questioned.

"Yes. See, Infinity don't tell everything."

"Hmph! The nigga told me he don't get high off his own supply."

"What you think the nigga in the rehab for?"

"He told me it was for smoking weed."

"Smoking weed my ass. That nigga smoke crack and snort coke." Tanisha could tell Venom was already head over heels for Roscoe and there was nothing she could do to change that. All she could do was tell her the things she needed to know to stay on top of her game, which clearly she had already fucked up.

"Bitch, I still don't know if Roscoe and Rodney are the same person. I can't believe this shit. You gotta give me some proof."

Sheiit! All you gotta do is take me with you when you go see him."

"Okay," Venom agreed.

It had been seven months since she'd been involved with Roscoe aka Rodney, and she was now four months pregnant and beginning to show, but pretending it was weight gain. Venom talked about all the women in her family that she could've inherited her weight gain genes from and knew it was a damn lie every time she spoke of it.

Chapter Twenty-Eight
BUSTED

A nswer the phone, bitch!" Tanisha shouted as Venom's phone rang. They stared at one another. It was killing Tanisha inside to blow that nigga's ass out the water.

"Slick muthafucka!" she mumbled. The palms of her hands were moist and her heart thumped uncontrollably.

"Hello?" Venom answered. She then put him on speaker phone.

"Hey ma," Roscoe answered.

Tanisha could tell by his tone that he was pleased to hear Venom's voice. It appeared as though he had a smile on his face from the way he spoke. Venom ate every bit of it up as she blushed. If she had been a white woman, her face would have been beet red. That nigga could charm the panties off Janet Jackson. The nigga knew just what to do and say to get a bitch to wet his dick up.

"What's up, ma?" he said. "You know a nigga miss you, don't you, girl? How's my seed doing in your belly?"

"She's fine." Venom chuckled.

The bitch is surely gone in the head over this nigga, Tanisha thought.

"What you mean she? That's Lil Rodney in there. Soon his dick gone be big like his daddy, and he gone be poking you telling you to let him up out of there," he joked.

"It's a girl, I can feel it," Venom said, rocking once on her feet.

"Well, I guess we'll find out when he get here since you told the doctor we want it to be a surprise."

Tanisha tilted her head, watching Venom in amazement. This bitch had been going to doctor appointments and shit with this nigga and lying like she hadn't made one doctor's appointment.

Tanisha thought, This shit gotta be deeper than what she's letting on.

"You right. We'll find out when she gets here." Venom blushed and carried on with the conversation as if Tanisha wasn't in the room. She stood and started pacing the floor. Venom still didn't acknowledge Tanisha until she started sucking her teeth as if something were stuck in it.

"What's that noise?" Roscoe asked.

"That was me sucking my teeth. I was eating some chicken and a piece got stuck between my teeth," Venom lied. She eyed Tanisha like 'shut the fuck up and be quiet so you could hear a mouse piss.'

"So baby, when am I gonna see you?"

"You dying to see papi, huh? You want me to give you some of this good loving?"

If she didn't know it was that muthafucka, she definitely now knew it was Roscoe when he said papi.

"Yeah, my kitten purring. Can't you hear it? Meow, Meow." Venom went along with his lead. She was dead ass serious.

"I can probably get out of here for a few hours if I tell the counselor I need to go to the hospital with my baby momma concerning the baby."

"Well do that, papi, 'cause I'm dying to wet that dick up real good."

"Okay, this is what you do. Hang up. Call here. Oh no, no don't do that. I'm going to call somewhere and act like I called home and got the news that you were threatening a miscarriage. I'll hit you back on your cell in a minute. I know the bitch at the front counter gone let me out 'cause she want some of this good dick, but don't worry, baby, it's all for you."

"It better be." Venom look liked she was agitated with his last remark.

They ended their conversation. Tanisha couldn't wait to tear into Venom's ass about all the shit she lied about. "So, you tryna set up house with this nigga? Y'all going to doctor appointments and shit together. You see how the nigga was getting ready to tell you to call the rehab center, then he changed his mind? Shit, you can't call there because the nigga name ain't no fuckin' Rodney. That's why the nigga changed his mind and didn't let you call. You try to be so muthafuckin' smart until you stupid."

"Girl, you still with that shit? How about we wait and find out when we meet up with him? How about that? Then we'll find out if the nigga's name is Roscoe. I know it's not. I'm not worried," Venom ranted, giving attitude.

It was definitely clear now that she was in love and hoping like a muthafucka that the nigga's name was Rodney and not Roscoe. The bitch was acting like a school girl in love for the first time. Tanisha still couldn't understand how Roscoe was the father of this baby. Hell, a while back Venom wished she could've blamed it on the dude at the car dealership.

I wouldn't put nothing past Venom. One minute she's all for pussy and can't get stuck on a man. The next minute she's lying for a nigga she doesn't even know. This bitch has really lost her mind, Tanisha thought. I can't believe my fuckin' ears. Especially from a bitch that has a sex addiction.

She'd heard those types of bitches didn't get hooked on one dick or one pussy for that matter. Maybe Roscoe was going in the Guinness Book of World Records as the man who changed a nymphomaniac into a housewife. Ha, imagine that shit.

"I'll tell you what. How about you look up the number to the rehab, call and ask for a Rodney. Do you know Rodney's last name?" Tanisha asked.

Venom dropped her head and shrugged her shoulders. She didn't have a clue what his last name was. Damn, how a bitch get pregnant, take a nigga to her doctor appointments with her and still don't know the nigga's name? Damn, did the bitch ever stop to think if he was going to give the baby his last name? Tanisha could understand if this was a one-night stand type of shit.

"I tell you what. Let's call the rehab and ask for a Rodney and make up a last name and see if we get anywhere from there." She looked to Venom and waited on an answer. After a few seconds Venom looked up.

"Okay, that won't hurt. We can try that," Venom said. She called information on her cell phone and got the number.

"Here goes nothing." She put the phone on speaker and began dialing the number. Tanisha sat there waiting, while impatiently massaging her knee caps. She was anxious to blow Roscoe's ass out of the water.

"Hello. Is Rodney Williams able to have visitors

today?" Venom asked as she began to chew on her nails.

"Hold on just a minute," the receptionist said.

They waited for about eight minutes. Tanisha knew their wait was so long because they didn't have anyone there by that name. How in the hell was she going to find someone she didn't have checked in?

"Hello. I'm sorry, but we don't have anyone checked in by the name Rodney Williams. Actually, we don't have anyone here by the name Rodney. Maybe you need to check with another facility." Clearly the woman had checked thoroughly and found no sign of Rodney just like Tanisha thought.

"Thank you," Venom said and hung up her phone.

"I told you that's Roscoe that you're dealing with." Tanisha pointed. "Now, I'm going to call there and ask for Roscoe Lopez, which is his real name." She dialed the number after putting her cell on speaker. The same woman answered.

"Hello?" Tanisha said politely. "Is Roscoe Lopez on the list for visits today?" It took the receptionist all of about thirty seconds before she returned to the phone.

"Hello," the receptionist said. A lot of noise could be heard in the background.

"Yes, I'm here."

"Yes, he's on the list for visits today, but he had an emergency and won't be able to get any visits."

In the middle of the woman talking, Venom's cell began to ring. They both glanced at the number. It was Roscoe. Tanisha immediately hung up her call without a second thought.

"Answer the fuckin' phone!" she yelled at Venom, sitting next to her looking like she'd lost her best friend. She stared at the phone, still nibbling on her fingernails.

"Hello?" she answered.

"Hey baby, what's up? You can come pick a nigga up. I took care of everything."

Venom sat dead silent. Tanisha gave her a boost by poking her in the side and pointing toward the phone for her to respond.

"Baby, you there?" He waited for a response.

"I'm here, baby," Venom said, barely getting the words out. "I'm okay, baby. I just feel a little ill, probably 'cause I'm missing you like crazy." Venom spoke with disappointment. She now knew that Tanisha was telling the truth.

"Damn baby, you don't need to be feeling ill 'cause I wanna beat that pussy today. I thought you said you want papi to slip and slide in it."

"I do, baby," she responded seductively.

"Let me hear you say it then."

"I wanna wet papi's dick up. I want papi to beat this pussy real good," she moaned.

"Now that's papi's girl right there. Now come pick me up. I'll be waiting at the gas station. The same one you always pick me up at." He laughed and hung up the phone.

Venom pressed end on her cell and the two women started plotting to set Roscoe's ass up.

"Hey, wait a minute. I got plans tonight. I need to call my friend and cancel." Venom got up and walked out the front door. Apparently, she didn't want her to hear who she was talking to. Little did she know Tanisha had to call Delicious and get a rain check, too. She dialed his number as soon as Venom walked out the door. It took him a minute to answer the phone.

"Yeah, hold on for a minute, Tee." He clicked back

over to his other line. She held on about three minutes then hung up the phone. He's got her on hold too fuckin' long, she thought. She could hear a bit of agitation in his voice when he told her to hold on. Delicious must've been trying to talk Venom out of canceling on him. The bitch didn't need to go to no party anyway with a baby.

Tanisha's cell began to ring as Venom came back into the apartment. It was Delicious.

"I'll be right back. I have to take this call," Tanisha told Venom and headed to her bedroom for privacy.

"What's up?" She gave no indication that she knew Venom had just canceled on him.

"What's up with you? I had a very important call on the other line. What's been going on with you?"

"Not much. I'm just gone cut to the chase, I'm not gone be able to do that party tonight. I have more important things to handle."

"Shit, man, don't do this to me. I got too much money riding on this shit. C'mon, Tee, don't do me like this." She could hear the desperation in his voice. "Fuck, man! My other girl just canceled on me too, and she was gone be the life of the party. C'mon Tee, what I need to do to get you to change your mind?" he begged.

"It ain't nothing you can do to change my mind on this one. I hate to cancel on you, but I never felt it was a good move for me anyway. Man, I'm trying to get my life together."

"So what you saying? You gone stop dancing at the club, too?"

"No, no. Hell naw, I'm not saying that. I'm gone keep dancing at the club, but I'm gone try to get in school and do something with myself. I need that money from the club to pay for my schooling. You're the one that told me

TD not gone do everything for me and I need to do some things for myself. I can't sit around and wait on something to come to me on a silver platter. I been through too much and seen too much not to do something with myself. I need something positive in my life. Too much negative shit been going on. First thing Monday morning I'm going to the college to take a placement test so I can get my life on the right track. I hope you feel where I'm coming from."

"Damn, I understand you, but that other chick ain't trying to do shit with herself. This is what she best at."

"What other chick ?" she asked.

"The girl Venom I told you about," Delicious said.

"Oh, why did she cancel on you?" Tanisha asked, playing dumb.

"She really didn't say much. She just said she wasn't gone be able to do it. She did sound a little frustrated though. I hate she did that shit, but she's never canceled on me before. She was always game for a party with lots of money and lots of sex. I can't be mad. I'll just have to find some more girls to do the party."

"Why don't you ask some of the other girls from the club?"

"Are you crazy? They talk too much."

"What you mean they talk too much? They work at the club. Is this party shit supposed to be a secret or something?"

"Put it like this. Boss don't know everything I do. Like I told you before, I do the job he asks me to do, then I do my own thing on the side."

"Oh, I see. You don't want Boss to know. I get it. Your secret is safe with me. Hey, I'm gone have to talk to you later. I got some business to handle."

"Okay Tee, but if you change your mind, you know where I'm at."

"It won't be tonight. In fact, I don't think it'll be any other night. I'll see you at work Monday night." She hung up without giving Delicious a chance to say another word. She walked back into the living room. Venom was curled up on the couch about to go to sleep. "Oh hell naw, get your big belly ass up. Let's go bust your baby daddy!" She grinned.

Venom rose from the couch with a 'what's so funny' look on her face.

Chapter Twenty-Nine
ALL A NIGGA KNOW

As they got in the car, Venom hunched over grabbing her stomach. "My stomach is cramping like hell!' Venom groaned.

"Here," Tanisha said, retrieving two Tylenol from her purse and giving them to her.

"Thanks, but I don't need them right now," Venom stated. "The pains come and go, but it isn't severe. Tanisha could only guess they were false labor contractions. She guessed all women had them during their pregnancy.

It's a shame I'll never get the chance to experience that, she thought.

Before approaching the gas station where Roscoe was waiting Tanisha climbed into the backseat so he couldn't see her. Venom was turning in the gas station. "Do you see him?" she asked.

"In the flesh." Venom focused straight ahead. Tanisha put a jacket over her head and a few clothes on her body that were lying on the backseat of the car. The car door opened and Roscoe got in.

"Hey, baby girl, what's up? You got what I asked you to bring me?" Tanisha peeked from under the jacket and saw her slide him a sack of cocaine. He stuck his finger in it and put it on his tongue. Then he rotated his tongue in his mouth, testing it to see if his tongue would get that numbness that cocaine is supposed to give.

"Baby, this that good shit. Them niggas gone love this shit!" he said.

"Tell me something," Venom said while pulling out of the gas station.

"Anything you wanna know, baby."

"What's the reason for going to rehab if you still gone do drugs?"

"Shit, it's simple. Everybody do it for different reasons. Some niggas do it to really get off the drugs. Some do it to keep them white folks off their ass, and others do it 'cause they initially thought they were strong enough to get off the drugs. Fact is, you gotta be stronger than a muthafucka, 'cause drugs are everywhere you go. That temptation is a muthafucka."

"Well, if you know that, why do you continue to feed off their weakness while trying to get money? I know it's another way for you to get money."

"Yeah it is, but this what a nigga used to. This all a nigga know. Sometimes what a nigga know may not be the best for a nigga. A nigga might need to get out there and learn some new shit, but this be a nigga's life and he be accustomed to it. A nigga have dreams and shit, but everybody comin' up outta the 'hood ain't gone be no rapper or be like that nigga that went to prison and wrote the book Cooked. You feel me?" He drew in a deep breath and let it out.

"I know if you apply yourself there's always a better way. I think y'all do it 'cause y'all afraid to leave the 'hood. Afraid to see what the world has to offer. I'll tell you one thing, the hood gone always be there if you need to go back to it."

"Girl, you talkin' like you been seasoned in the 'hood or some shit. What's up with that?" He let off a slight chuckle.

"Naw, I just got some cousins that grew up in the 'hood. Some still behind bars for this same shit. They claimin' that's all they knew. Some dead and some still out there nickel and diming just to make ends meet." Venom pointed to the bag of coke she gave Roscoe, disgusted that she was contributing to something she believed was the wrong thing to be doing.

"Well, what you bring it to me for?" He surveyed the contents in the plastic sack.

"'Cause if I don't you'll go get it from somewhere else."

"Exactly, you made a valid point. If I don't sell it to the users, they'll go get it from somewhere else, too." Roscoe smiled without conviction and kissed Venom on the cheek as he massaged her belly.

Venom pulled into the Radisson Hotel down by the river walk.

"What you gone do with that coke?" Venom asked.

"I'm gone sell it. What kind of question is that?" His brows narrowed, looking a bit disturbed by her question.

"I thought you might take a little bit every now and then. You did tell me that's the reason you were in rehab, right? "Venom hoped he would slip and change his story.

"Hell naw. I told you I was in for smoking weed," he replied with heavy bass in his voice.

"Well, how you know so much about people getting over their addiction?"

"Sheit! I've been around this shit all my life. I started

hustling on the street corners. After a while, I moved up in the game and then somebody robbed me for everything I had. I'm still feenin' to pay the muthafucka back that did it. The niggas might think they got away with that shit, but the shit is far from over."

"Don't you think you should let bygones be bygones? You about to be a daddy. You need to set good examples for the kid."

"Yeah, that means I'm starting off right by showing this lil nigga to man up and don't let no fool get over on him." He shook Venom's belly with his hand, still insisting that it was a boy in her stomach.

"It's gone be a girl I told you." She pushed his hand away jokingly, her smile gleaming.

"Girl, gone get the room so I can beat that pussy up." Venom was parked in front of the hotel office. The nigga still didn't look behind him.

From the floor of the backseat Tanisha thought, I could've blown this nigga's brains out if I was a robber.

Venom grabbed her purse, exited the car and went to get the room. Roscoe let his seat back and got comfortable as he fumbled with the disc changer. Tanisha continued to peep from under the jacket. She saw Roscoe open the sack of cocaine, stick a tightly rolled up bill inside. He took a toot in one nostril, then the other. He then checked the rearview mirror to make sure he didn't leave any residue on his nose.

Venom came back to the car twisting her ass and flashing the room key in his face, wearing a Kool-aid smile. Tanisha could definitely see that Venom was in love with Roscoe.

I'll be damned. He's done it again, she thought. Tanisha waited for Venom to give her a sign to get up, but she never did. Her backseat hide out gave her a front row seat to Roscoe's manipulating ass in action.

Venom parked in the closest space to the room she rented. Roscoe reached over to massage her pussy while circling her ear with his tongue. He slid a finger in her pussy and she began to moan. She didn't give a damn that Tanisha was in the backseat. At first, his hand moved in slow motion, then he started to move it faster. Venom moaned her pleasure even louder. Roscoe pulled his finger out of her pussy and licked her pussy juice from it. He unzipped his pants and shook his dick at Venom without saying a word. Obedient, she leaned over the seat and took him in her mouth as if this was a normal routine.

"Sheit girl, you suck a good dick. Fuck, this shit is good!" He grabbed the back of her head and slid some of the hair through his fingers taking a tight grip of her head. His face was all screwed up. "Damn girl, you gone make me cum. Shit, suck it faster," he insisted as he gyrated his ass in the seat. Venom obeyed.

"Aw shit! Shit, I'm cumin'!" His body started jerking. He pulled Venom's head off his dick and skeeted in her face. "Turn over in the seat so I can eat this pussy," he demanded.

Venom obeyed as she put her knees up in the seat. Her ass was tooted up in the air and her pussy was in his face. He leaned over from his seat, pulled her skirt over her ass, her panties to the side and began eating her pussy. He glided his tongue from her asshole to her pussy then pushed two fingers inside her pussy thrusting them in and out. "Damn, this pussy is good. Girl, I wanna put my dick in you." He put his tongue in her asshole and started tickling her clit with the tip of his finger. She moaned seductively with her face glued to the window pane. Roscoe ate her pussy as he too was on his knees in the seat of the car and started stroking his dick. It was still hard as a brick. He rattled Venom's clit with his tongue until the cum released from her pussy. He licked up every drop. "C'mon, suck it for papi." He stroked his dick.

"Let's go inside the room," Venom suggested.

"I wanna stay right here. I'm loving this shit. You think somebody watching?"

"I don't know," Venom answered.

"Well, know how to suck this dick." He stroked himself faster as he relaxed back in the seat. "C'mon." He grabbed the back of Venom's head, pleading with her to suck his dick again. Venom took him in her mouth. He moaned and his chest heaved rapidly. "Girl, you got the best head I ever had. The best, girl. You the fuckin' best!" His eyelids were clenched together.

"Better than mine, muthafucka?" Tanisha screamed as she threw the jacket off her.

Chapter Thirty
IF IT BE YOUR WILL

T rying to keep her thoughts off the phone call she received from Roscoe, Infinity lay quietly in the dark of the hotel room where TD left her without any notice. Her heart was torn to pieces and her eyes were bloodshot from all the constant crying. Thoughts of her past and present relationships encompassed her head. What had she done wrong to deserve so many heartbreaks and disappointments in return? Most of all, she still despised Tanisha, who she felt was the cause of her losing Roscoe and now TD. She picked up her phone and called Armani to come and keep her company because she felt she needed to share her feelings with someone before she had a nervous breakdown. She dialed Armani's cell phone several times but got no answer. Eventually, she dialed the house number.

"Hello?" an unfamiliar masculine voice answered.

"Where is Armani?" Infinity sat up straight on the bed. A man had never answered Armani's phone. "Who's speaking?"

"I'm her husband, Cliff."

"Cliff! What the fuck are you doing in Armani's house answering her phone?" Infinity's brows wrinkled.

"What do you mean? That's my wife," he said as if Infinity were somehow mixed up.

"Are you fuckin' crazy? She's not your wife anymore. Where the fuck is Armani?" she screamed. Her heart beat tripled as she realized Armani was in danger.

"The paramedics are taking her to the hospital," Cliff said calmly.

"For what?" Infinity questioned. Instant nervousness gave birth to her tone.

"She's been shot and it's not looking good."

"What hospital are they taking her to?" Infinity shouted in a panicked voice as she rushed to put on her clothes.

"Medical College." The phone went dead.

Twenty minutes later, Infinity stood in the entranceway where they unloaded the gurney. She was looking from left to right like she had lost her child and was trying to figure out which way to step next.

The man Infinity saw exiting the ambulance with the EMTs and Armani's bloody body couldn't possibly be Clifford. He looked like a homeless wino or crack addict that had been sleeping under bridges or the kind of person who snuggled up under some other homeless person trying to keep warm around a burning fire in an aluminum barrel on a cold winter night.

The police arrived shortly after. Infinity rushed up to the officers ranting and raving. "Why do y'all have this man around my friend? He's the reason she's lying on this gurney and can't talk. He's not her husband. She divorced him a long time ago and there's a restraining order against him. Are you guys nuts? And y'all are supposed to protect the innocent! You're really doing a hell of a job, I can tell you that. I can't wait to report you muthafuckas." Tears drenched Infinity's sullen face.

The police officers all looked at one another. Then they looked at Cliff. "Is there any truth to this, mister?" the older cop with the salt and pepper hair asked.

"Answer her!" the officer yelled.

"Yes and—" Cliff said. Before he could get the word 'no' out, they were already reading him his rights and slapping the cuffs on. Then he was thrown in the backseat of the police car.

Infinity was still ranting, very upset and afraid for Armani. She didn't know what the outcome would be. Her last visit to the hospital was when her brother, JJ had been shot. Now he was paralyzed and unable to walk. She wondered if the same thing could happen to Armani. She then quickly erased the thought from her head.

"Ma'am, calm down. We'll take care of it," the salt and pepper headed officer said. "He'll get what he has coming to him."

"He needs to be behind bars!" Infinity glared at Cliff sitting in the backseat of the police car. Cliff only stared back.

The emergency staff rushed Armani to a room in ICU after removing the bullet from her stomach. The one that went into her chest went straight through and didn't puncture any arteries. They allowed Infinity to sit with her until 8 PM when visiting hours ended, then she had to go.

During her stay, Infinity prayed for Armani and told her how sorry she was for all the times she'd treated her badly as she held her hand. "If you just wake up or squeeze my hand just a little I'll feel better." Armani didn't budge. She lay there like a corpse with tubes running through her body. Infinity continued to sob.

"Visiting hours are over, Miss," the nurse advised.

Infinity cried out, "God, please help her!" She held the rosary tight in her hands as she looked to the ceiling. "Dear God, please don't let her die if it be your will." Infinity laid her head on Armani's chest for a few seconds, kissed her cheek and exited the room.

"Excuse me, ma'am," the nurse said as Infinity turned to walk away.

"Yes," Infinity answered as she stopped but never turned around.

"Will you contact her next of kin? We have no record of anyone but her husband." The nursed proceeded to walk toward Infinity.

"They're dead," Infinity said as she dropped her head and walked off.

Chapter Thirty-One
KARMA IS A MUTHA

"W hat the fuck?" Roscoe yelled as he looked Tanisha dead in the face and then back at Venom. She almost choked on his dick when he jumped in shock.

"Better than mine, muthafucka? You heard me!" Tanisha glared at him with disgust. He zipped up his pants and buttoned them.

"Vee, what the fuck is going on here? You hanging out with crack heads now or you serving this bitch the shit you supposed to be bringing me?" Roscoe acted as if Tanisha was a nobody, a person who meant absolutely nothing.

Venom frowned. "No, I'm not serving her. She's my friend. We've been friends for a while now. She was telling me that your name isn't Rodney; it's Roscoe."

"Okay, so is this supposed to be some type of setup shit or something? Huh?" he yelled. Venom still didn't answer.

"With friends like this crack head bitch here, you never need any enemies. You gone go against ya baby daddy for this crack head?" Roscoe chucked his thumb at Tanisha.

Venom crossed her arms over her chest. "Well, is she telling the truth? Is your name Roscoe? Are you married to Infinity?"

Roscoe nodded and crossed his arms. "Oh, so I see. This is the million dollars question today. It don't matter what I tell you. It looks like you gone believe what this crack head tells you. Just take me the fuck back where you got me from 'cause I'm getting madder than a muthafucka right now. Neither one of y'all bitches ain't gone like it if I get outta control." He breathed harder.

"So you do know her?" Venom didn't let him steer her away from her questions.

"Yeah, I know the crack head. I used to let the crack head suck my dick," Roscoe spoke with a straight face.

"Now, the crack head found out I'm in love with you, and the crack head wanna hate. I just served the crack head the other day. She didn't tell you that, did she?" Roscoe glared back in Tanisha's direction.

Roscoe lied, but he was convincing enough to make Venom ponder. He had already planted seeds in her head about people being on drugs and how they'd relapse. Venom gave Tanisha a strange look. It was as if she wanted to believe him.

"Don't fuckin' look at me like that! You know I don't do no fuckin' drugs anymore," Tanisha said, seething with anger. "This nigga is trying to play on your intelligence, and you're letting it happen. He's manipulating you, girl. You need to wake up and think, bitch, not smell the muthafuckin' coffee."

"Is he trying to manipulate me or are you trying to manipulate me?" Venom asked her.

Tanisha's mouth gaped open. "Bitch, I can't believe you have the audacity to ask me some shit like that. You know this nigga grimy."

She hated having to explain herself in front of this

low-life ass nigga.

Roscoe grabbed Venom's hand. "Baby, put this crack head out so we can continue with what we planned to do. I know you didn't pay for that room for nothing."

"Listen, muthafucka! I'm not gone be too many more of your crack heads," Tanisha threatened.

"Oh yeah. What you gone do? Have me set up? You probably the bitch that had me set up and robbed before."

"Naw, muthafucka, I think you need to talk to your wife and her brother about that shit."

"My wife? What you say, bitch?" He leaned over the backseat.

"You heard what the fuck I said, bitch." She poked his nose with her right index finger. "Your wife and her muthafuckin' brother. You really thought JJ was gone let you get away with fucking Madison and getting her pregnant? Be for real, dirty ass nigga. That robbing shit ain't my style, so you can't put that shit on me, nigga."

Venom stared at them going back and forth word for word. She knew now for sure Tanisha was telling the truth.

Roscoe turned to face Venom as he rubbed her belly and kissed her on the neck. "Baby, put this crack head bitch out your car."

Tanisha sat right there to see if Venom was going to take this nigga's side over hers.

Roscoe got out the car and gave Venom a 'what the fuck you waiting on' glare. Venom sat there for a few more seconds, thinking. "Tanisha, I don't mean no harm, but this my baby daddy. I can't choose you over him. I don't owe that bitch Infinity nothing 'cause for real, I didn't even know they used to get down like that."

"I'm not saying you owe Infinity anything, but if you

think about it, it is fucked up."

"Look who's casting stones." She snapped her head back, looking at Tanisha suspiciously. "You probably want him for yourself. That's why you tripping so hard."

Tanisha looked at her in disbelief. "I don't want this nigga. This nigga played me just like he playing you. You'll soon find out."

"Tanisha, you gotta get out, man. I hope you got money to catch a cab back home. I'm sorry, but I gotta roll with him on this one."

"What did you just say to me?" she asked angrily as she mean mugged Venom.

"You heard me. This my baby daddy we talking about," Venom said with a dead serious look on her face. Tanisha couldn't do anything but smile a hurtful smile.

"So, what about Jazzy?" she asked.

"What about her? Just get out and go. We got things to do."

As Tanisha opened the back door and stepped out of the car, Roscoe gave her a superior look and then laughed.

"Remember, what makes you laugh now will make you cry later on, muthafucka," Tanisha said, slamming the door. She was angry as hell, but she had to respect the game. Tanisha started to walk away, but was still feenin' for some get back. She politely stopped and turned back to Roscoe and said, "I know more than anything that it's killing your ass on the inside to find out JJ was the one that robbed us in the apartment when those niggas ran that broomstick up your ass. You can pretend like it's not fucking with you, but I know it's eating your ass up on the inside. Ha! So I get the last laugh, muthafucka."

Roscoe grinned slightly, nodded his head once with

his eyes shut and slammed Venom's car door. Venom exited the car and they went to their room like a married couple on their honeymoon like nothing had happened.

Tanisha grabbed her cell phone from her purse and called a cab. Now she understood why people always said they'd take their own car. She couldn't believe that bitch tripped on her like that.

"It's all good though 'cause it happens to the best of us. Karma is a muthafucka!" she said aloud.

Chapter Thirty-Two
DAMSEL IN DISTRESS

Infinity wanted as many details about Armani's shooting as she could possibly get. All Cliff's arresting officer told her was that Cliff broke into Armani's house, held her at gun point, sexually assaulted her and they ended up struggling for the gun and it went off, striking Armani. Cliff was convinced that he could pick up the pieces and start over although he was strung out on drugs and his marriage to Armani had ended a while ago.

Although Infinity didn't want to, because her relationship with Jazzy had always been a tense one, she called Jazzy to find out where she was so they could talk in person. Infinity knew Jazzy might have access to the kind of information she wouldn't be able to get on her own. And even if Jazzy didn't have access, there was always the possibility that she knew another cop who did. Jazzy told her where she was on her way to have lunch, but Infinity's visit would have to be brief.

Infinity arrived thirty minutes later and found Jazzy sitting at a large round table with several officers. Jazzy waved her over, wondering what could be so pressing that it couldn't wait. Infinity took a seat and said hello to everyone after Jazzy made introductions.

"I'm on the job, so call me Sergeant Miles," Jazzy told Infinity.

Infinity nodded, watching everyone at the table having fun and belting out a good laugh. Jazzy cracked up after someone told a joke and removed her key chain from her pocket and placed it on the table.

"Sergeant Miles!" the tall distinguished Captain said, ignoring the strange look on Infinity's face.

"Yes, Captain Langston," Jazzy responded. Captain Langston took a hold of her key chain and stared at the picture dangling from it. It was a picture of Jazzy and Venom at the county fair. Jazzy stood behind Venom with her lips placed on the left side of her neck and arms wrapped around her.

"Is this your partner?" Captain Langston asked, puzzled about the woman on the picture with Jazzy. He'd instantly recognized the woman he'd been secretly seeing behind his wife's back, Venom. He knew that face and those lips anywhere.

"Yes, she is." Jazzy gently took the key chain from the captain's hand and admired it as a glow came upon her face and a sparkle to her eyes.

"Sergeant Miles, I really need to speak with you," Infinity said in a low whisper, shifting her body from one side to the other.

"What is it about?" Jazzy asked.

"Armani."

"So, how long have you been partners?" the captain interrupted Infinity with a pondering look.

"Excuse me, but Sergeant Miles, I really need to speak with you, in private." Infinity insisted as she stared into Jazzy's eyes and Jazzy stared back.

"How long have you two been together?" the Captain asked rudely interrupting again, anxious to get some answers about her partner.

"I don't mean any disrespect, but could your questions wait about her personal business, so I can speak with her for just a moment." Infinity beamed in on Captain Langston as she demanded her moment with Jazzy.

"Just a moment Infinity and I will answer all of your questions." Jazzy assured Infinity so she stood there waiting patiently hoping to get some answers about the shooting. Jazzy didn't want to be disrespectful to her Captain, but she thought about what Infinity had said about him asking her about her personal business.

Changing the subject, Jazzy touched an unusual looking zit on the captain's face. "What is this?" she asked.

"I'm not sure," he replied, quickly moving her hand.

It was barely visible through his immaculate beard, so it was a possibility that it could've been a small bruise or scar. The other officers talked among themselves about his sudden change since his two month absence. He was still as handsome as he'd always been, but not as healthy once he came back on the job from sick leave.

"You never answered my question," The captain looked at Infinity, he didn't forget about the smart comment she'd made about Jazzy's personal business, but neither did he care, he also wanted answers.

"Oh, we've been partners for a while now. Actually, we're planning a wedding and I'd like to invite all you guys if you'd like to participate." Jazzy was being polite to her coworkers, which was a side Infinity had rarely seen.

"I'd love to come. Give me the invitation. Don't mail it 'cause the wife isn't big on gay relationships," the captain responded as he grinded his teeth together.

"Me too," the rest of the crew all chimed in unison.

"Let me see the picture of your partner," Sergeant Rogers said as he reached out his hand to Jazzy.

"No, don't show Rogers. He's always a jokester. We never know when to really take him seriously."

"Yeah, the rookie is still wet behind the ears," another officer said.

Jazzy stared at Roger's, unsure about passing him the key chain because she didn't want her and Venom to be the butt of his jokes.

Jazzy handed Sergeant Rogers the key chain . He stared for a minute. "Hey! I know this chick! I gave her some of this good loving before and she gave me some real banging lip service." He smiled.

Everyone at the table laughed except Jazzy and Infinity.

"Not that chick. She don't do men." Jazzy snatched her key chain from Sergeant Roger's hand. She didn't find it the least bit funny. She loved Venom more than life itself and cared less to hear a joke like that about the woman she loved.

"Yo, Sergeant Daniels, you remember that chick I told you I boned at my pops dealership?" Rogers said.

"Yeah man, I do remember you telling me that," Sergeant Daniels said. Everybody at the table looked around at one another not believing their ears and, Inifinity's ear was wide opened as well.

Captain Langston was the only one distant from the group, but was taking in Sergeant Rogers.

"Yeah, I remember."

"Have you ever seen Sergeant Miles' woman before?"

"No, she's never shown me any pictures before. She might have mentioned something about her every now and then."

"Okay, so if you look at the picture, can you tell if she's the woman that I described to you?" Sergeant Rogers asked.

"I'm sure I could," Daniels replied.

"Let him see the picture, Sergeant Miles," Sergeant Rogers insisted.

Reluctantly, Jazzy passed the picture across the table with shaky hands. She was nervous and a bit hurt that this could possibly be true.

"What do you think, Sergeant Daniels? Does she look like the woman I described to you?" He slid so close to him he could have kissed him.

"Damn' no wonder she never called you back!" Sergeant Daniels said after seeing how beautiful Venom actually was. That pissed Rogers off even more. Sergeant Daniels looked at the picture, then at Jazzy. He saw the pain in Jazzy's eyes as if fire was boiling up inside of her.

"I'm not sure if it's her or not," he lied and passed the picture back to Jazzy.

"What the fuck you mean you're not sure?" Sergeant Rogers rose from his seat knocking his cup of coffee to the floor.

"Calm down, Rogers," Captain Langston said gently as he scanned the room. "This is not the place for you to be getting out of character. You see what you're wearing?" he said, referring to his police uniform. "You're supposed to represent for everybody else. You're an officer of the law. Now be seated!" Captain Langston demanded.

Sergeant Rogers exhaled heavily and sat back down at the table. "I'll tell you what. She has a tattoo of a black panther with red eyes and red nails on her right ass cheek. If you say that ain't true you telling a damn lie!" Rogers leaned across the table and peered into Jazzy's eyes.

She sat in a trance, knowing now that he was definitely telling the truth. Captain Langston already knew she was the same woman he was thinking about, but he knew for sure now because he had a vivid memory of the tattoo.

Jazzy stared at Rogers. How does he know what's on her body? Jazzy thought. "Why are you telling me these things, Rogers? Do you know that I'm in love with this woman?" Jazzy pointed to Venom on the key chain.

"You should've kept her on a leash." With a smug look on his face he picked his teeth.

"What the fuck you trying to say, Rogers?" Jazzy asked in a soft tone as a tear slid down her face.

"You know how you women call us men dogs? Well she's an untamed one. You need a thick leash. I advise you to spend your entire paycheck on one." Jazzy swung at Rogers, but Captain caught her arm. He maneuvered and smiled at Jazzy. She snatched her arm away and dashed to the ladies room.

Jazzy was in the restroom crying her eyes out. She couldn't get a hold of herself.

"Jazzy, are you all right?" Infinity asked..

"I'm fine," Jazzy replied in a trembling voice.

"No, you're not fine, look at you. I've never seen you like this before." Infinity said wrapping her arms around Jazzy.

"I've never had to go through anything like this."

"Baby girl, there's a first time for everything, but you're stronger than this, baby don't let anybody see you sweat. There's one thing that I know about you and that is the fact that you're a strong woman and you can weather any storm. I hate to admit it, but you're stronger than me ninety percent of the time." Infinity stepped back and took a look at Jazzy. Jazzy gave off a slight smile. Now pull yourself together, I was always taught that sticks and stones break bones but words never did. You don't know if he's telling the truth or not."

"Girl, you're crazy talking about some sticks and stones," Jazzy let off a wide grin, "But you're right let me pull myself together. I look pitiful huh?"

" No, you don't look pitiful, you're only human like the rest of us that fall in love and end up hurt. It's nothing to be ashamed of, at least I don't think so. I've had my fair share of heartache and pain."

"You're right," Jazzy laughed as she put cold water on her face.

"What's funny?"

"Me agreeing with you out of all people."

"It's okay it happens sometimes."

They both laughed and gave one another a warm embrace.

"So what's up with Armani?" Jazzy asked collecting herself and tightening up her clothes.

"She got shot, and the police won't tell me anything, well nothing significant."

"You want me to find out some information for you huh."

"Well, yeah, she our friend and I really need to know what happened."

"Girl no problem, you should've just told me that in

the beginning, hell maybe I wouldn't had to hear everything that I just heard about Venom."

"Some things come out for a reason baby girl, some things happen for a reason" Infinity gently rubbed her hand along Jazzy's arm in comfort. " Now let's go out here and you be the woman that you know you are." Infinity insisted.

"I thought I was gone have to come get you for a minute," Sergeant Daniels said when she returned to the table with Infinity on her side.

"Naw, I'm good," Jazzy said.

Jazzy walked over to Sergeant Rogers and said, "You know what? I'm not mad at you. I take the blame for everything my girl did. It was all my fault for neglecting her by working too many hours. Be looking for your invitation to the wedding. That is, if you still want to come. Since I've been on the force I've learned that people have motive for everything they do. I know you had motive for telling me and apparently you're hurt. I'm sorry about that too. You can blame me for that as well." Jazzy spoke as if it wasn't bothering her one bit. Everyone stared. Infinity smiled as Jazzy redeemed herself.

"I got the check. Let's go, Captain, we got some criminals to put behind bars." Jazzy smiled as she took the check and paid it. Everyone got in the cars they came in. Infinity drove off in her Range Rover.

Too many painful thoughts about Venom entered through her head.

The worse part of it all was that Venom cheated with one of Jazzy's co-workers, and a man at that. She thought of all the times Venom sat in her face and lied about how she'd never sleep with men and how degrading it was for

Jazzy to even question her about it. As Infinity was pulling out the Radisson's parking lot, she noticed Venom's car. What the fuck, now this is too much in one day. Jazzy slowed her car down and pulled into a parking space. Infinity noticed her pulling over and pulled over beside her. "Are you okay?" Infinity asked.

"I'm okay," Jazzy let off a fake smile.

"Oh, I was just checking on you, I saw you pull over, I think, I'm going to call it a night. Call me when you get the chance."

"I sure will." Calling Infinity was the furthest thing from Jazzy's mind, all she was worried about was Venom, she couldn't help who she was in love with and her heart was in control.

*****

"Thank you for calling the Radisson. How may I help you?" the receptionist said.

"Could you ring Veronica Long's room for me, please?" Jazzy asked, giving Venom's birth name.

"Hello," Venom answered, breathing hard.

"So I see you're really busy, huh? You really had me fooled. I want you to know that karma has no respect and you will get your day." Jazzy hung up the phone without letting Venom get a word in.

Jazzy sat in the car staring at her cell phone, waiting on Venom to call her back and give her some type of explanation or something. Venom never called, and Jazzy sat there for another five minutes.

Chapter Thirty-Three
STREAK OF BAD LUCK

After visiting Jazzy, Infinity went to the hospital to see Armani then straight home from the hospital. She dropped everything at the door except her cell phone, poured herself a bottle of wine and removed all her clothes. She lit some candles around the Jacuzzi and filled it to capacity with water. She stared at her cell phone, hoping TD would call at any minute. Infinity eased her body down into the water and lay her head back. As soon as she got relaxed, her phone began to ring.

She looked at the number. It was unavailable. "Hello?" she answered.

"This is a prepaid call. You will not be charged for this call. This call is from . . . JJ. Press seven to block this call or five to accept it," the federal prison operator stated. Infinity contemplated whether to accept the call or not. After a sip of wine, the operator began speaking again and in the middle of the operator speaking Infinity pressed five.

"What's up, sis? You leave a nigga hanging like this? A nigga only hear from you every now and then, and you leave a nigga hungry up in this muthafucka. You send a nigga money only when you get ready to do it. What the fuck is up, sis? You smoking dope or something?" Jimmy Jr. spouted off, but Infinity really wasn't hearing what he was saying.

"Are you listening to yourself? You need to calm the fuck down, nigga. I don't know who you think you are, but you got the game fucked up." Infinity took another sip of wine and rested her head back on the spa pillow. Jimmy Jr. stayed silent because Infinity's reaction shocked him. "Now nigga, listen to me. Right now is not the time to be calling me with this bullshit 'cause if you keep fuckin' with me you won't get another dime. Now, let's start this conversation over." Infinity took another sip of wine from her glass and set it back down.

"Man, sis, I'm just saying . . . you leaving a nigga hanging."

"JJ, the first thing you're supposed to do is ask me how I'm doing. That would be the right thing to do."

"C'mon, man. How you been doing, sis? What's good witcha? I don't want to argue with you. You know a nigga only got fifteen minutes on the phone." Jimmy Jr. calmed his tone to satisfy Infinity. He knew she was his only financial support from the streets and he definitely didn't want that to be jeopardized.

"That's more like it. JJ, I know I don't be sending the money when I say I'm going to send it, but you do get it."

"Man, commissary be closed when I do get the money. Then I have to wait until the following week. A nigga don't wanna be starving in prison and shit. You don't know how this shit go 'cause you never had to go through this shit, sis, damn. I don't mean to be trippin', but a nigga get frustrated in this muthafucka. You know I gave you everything I had and some."

"Shit nigga, everything you gave me was already mine. You took it from my husband."

"Yeah, you right about that, but are you woman enough to handle your business if the nigga come at you about it?"

"Why would he come after me about it? He don't even have a clue who the niggas was that took it. He thought the bitch Tiny had something to do with it."

"Naw sis, that nigga know that bitch wasn't smart enough to set no shit up like that. Word is the nigga still feenin to find the niggas that took his shit. I ain't out there to protect you if word gets out, so you better stay strapped. From what I hear the nigga ain't working with a full deck these days. Real talk, sis, you gotta watch your back."

"Romelo ain't gone fuck with me, JJ," Infinity spoke with confidence.

"Sis, I wouldn't be so sure about that."

"Can we talk about something else? I don't wanna talk about him. Didn't you just say that you only have fifteen minutes on the phone?"

"Yeah."

"Okay, well let's make the best out of it. How are your legs?"

"Good question. I've been doing physical therapy and guess what?"

"What?"

"I'm able to stand. I'm taking baby steps with a walker, but that's a start. I thought I was going to be down in that bed for the rest of my life. I guess God does look after 'hood niggas, too."

"When did you realize you were getting your feeling back?"

"Strange, but one day I was sitting in my wheelchair and a fine ass nurse walked by and my dick got rock hard!" Jimmy burst into laughter. "No, seriously, sis, I was sitting in my wheel chair in front of the television and I felt my feet getting cold. The nurse thought I was losing it and the doctor really thought I'd lost my mind. The doctor took me in for an examination and just as I said, the feeling was coming back. Ain't that a bitch?"

"That's good, JJ. I'm very happy for you."

"So what's good in your life, sis?"

"Not much, love just seems to spark in everybody's life but mine."

"Sis, I don't mean to cast no stones, but I was reading a book the other day about people getting their karma. Maybe you having this streak of bad luck because of something you did in your past."

"Oh yeah, like what? I never cheated on my husband and I never disrespected our parents."

"You right about all that, but—" A beep chimed in, indicating that the call would soon be terminated. "You hear that, sis? The phone gonna hang up in a minute."

"Okay, what were you going to say?" Infinity was anxious to hear what Jimmy Jr. had to say.

"Do you remember when you were sleeping around with that married man before you got with Roscoe. Remember how it tore his family to pieces? The sad part about it is the nigga wanted to leave his family for you and you didn't give a damn about him."

"Hello, hello!" Infinity yelled. The fifteen minutes were up and the phone call was terminated.

Infinity grabbed her glass of wine and finished it all in one gulp. She relaxed her head and closed her eyes as she thought back to when she had the affair with the married man. Marvin Butler was his name. He was a well kept gentleman and very organized. He was the perfect family man except when it came to his appetite for young, attractive women. Infinity was the perfect catch for him and he was definitely the perfect catch for her. Infinity was young, spunky, and quick with words. She could talk herself into getting anything she wanted. Her mom and dad gave her anything she wanted that was within their means, but never would they pay a thousand dollars for a pair of designer pants and a shirt with the name Gucci written on it where you could barely see it. On the other hand, Marvin would pay two thousand dollars for it if he had to. All he wanted was a piece of young ass to make him feel young and alive again.

Someone to make him feel like he still had it. To Infinity he had a nice size dick, but his back wasn't as strong as an athletic seventeen year old. When she had her meetings with him, she'd make him feel like he had the best dick in the world and fake multiple orgasms in all of the five minutes that he lasted. She'd cry during sex and tell him how much she loved him. She'd tell him how she wished she had him all to herself and knew she didn't give a damn about nothing but the money he gave her. During their sexual encounters, she couldn't wait to get the fuck up, get her money and get the hell on.

"Shit." Infinity quickly raised up from the water and mistakenly knocked the wine glass on the floor breaking it. "Is this my karma for that old ass shit? Can't be." She rubbed her hand through her hair, aggravated with herself. Her cell phone began to ring again as she realized it had fallen on the floor. As she rushed to pick up the phone, she'd forgotten about the broken glass and stepped right on a piece and nicked the heel of her foot.

"Shit!" she hollered as she answered the phone.

"What's that all about?" It was prince charming himself.

"Oh nothing," Infinity said as she pressed her washcloth up against her foot, applying pressure to stop the bleeding. She was ecstatic to hear TD's voice on the other end of her phone.

"If it's nothing, why did you say shit when you answered the phone?"

"Actually, I cut my foot on a piece of glass."

"How did you . . . never mind. I called for business. Is your foot that bad that you can't handle business? If so, I'll find somebody else.

"No, no, it's not that bad. What do you need me to do?" Infinity asked desperately. Anything to be in his presence was fine with her. If she had cut off half her foot, she still would've found a way to sew it back on.

"Meet me at Chocolate Castle tomorrow night around nine or ten o'clock. Don't cause no problems before I get there." He remembered the last incident that had taken place.

"I won't cause any problems. I'll be on my best behavior."

Infinity didn't get a response. TD hung up the phone after he told her what he wanted. Infinity didn't care, she was excited for the call itself. Infinity bandaged up her foot, cleaned up the glass, and got ready for bed. As she lay in the bed, she received another call from Jimmy Jr. He wanted to make sure she sent his money for commissary. As soon as she got off the phone with him she called Western Union and sent the money from her debit card. Seconds after the transaction was completed the phone rang again. The recording from the prison began and she pressed five before the recording allowed the name to be heard.

"Hey, I only have one minute on the phone, but yo' brother told me to tell you that he's sorry to hear you are always getting stabbed in the back."

Chapter Thirty-Four
SAVOR THE MOMENT

Tanisha finally made it to her apartment, kicked off her shoes and laid across the couch. She couldn't believe that bitch put her out of her car for that stank ass nigga. The bitch gone get hers though. All dogs have their day and karma don't have respect for no bitch. Fuck! My feet hurt like a muthafucka. That was a long walk home. She waited on the cab for almost an hour and it still was a no show. She didn't know how she was going to dance at the club tomorrow with aching feet. Shit! What the fuck is that? A noise echoed from the bedroom. Tanisha's heart pumped furiously. Should she haul ass back out the front door or see what the hell was going on? She decided to take her chances and see what or who was in the apartment. Tanisha crept down the hallway and glanced down at the floor near the entrance of the bedroom. The light repeatedly flicked on and off. She stood there for a second and twisted the knob. She waited a beat, then pushed the door open. There stood Mr. Sweet Dick himself in his birthday suit.

"How in the hell did you get in my apartment?" she asked with a slight smile, relieved that it was him.

"Really, it's my apartment. You're just renting," Mr. Sweet Dick said.

"Oh really?"

"Yes, really. I thought I told you I own these apartments."

"Oh really?" Tanisha stared at him.

"Yes really, and why do you keep saying oh really?"

"I don't know, maybe because you're standing here naked with a pair of baseball socks on in my apartment. Or maybe because you always seem to pop up out the middle of nowhere. Take your pick as to why."

I thought you liked to see me in my birthday suit! I sure like to see you in yours!"

"I do like to see you in your birthday suit, but not tonight. I have a busy day ahead of me."

"Why can't I join you in your busy day?"

"Are you sure that's something that you want to do?"

"Stop answering my questions with a question. Yes, I'm sure. We need to spend more time together. I haven't been seeing much of you lately."

"Maybe that's because you're a busy man."

"Or maybe it's because you're a busy lady." He rolled his tongue across his lips.

"It may be." She smiled, looking at his dick as it stood rock hard. He was so damn fine. She was glad that she had that effect on him, but tonight wasn't the night for sex. She guessed this would be the night she found out if he wanted her for who she was and not her body.

He pulled Tanisha to him as he cuffed her waist. "You look exhausted. How about I give you a hot bath, massage your body and put you to bed?" he asked as he massaged her neck with his tongue.

"Sounds good to me." She felt like she was being hypnotized by his tongue. He knew exactly what to do to turn her on. Her pussy moistened when his throbbing dick pressed against her stomach. Fuck it, I'm giving in, she thought.

Tanisha put her arm around his back and pulled him closer. The lingering scent of his cologne was even more of a turn on. He began to undress her and she stood there as he did as he pleased. When all her clothes were off, he left her standing there. Where is he going? Tanisha wondered. Then she heard the water running in the bathtub.

"C'mon baby. Let me give you a bath." He swiftly lifted her from her feet and carried her into the bathroom where he eased her down into the water. He'd poured Calgon bath beads into the water. The water temperature was perfect. He kneeled beside the tub and began to bathe her. Down her breasts and between her legs, he washed tenderly with the strokes of his bare hands. When he got between her legs she squeezed his hand with her inner thighs. He looked up at Tanisha and smiled. She wanted him so badly. He leaned over and kissed her twice on the lips, then inserted his tongue in her mouth. They began to make love with their tongues. Her body was so heated. Tanisha wanted to pull him into the water with her. In an instant he stopped and there was complete silence. He continued to bathe her without a word spoken. After he was done, he pulled the plug on the tub and helped her to her feet. He turned the shower on, rinsed her body and dried her off. Then he carried her to the bed, pushed her legs open and began to eat her pussy. His tongue jingled so fast against her clit she felt like she was about to have a heart attack. The more his tongue rattled against her clit, the wetter her pussy got. Tanisha tried squirming away, but he grabbed her legs and locked her in place with his arms, as his head stayed buried between her legs.

Tanisha's legs quivered and her breaths quickened. He eased off her clit and began to lay soft kisses on it. The feel of his lips was soothing. Her clit stood at attention, ready for more. As he felt her body calming down, he took her clit by force, flicking his tongue against it. In sixty seconds, Tanisha's juices flowed freely. He licked every drop and put her in the bed and pulled the covers up to her chin.

What is he doing? Now it's time to fuck me with some good hard dick. He crawled in bed behind her. She pressed her ass up against his dick, hoping he'd slip it right on in her pussy.

"Tonight was about you, not me," he whispered in her ear and patted Tanisha on the ass. He wrapped his arms around her and they spooned. Was he reading my mind? she thought. I guess it's not only my body he wants. Right as they both drifted into a deep sleep, her cell phone began to ring. "Do you want me to go get your phone for you, baby?" he asked, half asleep.

"No baby, don't get it. Let it ring. It's nobody." Tanisha was trying to savor the moment. She didn't give a fuck about no damn phone or who was on it. Again the phone started ringing. "Shit," she cursed, throwing the comforter off her and going into the living room to answer the phone.

"Hello?" Tanisha answered angrily.

"Girl, what's up?"

"I'm trying to sleep, that's what's up. Who is this?"

"Who do you think it is?"

"Bitch!" She realized it was Venom. "You got some muthafuckin' nerve to be calling here after the shit you pulled with that buster ass nigga." She tried not to talk so loud. She didn't want to disturb Mr. Sweet Dick.

"What? Girl, you would've done the same shit. You can't do for me what he can."

"You damn 'sho right about that!"

"Girl, I need a place to crash for tonight."

"You better take yo' ass home to Jazzy."

"She put me out."

"Well, you better take your ass back to that hotel room you had with that nigga."

"I don't wanna be by myself tonight."

"Oh well, a lot of people want things that they can't have. People in hell want ice water and can't get it."

"How do you know they want it? You been there before?" Venom asked, being sarcastic.

"Girl, fuck you and the people in hell that want the ice water, too. They in the same predicament you in."

"What's that?" Venom asked.

"Y'all fucked up and don't have no way to fix it."

"I'm still alive. I can fix my shit."

"Yeah right. I'd like to see that."

"Come get me and I'll show you."

"Come get you. Where's your car?"

"I left it, caught a ride with someone else and they put me out."

"Well, I'll just be damned. That's good for you. Karma struck quick. Girl, I got a man here tonight and there ain't no way in hell I'm gone let no bitch, especially you, sleep in my house while my man is here." Tanisha hung up, thinking, That bitch got some nerve.

Her phone rang again and she turned it off. Tanisha got back in bed and went to sleep with her arms wrapped around Mr. Sweet Dick.

Daylight struck the sky, and Mr. Sweet Dick served her breakfast in bed. They both showered together and he stayed with her all day like he said he would. Their first stop was at Augusta State University. Tanisha went in with him right by her side and registered for classes. They held hands and strolled the college grounds like two teenagers. She felt it was possible to fall in love with him and she also felt that he was falling for her too. She could've been wrong, but her gut told her that she was right. As the day went on, they told one another their life stories and got to know one another better. They were having so much fun that they lost track of time. She had to go to work and needed a way to get rid of him. The last thing Tanisha wanted him to know was that she danced at a strip club and she had to get to work. She knew if he found out he would want her to quit her job. Tanisha's days of depending on a man were over. Roscoe taught her that lesson and experience was definitely the best teacher.

Chapter Thirty-Five
JUST WATCH YOUR BACK

Tanisha felt like a new woman and finally she really felt that her life had started to take a turn for the better. She had a good man in her life and some good dick to go along with it, she had no complaints. I guess you do have to go through something to get somewhere. Tanisha thought to herself.

"Hello? Tanisha?" Venom answered.

"Yeah, call my phone back in twenty minutes and ask me to take you to the emergency room," Tanisha said.

The bitch had the nerve to act funny at first. "Call your phone back? After all the bullshit you just said to me," Venom said. "Do you know while I was sleep I woke up to a nine millimeter staring me in the face?"

"Hmmm, I can hardly imagine why," Tanisha said sarcastically.

"I asked Jazzy what the fuck she was doing and if she was crazy. I was scared shitless, but tried to hide it."

'No, I'm not crazy, but I think you are. Bitch, didn't I just catch you dead to the wrong?' Jazzy asked, chewing on her bottom lip.

'How did you catch me dead wrong? You didn't even give me a chance to explain before you hung up the phone,' I told her.

'Well, now is your chance.' I knew Jazzy wasn't gonna believe shit that came out of my mouth, but I tried to explain anyway and she slapped the shit out of me. Three times. Then she backhanded me for lying. I grabbed my face and started sobbing. I knew my spot was blown the fuck up.

"You a nasty bitch. I trusted you. Pack your shit and get the fuck out of my house before I splatter your muthafuckin' brains all over these walls! Oh, on your way out check out my windshield. That's the work of the nigga you fucked at the dealership and tried to play him."

"Oh my God! She found out about the salesman where we got my car!"

"I begged her to let me explain, but she kept cursing me out.

"Bitch, you can't explain a muthafuckin' thang. Get the fuck out. Here, let me help you.' "Jazzy went to the front door, opened it and started throwing my shit outside. Some of the neighbors heard all the commotion and came to their doors. Others just peeped out their windows. They probably felt I was getting exactly what I deserved. A few of them saw me sneak my coworker Dameon in a lot of times."

"Dameon? Would this be the same Dameon that works at Chocolate Castle?" Tanisha asked, not believing her ears.

"Yeah, he always paid for the pussy though. All the time. Anyway, we were fucking one day and Jazzy came home, but I got him out just in time and she never knew a thing. And it wasn't just him. There were others. Remember I told you I like to feel like I'm in control of men. Well, while Jazzy was working long hours, and I was too, in a way."

Tanisha shook her head the entire time while Venom spoke.

"So anyway, she was like: 'Get out, bitch!' and stood in the doorway as I gathered my things and put them into my car. Jazzy still had her nine millimeter in her hand. She looked like her temper was seconds away from exploding. Even though I was scared, I still wanted to know if this was really the end of us.

"Are you sure this is what you want because there's no coming back?' I asked her as I proceeded to walk out the door.

"The bitch smacked me twice and backhanded me twice too. I flinched; that shit hurt. Jazzy finally said, 'I'm sure, bitch, and don't you ever come back. Take this too, bitch.' Jazzy took the ring off that I gave her and threw it. 'Trifling bitch! Bitches are no better than the niggas,' Jazzy hollered. She went inside the apartment and slammed the door."

"And I guess you want me to feel sorry for you now, huh?" Tanisha had to remind the bitch how she treated her when she was with Roscoe's sorry ass.

"Fine, I'll help you out." Venom finally came to her senses and decided to help her out. Tanisha didn't tell Venom all the details because she was too grimy. She told her only what she wanted her to know. Tanisha was very familiar with the analogy: Never let your left hand know what your right hand is doing.

Twenty minutes later, she and her date were in the car on the way back to her apartment and her phone rang. "Hello?" she answered and waited long enough for Venom to tell her what she wanted to hear. Which wasn't what she expected.

"I'm at the emergency room.

"Emergency room? What's wrong? Is it the baby?" she asked, glancing at her date. Tanisha should've won a Emmy for the way she responded.

"I'm bleeding."

"Bleeding. Oh my God!

"Okay, I'll be there soon."

She couldn't believe the bitch was still at the Radisson. She almost fucked the entire call up when Venom said she was at the Radisson. Damn, we put the shit on the baby. Shit, we're not supposed to do no shit like that, Tanisha thought.

"Baby, what's wrong?" Mr. Sweet Dick asked.

"My friend is pregnant and she's having some bleeding. She needs me to take her to the hospital."

"Do you want me to take you ?" he asked.

"No, you don't have to take me. I'll be fine."

He pulled up to Tanisha's apartment, and she gave him a quick kiss on the lips and jumped out the car. She didn't even want him to attempt to get out the car. She went inside her apartment, peeped out the window to make sure he was gone and jumped in the shower. As she was getting ready for work her cell rang. "Hello?" she answered.

"Damn, did you forget about me?" Venom asked.

"What do you mean, did I forget about you?"

"I'm still sitting here. I told you where to pick me up at."

"At the hotel?"

"Hell yeah."

"You mean to tell me you're still at the hotel?"

"Where else would I be? You coming or not?"

"Yeah, I'll be there in a minute." Tanisha hung up the

phone and continued to get dressed. She snatched up her purse, her keys and headed for the car.

Tanisha flew like a bat out of hell trying to get to Venom. She didn't want to be late for work. When she reached Venom, she rushed to the car, got in and slammed the door. "Damn bitch, me or my door ain't the one that left your ass at the hotel." Tanisha looked at her and brushed the shit off. She wasn't about to let Venom get her upset.

"Where's your car so I can take you to get it?"

"It's at the BP gas station on Deans Bridge Road. That's if the police didn't tow it," she said with an attitude.

"Well damn, how long it's been there?"

"Just since last night."

"So, have you called Jazzy?"

"Every five minutes. I keep getting voice mail. She's mad and she didn't even catch me doing nothing."

"She had to have caught on to something." Tanisha gave her a 'don't give me that bullshit' look.

"All she did was call the hotel when I was with Roscoe. She didn't even give me a chance to defend myself before she hung up. When I got home I told her that I got the room for you."

"You did what?" Tanisha was shocked that she'd said that. She didn't want to be a part of their bullshit.

"Yeah, it was the first thing that came to my mind. I thought you told her because I put you out the car."

"I can't believe you. You get yourself into some shit and blame it on me. I should've left your ass at the hotel!"

"Tee, don't act like that."

They arrived at the gas station, and Venom's car had

busted taillights and the trunk was dented. Tanisha didn't even bother to ask her why. Venom hopped out and Tanisha kept it moving without a second thought.

When Tanisha arrived at the club, the parking lot was packed to its capacity. Cars were even lined up near Ninth Street and James Brown Boulevard, which was the side street of the club. That was unusual considering it was a Monday night. Chocolate Castle usually had a nice crowd but not this big.

She parked her car and went straight to the bar, expecting Delicious to be there but he wasn't. There was a woman bartending that she'd never seen in the club with tits that looked like a size 44G and a long jet black ponytail. Tanisha suspected she was another one of TD's girls filling in for Delicious. She ordered a drink and waited to strike up a conversation with the bartender. More women were working tonight than she'd ever seen in Chocolate Castle since the first day she stepped foot in the club. Everyone appeared to be having a nice time. The music was booming, the plasmas on the walls were playing and everyone was drinking and feeling good.

"What's with the large crowd tonight?" she asked as she caught the bartender crossing her path. The woman stopped dead in her tracks. "Excuse me, I don't mean to be rude. First, what is your name if you don't mind me asking?" Tanisha said.

"It's Sasha, don't worry 'bout it." She was very nice and friendly. Tanisha could tell she was a gossiper when she started talking.

"I hear it's TD's brother's birthday. They invited all the big ballers out tonight to celebrate. I hear his brother had a hard time last year. They say he lost his wife and kids in a fire, or something like that. Don't quote me on it though. They say TD's tryna show him the birthday party of a lifetime. I dunno, but it seems like he showing him more than a good time to me. I wish I had a brother to throw me a party like this." She washed the counter to make it seem as if she was working while she conversed with her.

"I thought he didn't have any brothers or sisters?"

"Gurl, TD is a man of many hidden secrets. You never know what to expect outta him."

"So where's Delicious?" I asked curiously.

"Gurl, dunno. They say nobody has heard from him since Sunday night. Rumor has it that he's been doing his own thing on the side and he thinks TD don't know 'bout it."

"His own thing like what?" Tanisha played dumb.

"Gurl, they say he been tryna take TD's gurls from da club and have 'em doin' parties for other people."

Tanisha eyes bucked in shock. Sasha thought they bucked because this was new information. "Oh yeah, gurl. One of the gurls told TD on him a while back. TD don't just go off what nobody say; he do his own investigation before he step to you. Gurl, TD don't play no games when it comes to his biz, money, and being loyal."

"Damn, do you think TD gone do anything to Delicious if all these allegations are true?" Tanisha asked.

"Gurl, you dunno who you working for, do you? Gurl, messing with TD and his money is the wrong thang to do. He don't play that shit when it comes to his money! Nice talking to you. Maybe we can talk later. I gotta serve these customers and get this money." She turned to serve another patron. Sasha's ass was just as huge as her tits.

Where in the hell did TD get her from? she wondered.

Tanisha headed for the dressing room and to her locker. She was humming a tune playing in the club as she unlocked her locker. There were dancers standing to the right and left of her. Everyone was changing their outfits and fixing their makeup. Tanisha opened her locker and a plastic sack with crack and a crack pipe fell to the floor. She looked around and hurried to pick it up, hoping no one saw her.

"You know if TD find out that you're smoking dope, you're gone," the dancer next to her leaned over and whispered.

"I don't smoke dope. I don't know where this came from." Tanisha had the sack cuffed in her hand where no one else could see it.

"Are you sure? 'Cause the talk around the club is that you're a retired crackhead." The dancer continued to keep her voice low.

"Hmmm, oh yeah? And I wonder where that talk came from?" Tanisha's mind went to Infinity. That bitch been setting me up all this time. I guess it can't get no worse than this. The bitch either want me to get fired, get back on dope, or both. I know the bitch can't stand me around TD. The bitch so busy trying to find out if me and him got something going on.

"I don't know where the talk came from, but I heard it through the grapevine."

"That grapevine is a muthafucka."

"Yeah, it is girl. You just watch your back. I'll talk to you later. It's my turn to hit the stage." She closed her locker, secured it, and headed for the stage.

Damn! Tanisha stood there rubbing her head. She broke into a cold sweat. She put the dope in her purse and put it in her locker.

Tanisha's cell began to ring. It was Mr. Sweet Dick himself. She went into the bathroom stall to answer it, lessening the sound of the background music.

"Hello?" she answered.

"Hey love, I just wanted to call you and tell you that I love you."

"You what?" She couldn't believe her ears. Her heart dropped to her stomach to hear those words.

"I said, I love you. I've fallen in love with you."

"I love you, too. I've fallen in love with you, too. You don't know how relieved I am to hear you say it first."

"Baby, always remember time waits on no man. The next time you feel something like this you need to express it. Don't wait on the next person because you're scared. You might miss out on something."

"I know. It's just hard for me. So you love me?" Tanisha yelled out in laughter.

"Yes, I do." He laughed at her reaction.

"Okay baby, as soon as I'm free I'll call you."

"Okay, no problem." They both hung up with an I love you.

She burst out of the bathroom singing, "Mr. Sweet Dick is in love with meeee . . ."—and ran dead into Infinity. Their eyes locked on one another. She gave Tanisha a devious smirk and walked past her.

"Now where did this bitch come from?" she mumbled to herself. Tanisha knew for sure now that the bitch planted the dope in her locker.

Chapter Thirty-Six
MEANT TO BE

Tanisha was preparing to tame the stage. She put her outfit on, wrapped her two braided ponytails with red ribbons and made sure her makeup was in place. The DJ called out to let Tanisha know it was her turn to shine and she took the stage. Someone in the club requested that she dance off all slow songs. Whoever this mysterious man was, he always seemed to get his way. He also always left her a nice stack of money every night before she left the club on the nights she worked.

The DJ started the song and Tanisha began to hypnotize the crowd as she always did. More men crowded the stage than ever in her history of dancing. Not that she had a long history, but she was good at what she did when she did it. Twenties, fifties and hundreds were the only thing hitting the stage. As she danced, Tanisha caught a glimpse of Infinity coming toward the stage. As she approached the stage she kissed something cuffed in her hands and threw it onto the stage. Tanisha continued to dance but looked down at what she threw. Infinity threw a handful of pennies onto the stage. Tanisha held her composure as she wound her body. She stared in Infinity's direction wearing a beautiful smile on her face. Be jealous, bitch, she thought. As she went up the pole and slid down upside down she saw Mr. Sweet

Dick walking to the stage dressed in a black linen suit and matching gators. Tanisha almost choked. She was heartbroken instantly. He'd just told her that he loved her and now he saw her showing her body for money. Tanisha never took him for the type that hung in strip clubs. She thought she could hide her dancing until she finished school. He sat in a chair center stage and pulled out a wad of hundred dollar bills.

Tanisha saw him look over at the DJ and nod his head. Then the tune "Bump and Grind" by R. Kelly began to play. Tanisha began to dance like she'd never danced before. She gave him her undivided attention and got lost in the music and the thought of hearing the words 'I love you.' She wondered if this had changed his mind. Toward the end of the song she saw the crowd's attention go elsewhere. She put her hand behind her head as she circled the stage and gyrated her hips.

As she turned, her eyes hit one of the plasma screens. There Tanisha was, having sex with two men. She was sucking one guy's dick and the other one was thrusting roughly in and out her pussy. She thought things couldn't get any worse.

Tanisha turned back to see the expression on Spencer's face and his seat was empty. She scanned the room everywhere for him and he was nowhere in sight. Suddenly, all the plasmas went blank and the lights came on in the club. "The party is over. The muthafuckin' party is over! Everybody clear out!" Spencer shouted.

Tanisha wondered where he got the authority to end a party in TD's club. He had really fucked up. A few minutes later, TD came walking in rubbing the bottom of his chin. He was dressed in a lime green linen suit with a pair of matching gators. He had a thick platinum link on with the matching pinky ring. It looked identical to the jewelry that Spencer was wearing.

Infinity ran up to him. "I've been waiting on you all night," she said.

"Not now." He pushed her away and headed over to where Spencer was.

Infinity walked over to Tanisha. "I knew you was fucking my man all along, you trifling bitch."

"I'm not fucking your man, bitch," Tanisha shot back.

"Oh bitch, I heard you say Mr. Sweet Dick, I love you, when you were coming out the bathroom." She stood with one hand propped on her hip.

"Bitch, Mr. Sweet Dick is my man. You got your people fucked up." Tanisha was getting heated.

"So you wanna take TD like you did Roscoe and fuck his life up, too? Bitch, if that's what you think you got another thang coming."

"What are you talking about? I don't want TD, and you're right, he is your man if that's what you say!" TD was nobody's man and he chose his woman on a daily, weekly or monthly basis.

By the time their argument got heated, TD and Spencer walked over to them. Everyone had left the club except Tanisha, Infinity, the DJ, four of the bouncers, and the bartender, Sasha.

"Infinity, I told you time after time that you never mix business with pleasure. Now I know you put that DVD in to humiliate Shanoah. I've been hearing about the DVD for weeks now. Word on the street is that you drugged her at a party. Then you paid two guys to have sex with her so you could tape it. Haven't you gotten enough yet? You continue to disappoint me. You gotta let this hatred go that you have in your heart. It's not going to get you anywhere in life. I want you to know everything that you do to somebody always comes back to get you one way or another. I'm a poster child for that; it's called karma." TD unbuttoned his shirt.

"You see this?" He grabbed Infinity's hand and pulled her closer to him and pointed to his tattoos. "Touch them!" he yelled with bass in his voice. Infinity trembled. She gently rubbed her hand across his chest. There were seven tombstones tattooed on his chest.

"Why am I rubbing this? I've seen them before," Infinity said.

Spencer stood there with his hand behind his back. Tanisha was ready to get the hell out of dodge, but didn't know how TD and Spencer would react so she stayed put.

"Of course you've seen them before, but do you know what they stand for?" TD asked in an agitated voice.

"No, I don't know."

"Well, the tombstones are for seven people I lost that I loved. The scars underneath are the seven bullet wounds. These bullet wounds came from someone retaliating after they accused me of killing seven people that they loved. They wanted to take my life because they wanted revenge. I had to learn the hard way. When things like this keep going, nobody wins." He pushed her hand away and buttoned his shirt back up.

"Do you wanna lose your life over nothing? Do you?" he bellowed. Then he rubbed the bottom of his chin as sweat formed on his nose. She dropped her head like a two-year old.

"No." She barely let the word come through her lips.

"I didn't hear you. Speak louder," he demanded.

"No," she spoke up.

"I thought so. Now apologize to this young lady for

what you did."

Infinity looked at Tanisha with disgust in her eyes and said, "I apologize."

Tanisha knew it wasn't sincere. Then Infinity said something in Spanish that none of them could understand.

"I guess using The 48 Laws of Power as your Holy Bible didn't work for you, did it?" Tanisha whispered to Infinity and walked away, headed to the dressing room. Once she got in the dressing room she broke down in tears. She felt so embarrassed. There was nothing she could do to defend herself. Tanisha's mind wandered as she searched for a way to cure her pain. The crack in her purse came to mind. She'd fallen weak. She'd taken too much. All she could think was if she just took one pull, it would take away all the pain. Long term or how far she'd come didn't register. All she thought about was right then and there. Tanisha took the crack sack out of her purse and dropped the purse on the floor. She searched the locker room high and low for a lighter, a match, anything to spark a fire. Finally, she found a lighter in one of the girl's jacket that she knew smoked cigarettes.

Wasn't a soul in sight. She sat in a chair and at that moment she felt like G-Money on New Jack City. She had fucked up her life and humiliated herself in the worst way. What else did she have to lose? She packed the glass pipe with crack, put the pipe in her mouth and flicked the lighter. Before she could inhale, she saw a pair of black alligator skin shoes standing in front of her. She looked up with the crack pipe clenched between her lips. It was Spencer. "Is this what you wannna do with your life?" he asked as he snatched the crack pipe from her lips and held it in his hand.

"No, this isn't what I want to do," she said as she slowly stood to her feet.

"Is this going to be your solution to all of your problems?" he asked, shaking the crack pipe in her face.

"No," Tanisha cried softly.

"What reason do I have to believe you?" He cuffed her chin in his hand and peered into her eyes. The hurt was evident in his disappointed eyes as he caught her about to relapse on dope. She thought about rehab when she and Spencer first met. She remembered telling him how she wanted to get off dope and stay clean. Tanisha told him how she'd kicked the habit and wasn't going back to crack. Now there she was about to sell her soul to the devil once again. Her heart bled. A massive power of shame took over Tanisha's entire being. She was caught red-handed.

"Do you hear me talking to you?" He shook her chin in his hand and squeezed it. At that moment Tanisha could tell he really cared for her. It didn't matter to him that she had been on crack in the past. One of his eyes began to tear. She tried not to notice, but it hit her like a ton of bricks. A man isn't supposed to cry, she thought as she held her head down, but here was a man forming a tear for her.

Spencer removed his hand from her chin and took two steps back. "Don't you want a better life than this?" He shook the crack pipe at her, threw it on the floor and smashed it with his foot. "Do you!" he yelled.

"Yes," Tanisha said softly.

"Well, this is your one chance to choose and there's no turning back. Do you wanna be on the same shit for the rest of your life, or do you want a better life for yourself? Because if you continue to take this path, that's exactly what you'll be doing. It'll be one quick high after another. You'll be stealing, turning tricks and whatever else dope fiends do to get high. On the other hand, you can come with me, be loved unconditionally and live life fruitfully." He stuck his hands back into his pockets, fumbling with something.

"You mean to tell me that you still want me?" Tanisha was confused. She thought he didn't want anything else to do with her. She assumed the dancing had done it and getting caught with the dope added fuel to the fire.

"Of course I want you. I want to have you as my woman. I'm in love with you." He smiled, pulling Tanisha to him and stroking the back of her head. She grinned like a Cheshire cat. She was so relieved, but still felt embarrassed like a muthafucka on the inside. "I have something for you," he said as he took his arms from around her. Spencer put his hands back into his pocket and pulled out a small black velvet box. He then looked at Tanisha and smiled. Her heart beat increased speedily. She was hoping that what she wanted to be inside the box was actually in it. He opened it and there was a pair of emerald earrings. They appeared to be the same earrings that TD wore in his ear. The ones he said he'd never remove until he found the woman of his dreams. The woman he was going to marry. Tanisha stood there in awe. Tanisha looked confused. "What's wrong? You don't like them?" Spencer asked, holding the box in his hand.

"No. Nothing's wrong. I love them."

"If you love them, why are you looking like that?"

"The truth?" she asked.

"Yes, the truth."

"They look like TD's earrings."

"They were." He smiled.

"What do you mean, 'they were?'"

"He gave them to me."

"Why?"

"Because he didn't find the woman of his dreams and I did. He gave them to me as a birthday gift."

"Why would he do that?" Tanisha was confused.

"He's my brother," he said with a serious face.

"Your what?" Her forehead wrinkled in confusion.

"My brother."

"Holy shit! He's your brother." Tanisha was shocked.

"Yes, he is. Don't be so surprised," he replied with a smile that appeared to be permanent.

"How?"

"Papa was a rolling stone," he joked.

"So you mean to tell me that you knew I was dancing too?"

"Of course I did. I was the one who sent you all the roses. I was the one requesting all the songs. I was the reason you got the job and the one leaving you all the extra money. The first night you came in I was sitting in the office. I came out when Dameon told me there was a woman inquiring about a job. I thought I recognized you. I didn't know for sure so I got Dameon to get more information on you. When I found out it was you, I knew you were meant for me. That's when I started bombarding my way into your life. I'm also the one that sent all the stuff to your apartment."

She couldn't believe her ears, but she was thrilled and relieved. She found herself over talking him.

"When I left rehab I thought about you all the time. I said to myself if it was meant to be we would meet again.

You were so nice to me. That meant the world to me. You were mourning the loss of your family and still had time for me. The story you told me about them burning in the fire never left me. My heart ached for you. The bartender told me TD's brother lost his family in a fire! At that moment I had no clue that you were his brother. I don't know why I didn't put two and two together."

"It's okay. I'm better now and rehab really helped me. I haven't taken a drink since I left there."

"That's very good." Tanisha stroked his chest. "Very good!" Out of all the times Spencer and Tanisha spent together she never mentioned his family. She didn't want to reopen old wounds. Instead, she decided to wait for him to initiate the conversation if he wanted to. It wasn't her place to do so. Besides, she was only enjoying the moment.

"This is very good, too," Spencer said as he softly put one finger on her lips, referring to being there with her.

"Here, hold this." Spencer gave her the black velvet box, then removed her ponytail from around her ear. He took one earring, placed it in her ear and did the same with the other. Taking the box from her hand, he pushed it back into his pocket and took hold of her hand and walked her over to the mirror. Spencer stood behind Tanisha with his chin resting on her shoulder and his arms wrapped around her waist.

"You're beautiful," he said and kissed her neck.

"Thank you," she replied with a heart full of love and joy. He turned her around to face him.

"I have something else for you." Spencer pulled what appeared to be the same black velvet box from his pocket. He knelt on one knee and looked up at Tanisha.

There's nothing else in that box, she thought to

herself. He took her hand, kissed it softly and released it. He opened the box and displayed the biggest emerald ring she'd ever seen with a platinum band. Hell, it was the only emerald ring she'd ever seen. "Will you marry me?" he asked Tanisha. She stood there with her mouth gaped open, eyeing the ring. Spencer stood to his feet, got an aggressive grip on the back of her neck and began to kiss her passionately. Tanisha felt caught up in the moment. "Will you marry me?" he asked again as he began to lay soft kisses on her lips.

"Yes," she responded and slipped her tongue into his mouth.

"Baby, we have to go. My brother is waiting."

"Why didn't he come and say something?"

"He doesn't get in my business and I don't get in his."

Tanisha didn't say another word. They began to walk out of the dressing room. "Wait, one more thing."

"What is it?" She smiled with excitement, wishing at that moment that Frenchy was still alive. Tanisha would have loved for her to see how her life took a turn for the better.

"The ring. You forgot to let me put the ring on your finger."

"Oh," she replied, stopping dead in her tracks and letting him slip the ring on her finger. It was a perfect fit.

When they walked into the club, TD had Infinity wrapped in his arms consoling her. She was crying, but for whatever the reason she didn't know. And really she didn't give a damn either.

"You ready to go?" Spencer asked TD.

"Yeah, I'm ready," TD responded.

When Infinity held up her head, her eyes landed directly on Tanisha's ears. She could read her thoughts as well as see the anger growing in her eyes. TD told everyone else in the club that they were leaving. He also told them to close and secure the club. Infinity and TD walked ahead of Tanisha and Spencer. Infinity looked back and gave her a slight grin. Her eyes were fire red. Tanisha sensed the animosity still between them.

"Get the things you need out of your car. You're riding with me," Spencer said. Tanisha went to retrieve the things from her car and proceeded to walk toward Spencer's Aston Martin.

She had never seen this car before. Damn, he has a nice ass ride and everything else to go along with it, she thought as she slowly approached his car. Damn, I came a long way from being on dope. Shit, I know there's plenty of them bitches in the club that wish this could've happened to them, but it happened to me! Spencer was leaning against his car with his legs crossed, arms folded and smiling in her direction. He opened his arms and held them out to her. As soon as Tanisha got within arm's length of Spencer, two shots fired from a gun. She fell into Spencer's arms, feeling a burning sensation in her body.

In an instant, Spencer's smile disappeared. She saw a tear form in his eye. This time he couldn't control it from trickling down his cheek. "That bitch shot her!" Spencer yelled as he tightly gripped her body. "Call the paramedics, somebody please!" he shouted again as he lifted her from her feet and cradled Tanisha like a baby. Sasha was still there, and she opened his car door and he laid her on the seat.

The way Tanisha was facing she could see Infinity in her view, standing next to her Mercedes. She dropped the gun on the ground beside her. Infinity shivered, appearing to be in shock.

"Gurl you gotta hold on. Everything's gone be all right," Sasha said in her country southern accent. Spencer was applying pressure to her wound to minimize the bleeding. Tanisha still didn't think she was in any pain, but her body felt like it was on fire in the inside. The burning sensation was something new to her.

Five minutes after lying there and everyone surrounding her, they heard four gun shots and a man's voice say, "Bitch, you thought you and your brother was gonna get away with my money and dope, didn't you?" Roscoe had snuck up out the middle of nowhere and gave Infinity four bullets to the chest.

Infinity's body hit the hood of the car then fell limp to the ground.

As Roscoe tried to get away, TD pulled a gun from the holster underneath his shirt and shot four bullets into the back of Roscoe's dome.

Roscoe died instantly.

Chapter Thirty-Seven
ONE DAY AT A TIME

Six months later . . .

Tanisha survived being shot in her shoulder; the bullet hadn't hit any major organs. Infinity died three days later. TD stayed by her bedside the entire time. He held the look of a man that needed to say something that was never said. Her mom and dad were devastated. She had visitors non-stop and everyone blamed Roscoe. On the third day, the doctors told her mom that her lungs had collapsed and she'd never be able to breathe on her own. They then made the decision to pull the plug. No one ever told her family that she was the one who'd shot Tanisha because they were already dealing with enough.

When Roscoe was buried, Madison showed up with her son, looking identical to Roscoe. He looked as if Roscoe had given birth to him and not Madison. Nothing had changed about the bitch. She was still the same old cheap shoe wearing, bubble gum blowing bitch she'd always been. JJ tried to get released to go to Infinity's funeral but the Federal Bureau of Prisons wasn't hearing it. Infinity had a small, private, closed casket funeral.

After the funerals and the settling of the dust, Spencer and Tanisha tied the knot. The first day Spencer and

Tanisha were back from their honeymoon in Cancun, he served her breakfast in bed. He'd already moved her from her apartment and into a mini mansion. The two lay there and reviewed pictures from their wedding and reminisced. The wedding was beautiful. The colors were royal blue, cream and gold. TD was Spencer's best man and Sasha was Tanisha's matron of honor. Tanisha didn't know too much about her, but she didn't have to worry about her sticking a knife in her back. At least at the moment she didn't. Tanisha's mom even showed up. They hadn't been in contact for over a year. She had washed her hands of Tanisha after receiving heartbreak after heartbreak by Tanisha being in the streets on dope. Once Tanisha finally did get clean, her mom still didn't believe her. Her mom thought it was just a short intermission and she was going right back to it. Fooled her this time! Her mother had more faith in her now than she'd ever had in all of Tanisha's life.

As Tanisha and Spencer lay there going through the pictures, her cell rang. "Hello?" Tanisha answered.

"Hey girl." She could barely hear the voice on the other end of the phone.

"Who is this?" Tanisha asked, looking confused. The voice sounded like that of a sickly person. Spencer sat up in bed, his eyes locked on her.

"It's Venom."

"Venom?"

Spencer turned his back to her and continued looking at the wedding pictures. He'd heard all that Tanisha had been through with them and didn't want her having anything to do with them. Tanisha hadn't spoke to Venom since the night she was shot. She didn't know if she had been dead or alive.

"Yes, Venom," she answered.

"What's wrong?" Tanisha asked.

"I'm in the hospital and I need you to come get the baby," she said.

Tanisha wore a confused expression. Spencer sat back up in the bed and turned to look at her.

"Yes, I want you to come get the baby and keep the baby."

"Your baby?"

"Yes. Keep her and raise her as your own." She barely got the words out. Tanisha could tell that she was crying.

"Why? Why won't you keep your own baby?" she asked.

"I can't, because I'm not gone make it. . . . I have AIDS, Tee. I'm not gone make it."

"Oh my God. I'm so sorry." Tanisha began to cry. Everyone around her was dying. Now here was a child born that would never know her mother.

"Don't be sorry for me, Tee. Just come get the baby. She is gorgeous. I saw her," Venom cried aloud.

"Wait, but isn't the baby infected?"

"No, she's not infected. I had a cesarean. The baby is free and clear." Tanisha could hear the joy through Venom's cries. She was relieved the baby hadn't contracted the disease.

"What hospital are you at?"

"St. Joseph. You know where it is, right?" She gasped for air.

"Yes, it's not far from the Veteran's Hospital, right?"

"Right. I'll see you when you get here."

She hung up the phone, then Tanisha told Spencer everything that Venom told her. He knew how badly she wanted a child. He knew she couldn't have one, so he agreed to them raising Venom's baby as their own.

They hopped out of bed, got dressed, and headed to the hospital. Before they were able to enter Venom's room they had to get suited, putting on a mask, sterile gown, and booties over their shoes. Tanisha remembered these procedures from when Frenchy was on her dying bed. They were more of a threat to Venom than she would be to them. Her immune system was weak. They went into Venom's room and there she lay smiling at Tanisha with tubes running through her body.

"Hi, how are you?" Tanisha asked. She began to cry.

"I'm okay," Venom said. Tanisha went over to her and stroked her head.

"It's gone be okay. We're going to take good care of your baby." Venom smiled up at Tanisha as tears raced down her face.

"Tee, can I tell you something?" Tanisha grabbed a hold of her hand.

"You can tell me anything." A tear trickled down her cheek. She let it roll.

"The baby was always yours. From the moment I knew she was growing inside of me she was yours. That's the reason I didn't have an abortion. I knew how badly you wanted a baby. All the days I thought about having an abortion, I thought about you. I had no right to take a life. God gives blessing. I knew in my heart of hearts that you weren't going back to drugs. I could tell that you wanted a change. You did better than most, Tee. Look at you! You've got a husband!" They both smiled and looked at Spencer standing at the foot of the bed.

"That's what you always wanted. Now your family is complete. Go see your baby girl," she insisted with a half-smile, which was all she could give.

"Are you sure?" Tanisha asked as her heart flipped in her chest.

"Yes, I'm sure. Go, I'll be okay. I'll be right here when you get back." Her eyes lowered and her smile vanished.

Spencer and Tanisha went to the nursery to see the baby. They scanned all the names on the babies and finally found baby Long. They wanted to hold her. There was something definitely strange about this baby. The skin was light, but the eyes were blue. Tanisha thought the baby had been switched. Then she thought about Roscoe being the dad. It was a strong possibility, but Roscoe wasn't full blooded Puerto Rican himself.

Spencer and Tanisha finished visiting with the baby and went back to see Venom. Her eyes were closed and it was quiet. All she could hear was the beeping sounds of the machine. Tanisha walked over to Venom's bed, stood there and took in the features of her face for a moment. Then she stroked her hair and Venom slowly opened her eyes.

"Hi there," Tanisha said. Venom smiled.

"I know!" she said. Venom took in the confused look on Tanisha's face. A look her smile couldn't hide.

"What is it that you know?"

"About the baby, Tee. C'mon now! No! She's not Roscoe's baby."

"Well, whose baby is she?" Tanisha demanded to know who the maternal father was.

"Does it really matter? Or were you hoping she was Roscoe's baby?"

"Look. The least you can do is tell me who's the daddy."

"Okay. Okay, Tee. Levert Langston is the daddy. That's where she gets those blue eyes from. It's not like you know him anyway."

"Oh, I know him all right," Tanisha said sarcastically.

"How?" Venom wanted to know, almost demanding as if she had the strength.

"I met him one night with Armani. He was her sugar daddy."

"Her sugar daddy?" Venom tried to sit up, but couldn't.

"You heard me." Tanisha made herself clear.

"Oh my God! Noooooooooo," she screamed slightly and began to cough uncontrollably.

"Do you need me to get the doctor?"

"No, no, don't get the doctor. I'm okay." Her chest heaved.

"Well, what is it?"

"Levert Langston died three months ago of AIDS. Either I contracted the disease from him or he contracted it from me. I'm not gone lie, Tee. I don't know. You need to go see her."

"Are these the sincere words of a woman that never cared about nothing but an orgasm?" Tanisha joked.

"Tee, all bullshit aside. I wouldn't wish this disease on my worst enemy."

"I know you wouldn't. I just wanted to throw in a little humor." She chuckled, hoping to calm her down.

"You know the crazy part about all this shit? Levert used to work with Jazzy. He was her Captain."

"Small world, huh?"

Venom was trifling as hell, but this wasn't the time to cast any stones, especially from a glass house.

"Whatever happened to Jazzy?" Tanisha asked as if

she really cared.

"Well, she made detective like she wanted. She's gone straight. Strictly dickly now; at least that's what I've heard. She didn't want anything else to do with me anymore. I can't blame her. I had to leave a message on her answering machine to get tested when I found out I was positive. I take it she's in the clear 'cause the bitch probably would've tried to kill me before I died," Venom joked.

"Damn, a lot has happened in such a little time."

"I know, huh? Tee, make sure you tell the baby that I hope she turns out to be a better woman than me."

"Oh, she will! I'm not raising no whores!" Tanisha joked. They both laughed.

"I wanna thank you for every moment you were there for me. I'm so sorry I couldn't return the favor. I'm also sorry about that tape. Sorry I didn't tell you sooner."

"It's okay. Don't worry about it. That's water under the bridge."

"I know, right? It's just a lot of things I need to ask forgiveness for before I enter the pearly gates." After Venom's last statement a woman walked in and handed Tanisha a thick stack of papers.

"What is this?" Tanisha asked, looking toward Venom.

"It's all the paperwork you'll need for the baby. I signed them. Now, all you have to do is sign them. Then you can take your baby home with you." Venom began to breathe rapidly and pressed the nurse call button. The doctors and nurses rushed in.

"Back up, please," the nurse demanded.

Venom was staring into Tanisha's eyes. Then she motioned her over to her with her finger. Tanisha walked over to her bedside. "Take your baby. Leave and don't ever look back," she whispered.

Tanisha kissed her hand and put it on Venom's forehead. She walked over to Spencer, grabbed his hand, and went to get her baby. She never looked back.

Venom died later on that evening. The doctors did everything they could to get her blood to clot, but her body fought against it.

Chapter Thirty-Eight
THIS ISN'T FAIR

A few days later, Tanisha decided to check on Armani. Although she knew she wasn't her favorite person, she decided to take her chances. She'd been out of the coma for at least three months. Tanisha drove over to her house in her 745 Beamer, a wedding gift from Spencer. Dressed in a cream Chanel suit, matching purse, and peep toe pumps, she walked up on the porch and rang the bell. The house looked deserted from the outside. Finally, the door swung open. There stood a very handsome man. He was polite and took her straight to Armani, who was lying in her big California king bed with a red silk Victoria's Secret gown and robe. She appeared to be her same old beautiful self. Her eyes were bright and her skin was as flawless as ever. There was no sign of any virus from what Tanisha was seeing.

"Hi. Come in and have a seat," she said. Tanisha took a seat on the couch next to the window. Armani sat up on the bed.

"I was afraid you wouldn't want to see me," Tanisha said.

"Why would you think that?" Armani asked with a small smile.

"Because of Infinity and everything else that's

happened," Tanisha explained.

"Girl, I don't have any room to cast any stones. I had to learn the hard way that every woman's fate is held in her own hands."

"True," Tanisha agreed.

In the middle of their conversation, the handsome man dressed in a lab coat, a pair of slacks and some dress shoes came in. "Excuse me, is there anything I can get you ladies before I go?" he asked. Armani looked over to Tanisha.

"No thanks," she answered.

Armani nodded no. He kissed Armani on the lips and ran his hand down the side of her face. Tanisha felt the power of love enter the room.

"Okay, if you're sure you don't need anything I'm headed to work."

"I'm sure," Armani said as she grabbed his chin and kissed him gently.

"Have a nice day," the gentleman said as he exited the room.

"Who might that be? If you don't mind me asking."

"That's my husband, Cliff."

"Cliff?" Tanisha asked, looking confused.

"Yes. I decided to take him back."

"Why?"

"Because I love him and he loves me." Armani blushed.

"My God, what is happening around here? There has to be more to this story."

"Look at you. You're judging already from what you've heard. Before I told you who he was, you didn't have anything to say."

"I'm not judging. He just doesn't look like the person

that was described to me."

"That's because he's clean now and he's gone back to work. He wasn't always in the streets, you know? He did have a life before drugs and alcohol. You would know about that, wouldn't you?" Armani was being defensive yet sarcastic.

"Of course I know. I know that better than anybody," Tanisha spat back.

Armani got up off the bed and sat next to her on the couch. She stared at Tanisha for a moment. "I'm sorry. I'm sorry," she cried out.

"For what?"

"The tape. The fuckin' tape! I'm so sorry."

Clearly, Tanisha had forgotten all about the video. Spencer wasn't worried about it, so neither was she. He had gotten a hold to as many DVDs as he could from what she heard in the streets. TD sent threats out to everyone that even attempted to sell the video.

"It's okay. Don't worry about the video." Tanisha assured her that she wasn't worried about it. Armani continued to cry. Tanisha put her arms around her as she latched on to her.

"Tanisha, there's something I have to tell you," she cried.

"What is it?" she asked, stroking the back of her head. Her hair was long, silky, and jet black. Tears trickled down Armani's cheek.

"I have HIV." She sobbed in between sniffles.

Tanisha tried her best to look surprised. Now wasn't the time to say she already figured that. Even though she was positive, nothing about her physical appearance co-signed what she was telling Tanisha. Armani was very beautiful and her body was equally attractive. Any man would love to have her in his bed.

"Do you know where you got it from?" she asked, figuring Levert Langston was the only person responsible, and he had died about three months ago.

"It's gone be okay." Tanisha patted her back.

"Easy for you to say." Armani snatched away from her and went over to her dresser. She snatched open a drawer. "Come over here and look," she said. Tanisha didn't move. Armani began hollering and screaming.

"You were the one on drugs and selling pussy, not me!" she yelled. "Why don't you have HIV? This ain't fair. I don't understand." She dropped to her knees.

Tanisha went over to console her and sat on the floor next to her.

"Life isn't fair," Tanisha said. "Everything hasn't been peaches and cream for me." Tanisha cried with her.

"This isn't fair to Cliff. I didn't want him and now he still chooses to stay with me. It's not fair."

"Have you seen Cliff? I mean, have you taken a good look at him?"

Armani looked puzzled as she wiped the tears falling from her eyes.

"This is where Cliff wants to be. His entire world is better because of you. You give him hope and something to hold on to. Cliff had turned to drugs and alcohol when you left him. That isn't a nice place to be in life. Now you two are building together. You loved one another through the storm. Most people only hope for a love like that. Take it for what it is and live one day at a time." Tanisha couldn't believe the words coming from her mouth, but they were sincere and from the heart.

"You're right," Armani said as she got up off the floor and helped Tanisha to her feet. She picked up the phone and proceeded to dial a number as she smiled at her.

"Hi. What time are you coming home tonight?" she asked. Tanisha couldn't hear what was said on the other end. "Eight. Okay good. I'm going to cook dinner. Make sure you bring some condoms home with you. I love you, Cliff." Armani hung up the phone and looked at Tanisha.

"Condoms?" Tanisha asked.

"Yes, condoms. We have to have safe sex. I don't want Cliff to get HIV."

She and Armani conversed for a while. They did a lot of catching up. Armani ran her and Cliff's life story to her from the beginning to end.

She'd forgiven him for everything he'd done and learned to love him all over again.

Chapter Thirty-Nine
CHEATING SO SOON

Spencer," Tanisha called out as she walked into her house and threw the keys on the counter. No one answered. She didn't even hear the baby making a sound, but Spencer's car was home. Tanisha continued walking up the stairs. She checked in on the baby first, who was sound asleep. Tanisha went to her bedroom and pushed the door open. Her heart dropped to her stomach. She couldn't see Spencer's face, but when she heard the woman say, "Mr. Sweet Dick," and saw a woman riding him and their hips were gyrating in unison, her heart slipped from its place. There wasn't a condom in sight. The woman moaned in pleasure each time she gyrated her hips full circle.

"Ooow weeeee, Mr. Sweet Dick. It feels so good. You got my pussy so wet. Make me cum. Make me cum, Mr. Sweet Dick," the woman moaned. She had her hand placed on his stomach, riding him like she was in the Kentucky Derby.

Goodness! I just got my life together and somebody's fuckin' my man in my house already, Tanisha thought. She decided not to fight it. Tanisha guessed this was her karma. She turned to walk away and there stood Spencer holding the baby.

"So you're a peeping Tom now?" he asked.

My God! How happy she was to see Spencer's face. He burst into laughter at the relieved look on her face. Spencer grabbed her around the waist and they went into the baby's room and laid her in her crib and they walked out.

"You didn't think I would be cheating so soon, did you?" he joked.

"You better never cheat." Tanisha smacked him in the chest. "Sweet Dick. I knew for sure it was you."

"Didn't I tell you papa was a rolling stone. He used to tell us that if he didn't give us nothing, he gave us a sweet dick and every woman would love it. It's kind of a little joking thing me and my brother say every now and then." Spencer grabbed Tanisha's chin and began kissing her.

"I'll never say it again." She pulled away.

"Aww baby, don't be like that." Spencer and Tanisha started to tussle with one another and from her peripheral she saw the woman exit the room. She gasped. It was Jazzy.

The End.

READING GROUP QUESTIONS
STILL FEENIN' BY SERENITI HALL

1) Who was your favorite character?

2) Do you think Tanisha was being too gullible when it came to Infinity giving her a second chance after she'd been sleeping with her husband and all up in her face on a regular basis?

3) Do you think Armani and Infinity had feelings for one another?

4) Were the sex scenes too much or just enough?

5) Do you think Roscoe's character came back in at the right time?

6) Did you think that Tanisha was sleeping with TD? Did you remember Spencer from Feenin?

7) Do you think Infinity treated Jimmy Jr. right while he was in prison after he looked out for her?

8) How do you feel about Tanisha's new found love?

9) Did you ever suspect Jazzy being with a man?

10) Do you think the ending did justice?

About the Author

Sereniti is currently working on her next project and Lives in Augusta, Georgia with her two daughters. You can contact Sereniti Hall via email at: serenitihall@yahoo.com
On Facebook: Sereniti Hall on Twitter @Serenitihall

WAHIDA CLARK PRESENTS

BEST SELLING TITLES

Trust No Man

Trust No Man II

Thirsty

Cheetah

Karma With A Vengeance

The Ultimate Sacrifice

The Game of Deception

Karma 2: For The Love of Money

Thirsty **2**

Lickin' License

Feenin'

Bonded by Blood

Uncle Yah Yah: 21st Century Man of Wisdom

The Ultimate Sacrifice II

Under Pressure (YA)

The Boy Is Mines! (YA)

A Life For A Life

The Pussy Trap

99 Problems (YA)

Country Boys

UNCLE YAH YAH

21ST. Century Man of Wisdom

VOL 2

COMING SOON!

AL DICKENS

WAHIDA CLARK PRESENTS

COMING
SOON!

NUDE
Awakening
A NOVEL

VICTOR L. MARTIN

WAHIDA CLARK PRESENTS

TRUST NO MAN

A NOVEL

CA$H

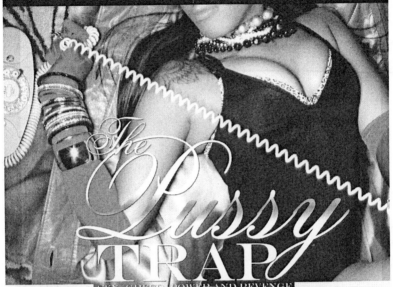